TIMELESS

A TROPICAL AUTHORS NOVEL

TROPICAL AUTHORS   NICHOLAS HARVEY
NICK SULLIVAN   JOHN H CUNNINGHAM
WAYNE STINNETT

DOWN ISLAND
PUBLISHING

Printed in the United States of America

First Printing, 2022

ISBN-13: 978-1-956026-95-5

Cover design: Harvey Books, LLC

Editor: Gretchen Tannert Douglas

"Time is the longest distance between two places."

Tennessee Williams, *The Glass Menagerie*

For Dawn Lee McKenna
An inspiration and friend to us all.
The storyteller we aspire to be.

PART I

PROLOGUE
GRAND CAYMAN, MAY 9, 1976

Woody Rains had always been a trusting soul. A former naval aviator, he believed in the Stars and Stripes, the Good Lord, and putting his family first. So, when an amiable man had approached him at the Opa-locka Airport in Miami, looking for a ride to the Yucatán Peninsula, Woody had volunteered a seat in the plane he was delivering. "I'm heading that way," he'd happily told the fella. Four hours later, with a gun pressed to his shoulder blade, storm clouds as far as the eye could see, and his fuel gauge on the opposite side of full, Woody questioned his judgment, and prayed to his Maker.

Amelia Earhart had made the Lockheed Vega famous when she'd become the first woman to fly solo across the Atlantic Ocean in a 5B. That was in 1932. Woody was flying the aluminum version, built by the Detroit Aircraft Corporation, and dubbed the DL1 Vega. A valuable, freshly restored antique aircraft he was being paid good money to safely deliver to the docks in Panama. From there, she would be transported by sea to her wealthy new owner in Australia. If Woody kept her in one piece.

"Little Cayman," the man who'd called himself Calloway barked.

Woody doubted his real name was Calloway. He doubted everything the swarthy man with thinning hair had told him. Six inches shorter than Woody's tall, broad-shouldered build, he knew he could take the man in a fair fight. But the gun heavily tipped the odds, and the peculiar layout of the Vega meant Woody was strapped in the lone pilot seat, forward of the bulkhead. His adversary was behind him in the cabin built to carry six passengers, along with an overnight duffel and an odd-looking watertight case he'd brought aboard.

"The storm is coming from the east," Woody shouted over the racket of the 450-horsepower Pratt & Whitney engine. "Since you insisted we turn back east, we're now too far from Mexico, we don't have enough fuel, and Cuba's not a friendly option. Little Cayman is farther east. Look for yourself," he declared, pointing across the dark gray clouds spread before them, bathed in the warm glow of the setting sun at their tail. Ahead and to the left, the clouds billowed in threatening mountains of charcoal, lit from within by bursts of lightning. "I'm not flying into that mess. Our only chance is landing in Grand Cayman."

Calloway shoved the barrel of the .38 against the back of Woody's head. "Fly this heap to Little Cayman or, so help me God, I'll shoot you."

Woody turned in his seat, forcing his eyes beyond the gun to stare at the man. "You a pilot?"

"Little Cayman, damn you!"

Woody laughed, "I thought not. Go ahead, shoot me. See if that gets you to Little Cayman. I'm confident God will give you no such help."

He faced the front and checked his heading, keeping the Vega aimed for Grand Cayman. Or, where Grand Cayman theoretically was, as all he could see was an ocean of gray cloud. They were 9,500 feet above the Caribbean Sea, staying a thousand feet above the stratus, the highest he'd care to go without supplemental oxygen. The air was thin in the unpressurized plane, and both men were breathing heavily. At some point Woody needed to duck through the cloud cover and hope he had enough visibility to sight the island. The orange and yellow hues tinting the blue skies behind them were a far cry from the rain-soaked shadows and darkness awaiting below.

"No radio," Calloway ordered. "We can land in Grand Cayman, but no radio communication."

"I need the lights on to land. If I don't let them know I'm coming, they won't know to turn them on," Woody explained in frustration.

"You said you've landed there before."

"Sure, I have, a few times. In daylight." Woody glanced at his 1964 Rolex Submariner, a treasured gift from his father on his twenty-first birthday. The day he'd joined the Navy. It was 6:45 p.m.

"Well, today you'll be doing it in the dark," Calloway replied, unrelenting. "Turn the radio off."

Woody turned the VHF radio off. "You know they'll notice an airplane landing, right? It's not like we'll sneak in. Someone's gonna hear us."

"Don't worry about that. Just remember," he said with another shove of the gun barrel, "I was never on this plane."

Woody figured a bullet was the surest way the gunman could keep him quiet, but before he could worry about that, he first had to land. He dipped the nose of the Vega, and within a few minutes, the old plane descended into the clouds. It was as though someone had thrown a sheet over the plane. Swirling gray hues whipped past the windshield, and the plane jolted and yawed in the turbulent air.

"God damn it!" came Calloway's voice from the cabin, and Woody hoped he'd cracked his head on the airframe.

Watching the altimeter carefully, and focused on maintaining wings level flight, Woody dropped through the blanket of rain clouds. The more they descended, the rougher the ride was getting, and moisture streaked over the glass. Occasionally, they dropped through pockets of tempestuous air, where it felt like the Vega was falling from the sky.

"We should have stayed up there!" Calloway screamed from the rear.

"Good plan," Woody shouted back. "That way we'd have farther to fall when we ran out of gas."

"Fuck you," came the terrified reply.

Woody couldn't help but grin. He'd prefer not to fly through heavy turbulence, but it sure beat having the Viet Cong firing 37mm shells at his A-4 Skyhawk. After years of flying everything from crop dusters to Navy jets, he'd learned to stay calm amidst the chaos. He wasn't worried about the turbulence. He was worried about finding dry land.

The Vega finally dropped below the cloud layer at just under a thousand feet. Rain lashed across the windshield, keeping visibility to a minimum, and Woody searched the seas from the side windows in the hope of seeing a sign of land. Grand Cayman was only twenty-two miles long and as flat as a pancake. There was no danger of crashing into a mountainside, but plenty of chance they'd miss the island entirely.

The rain suddenly abated, and Woody spotted lights in the distance like an oasis in the desert. The setting sun was mostly obscured by the rain and cloud on their tail, dusk providing barely enough light to make out the land. Approaching from the northwest, he would bank around and land from the west, into the easterly wind. Without radio communication with the airport, the tower had no reason to warn any other traffic of his presence. But there again, who in their right mind would be flying in this muck?

He hoped Kingston Center in Jamaica became concerned when Woody went radio silent. If they did, they may have prepared all the airfields in range for the possibility of his unexpected arrival.

With daylight fading, the lights out the port window along the shoreline of Seven Mile Beach were Woody's best reference. A concentration of lights to the south had to be George Town, and to his great relief, two lines of runway lights sparkled from Owen

Roberts International Airport. Either they were expected, or someone else was. He needed to watch for another plane.

Woody made a wide banking turn to set up his approach, dropping to five hundred feet as he neared the island. Kingston Center had to be going berserk trying to hail the Vega. He had the plane's lights on and hoped the control tower at Owen Roberts spotted him. They'd figure out there was a problem and have emergency services on standby. Maybe they'd reach him before Calloway made sure he'd stay silent, but he held little confidence they'd see his meager lights through the rain. Woody cinched his shoulder straps tight.

Hitting a bird was bad luck. Hitting a flock was a disaster. In a split second, the propeller buckled, and the windshield shattered. Pieces of pelican hit Woody on the side of his face and slammed his head against the back of the cockpit. The deep drone of the radial engine roared through the broken glass, joined by a deafening rush of unhindered wind. The entire plane violently shook with the unbalanced remnants of the propeller trying to rip the engine apart.

Barely conscious, Woody reached to the dash and killed the engine, straining to focus on the gauges as they descended toward the water.

Could he make the airfield? He knew he couldn't, which meant crashing the plane into whatever lay in the flight path. Buildings. Homes. People.

No, he needed to ditch in the ocean.

Blinking to clear the water and blood from his eyes, Woody squinted to read the altimeter. Dropping quickly, they were already below a hundred feet and airspeed was down to 86 mph. They'd stall at 59 mph, at which point they'd drop like a stone. He needed to be as close to the water as possible when that happened. Woody nosed the Vega down and picked up airspeed, hurtling toward the Caribbean Sea.

He thought about warning Calloway to strap in but figured if the idiot wasn't smart enough to do that, then to hell with the man. He momentarily considered nosing the plane straight into the surf and ridding the world of a shitty human, but he desperately wanted to live.

For Margaret.

For the kids.

He had so much to live for. Woody pulled up the nose with thirty feet on the altimeter and held the Vega level, waiting for the wings to stall.

With fixed landing gear which would hit the water first, Woody expected the impact to be rough, but nothing could prepare him for the violence of the crash. Crushed into the belts, every last drop of air was forced from his lungs as the wheels touched and pivoted the plane nose first into the ocean. A wall of water surged through the broken windshield and the plane launched into a cartwheel when the starboard wingtip struck the waves. Metal was shredded, torn and ripped from the fuselage as water sprayed, and the thundering sound of the Vega being decimated blocked out all else. Then, in an instant, everything came to a stop.

Woody hung against his belts and tried to catch his breath. He was alive. He looked around and all he could see and hear was water pouring into the cockpit. *Shit, if I don't get out fast, I'll drown after surviving an impact I shouldn't have lived through.* The lever on his five-point harness didn't want to release, and he realized too late that he was hanging with all his body weight against it. The mass of the engine was pulling the Vega down nose first. The lever gave way, and Woody dropped, bashing against the dash, his fall only slightly broken by the water filling the plane. His watch on his left wrist caught awkwardly on something and he noticed his headset plunging into the blackness of the water-filled cockpit.

Woody turned and looked above him. He could make out gray sky. The entire tail section of the plane had broken away. He grabbed the life vest from behind the pilot seat and pulled the lever to collapse the seat back. As Woody clambered through the small doorway into what was left of the cabin, he felt seawater surge all around him as the fuselage disappeared under the waves, leaving him bobbing alone in the turbulent sea.

He donned the life vest and for the first time since the impact, wondered what had happened to Calloway. Spinning around in the warm water, Woody spotted lights on the shoreline. Darkness concealed everything else. Within minutes of hitting the water, all trace of the Vega and the accident seemed to have disappeared. He listened for a voice in the night but all he could hear was wind, waves, and rain.

Woody started swimming toward the shore. Swells carried him closer as he rose up and down with the scattered lights on the coast disappearing as he sunk into the troughs. He couldn't believe he'd survived the crash. Again and again, he muttered his thanks to God for sparing his life.

He would see his family again.

Woody ran a hand over his left wrist. The watch was gone. He said another prayer, this time to his late father, hoping he'd forgive his son for losing the precious gift.

"How many more o' you gonna walk out da water?" came an island-accented voice that startled Woody.

He reached for the bottom with his feet and realized he could stand. Squinting, he saw the faint outline of a figure on the limestone rocks, known as ironshore. An orange glow from the man's cigarette partially illuminated his face. He was an older, dark-skinned local.

"I think I'm the last one, sir," Woody replied. Apparently, Calloway had survived the crash too. "Did you see the other guy?"

"He told me I didn't, but I s'pose I did," the man said.

Woody heard him set something down on the rocks before offering the pilot a helping hand from the water. He could see him more clearly up close. The man was a small-framed fella with a face wrinkled from decades in the sun. He guessed he was middle-aged but looked older. Woody was worried he'd pull the man into the water, rather than the other way around, but he accepted the man's help to be polite. The pilot clambered up the rocks as best he could, and sat down next to the stranger, exhausted. He noticed a fishing pole laid on the rocks next to the man.

"What did you crash out dere?" the man asked. "Make some awful noise."

"A really nice old airplane," Woody replied, taking a minute to catch his breath.

"Airport over dere," he said, pointing a thumb over his shoulder. "You come up a bit short, mister."

Woody managed a chuckle. "Yeah, thanks, I noticed. I had some trouble with a bird or six."

"Pelicans, I'd say," the man muttered. "Good riddance if yer ask me."

Woody thought using antique planes to take out pesky birds wasn't an efficient method and guessed the Australian owner would agree.

"Which way did the other man go?" Woody asked.

"He your friend?"

"He had a gun on me before we crashed, then left me to die in the wreckage afterwards," Woody explained. "So, no. He's not on my Christmas card list."

"Hmm," the man mumbled. "He said I shouldn't see where he gone."

Woody grinned and watched the glow of the man's cigarette brighten as he took another pull. "I wouldn't worry about him. If I find him, he won't be threatening anyone again. I plan on handing him over to the police."

"In dat case, he went up da shore right dere," the man replied, pointing over his shoulder again. "Carried some box wit him too. Reckon I'd have left dat behind if I just fell outta da sky."

That damn case. What could possibly be in that thing?

"You're bleeding," the man noticed.

"I believe I am," Woody replied, dabbing a finger to the sticky mess on his forehead.

"Guess we best get you fixed up den," the man offered, rising up surprisingly spritely.

"I'm sorry to interrupt your fishing," Woody replied, struggling to his feet. He was pleased to feel his Navy dog tag swing from his boot lace. His lucky charm had worked again.

The man held up a string with two small fish dangling from the line. "Got me a couple," he said. "Besides, dis for da wife's bruddah, 'cos he too lazy to catch for his self. Dis all he deserve."

"Where do you live, sir?" Woody asked.

"Dat shack down a ways. Wit der light on."

"Tell you what, fella. My money's a bit damp," he replied, pulling his soggy wallet from his pocket, "but I'd be mighty grateful if you'd share some water and maybe a bite to eat. I reckon there's not much to be done until daylight. Then I'll see about finding Calloway."

"Dat da udder man's name? Calloway?"

"So he said."

The man nodded and looked up at the bedraggled figure before him. "Will you tell the missus I was busy fishin' when you showed up?"

"Yes, sir, I'd be glad to," Woody replied.

"And I quit to help you?"

"That'll be the truth, and the story I'll tell," Woody assured the man.

"All right den."

The pilot extended a hand. "Woody Rains."

The man shook. "Arlo. Arlo Bodden."

1

PRESENT DAY

The building was a two-level stucco, typical of the Caribbean islands. Clean, tidy, with a crushed limestone parking lot full of vehicles. Unremarkable, except for the ornate pub sign hanging over the door. It was shortly after sunset when I pushed the door open to the cool blast of air-conditioning. Once inside, the Fox and Hare was a trip across the Atlantic to an old pub that wouldn't be out of place in the Cotswold countryside. Dark wood paneling, a large oak bar, darts, and warm beer on tap, alongside chilled island favorites. Even a picture of the Queen graced the wall behind the bar.

I scanned the busy room for a person I'd never met. When I'd searched for dive operations in the Cayman Islands, Mermaid Divers and AJ Bailey's name appeared in several articles. A long-lost U-boat discovery. Recovering the ancient Cross of Potosi. This guy seemed like a real Indiana Jones kinda dude. Except it turned out he was a she. A pretty good-looking young woman at that.

Pushing through the crowd toward the bar, a hand reached out and touched my arm.

"Eddie? Eddie Rains?" came an English female voice.

I turned and saw a smiling young lady with purple-streaked

blonde hair and a snug-fitting tank top revealing toned and artistically tattooed arms.

"You must be AJ," I responded.

"Yeah," she said and extended a hand.

I shook her firm grip and she nodded toward a long table with only a few open chairs.

"Come join us, the music's about to start."

I sat down beside her while she introduced me to her friends. An assortment of ages and nationalities smiled my way, and I greeted them all in turn. I knew I wouldn't remember any of their names. I had too much on my mind.

"Reg's wife Pearl is playing tonight. She's about to start," AJ explained.

A broad shouldered "old man of the sea" she'd introduced as Reg nodded my way, and I tried to look enthusiastic. In my fifty-three years, I'd deliberately avoided this island. I hadn't traveled all the way from North Carolina now to hear music. But I didn't want to appear rude. Pearl started playing and applause erupted throughout the pub. Twenty minutes later, the singer announced she was taking a break, and I had to admit I'd thoroughly enjoyed her set. Classic rock with a raspy powerhouse voice. Maybe I did need a few minutes to relax.

We all stood and congratulated Pearl as she joined the table, giving her husband a peck on the cheek. She was an attractive, shapely woman, I guessed to be in her fifties although she could easily pass as younger. She reminded me of Bette Midler in her heyday, until she spoke. Like Reg, she had a London accent.

I realized AJ was talking to me. "You've chartered the boat, so we can go anywhere you'd like. But you suggested in your emails that you had something specific in mind?"

It was still loud in the pub with excited chatter from the group at the table, and the busy crowd surrounding us. Not really the environment I'd envisioned in which to tell my story.

"Is there a quieter spot we can talk?"

"Not in here, really," she replied, standing. "But we can step outside."

I rose from my chair and noticed AJ made eye contact with a dark-skinned young man across the table. I tried to recall his name and failed. He took his arm from around his girlfriend and followed us through the crowd toward the door. I assumed he was coming along for protection as she was about to walk outside with effectively a stranger. Personally, I would have invited Reg along. He was probably sixty-something, but I wouldn't want to cross him. I'm six feet tall and in decent shape, yet I found him slightly intimidating.

"Thomas and I run Mermaid Divers together," AJ explained as the door closed behind us. "We'll probably alternate dives with you as one of us has to stay on the boat. He should hear the plan too."

I was wrong. The young woman was either sure she could handle herself, or trusting of me, which I hoped was the case. We sat on a bench, and I realized she'd been happy to let me think the two of them owned the dive operation. I knew it was AJ's company. Her inclusion of her employee spoke volumes.

I'd been practicing my speech for two weeks, ever since I'd booked this trip. There was so much to say, but I hoped I'd whittled it down to the necessary facts. My roller coaster of emotions weren't important. At least not to the two people sitting next to me.

I took a deep breath and began. "In 1976, my father died in a plane crash, here on Grand Cayman," I said, and a lump immediately formed in my throat.

Being without my father since I was eight years old, you'd think I could talk about him without getting upset. For many years I did. But hope will play tricks on your emotions. They were both looking at me with sympathetic eyes, so I pushed on.

"Four weeks ago, my mother, Margaret, passed away."

I'd become accustomed to pausing after those words, giving people time to offer their condolences, prayers, and thoughts. It was awkward for both sides, but common courtesy demanded the exchange. AJ looked me square in the eyes when she told me how sorry she was. I liked this young woman. She was probably a few years older than my own daughter, Molly, but their forthright honesty was similar.

"My sister and I had the unenviable task of going through our mother's possessions. Mom had been fighting cancer for almost a year, so she'd quietly made it a little easier by thinning down the old junk. But still, it took some time."

I reached into my pocket and pulled out a piece of paper, unfolding it and handing the photocopy to AJ. "This was amongst her personal effects."

She took the copy of the letter from me and began reading out loud.

My darling Margaret,

I hope to hold you in my arms before this letter reaches you, but in the event I'm delayed, I wanted you to know I'm safe.

I had to ditch the Vega. Just my luck, a bird strike on approach into Grand Cayman. I am devastated. A wonderful piece of history is ruined.

The good news is that I am fine, do not fret my love.

A man accompanied me on the flight. I must find him before returning home. There is so much more to tell, but it can wait until we're together again.

Hug our beautiful children for me. I miss you all so much.

As always, my Love is Timeless,
Woody

We sat in silence for a few moments while they both absorbed the words that had turned my world on its head.

"You said your father died in the plane crash," AJ finally said.

"That's what I've always been told," I replied. "The crash is on record. One fatality. No body ever recovered."

"Maybe he took off and crashed again," Thomas said, sounding skeptical.

"The letter was postmarked a day later," I pointed out. "From Little Cayman."

We all fell silent again, the humid night air making my shirt cling to my body. Or maybe the slim chance that my father was still alive was making me perspire. I knew that made no sense. He loved us and would have found a way back. If he could.

I reached into the chest pocket of my shirt and took out an old black and white photograph, handing it to AJ. "That's my father. My mother took this the day he left. We lived in Florida when I was a kid. That palm tree behind him was in our front yard."

AJ studied the picture and held it so Thomas could also see. "Handsome fella, your dad."

Thomas glanced back and forth between me and the photograph. "You look like your pap."

AJ gave me back the picture. "Was this letter the only contact?" AJ asked. "Any other correspondence or paperwork from that time?"

"That's it," I replied. "We searched, believe me."

"Did your mother not show dis letter to da authorities?" Thomas asked.

A legit question that only the person we'd just buried could answer. One of the few benefits of a prolonged illness is the time to share the important words with each other. I thought we'd said it all. One letter, at the bottom of a shoebox, told me there was much more left unsaid. She'd taken a secret to her grave, and now, I had so many questions.

"We have no way of knowing," I answered. "If there was an investigation, I found no sign of it on the Internet. I plan to visit the police during my stay and see if they have records from that time."

"I can put you in touch with a detective," AJ volunteered. "He's a friend."

"I don't mean to sound rude, you chartering da boat and all, but why are you here if da last contact was from Little Cayman?" Thomas asked.

Another good question, and one I'd fought over in my mind. "I want to find the wreckage of the plane," was my simple reply. "All I have directing me to Little Cayman is a postmark from 1976. The trail, if there is one, starts right here. If we find the plane, maybe we can find some kind of clue."

AJ shook her head, "You know that's the long shot of all long shots, right? It's most likely too deep to dive even if we could locate it. How big was this plane?"

She was being realistic rather than negative; our chances were slim at best. I took another piece of paper from my pocket with a picture of the Lockheed Vega.

"Cool plane," AJ commented.

"He made it to shore, so there's a chance he ditched over the reef," I said optimistically.

"These waters have been dived a lot," she replied. "Every inch of the island has been searched at some point. North of the flight path is a popular area with a dive resort. South of Sunset House is the fuel terminal where the tankers deliver petrol and diesel. That's not dived much now, but it was when they were installing the terminal. It would be amazing to think a plane had spent forty-six years unnoticed. It's far more likely the wreckage either sunk in the deep water or was dragged down there in a storm. Our little island is actually the peak of a mountain just poking out of the ocean. All around the island the seafloor slopes to about a hundred feet, then plummets to thousands."

"I'm aware. But I have to try," I said, knowing I sounded like a desperate man. Which I was.

"Did dey dive for it at da time?" Thomas asked.

I shrugged my shoulders. "I read a news article that said they did after the storm let up, several days later. A lot of the wreckage floated to the shore apparently. The divers found a wing section and the tail which they pulled out of the water. But no fuselage."

"Or bodies," Thomas pointed out.

I nodded, "Correct."

AJ smiled, "You have us chartered for two days. As long as we stay safe, and don't do anything illegal, it's your call where we dive. We've performed search dives before, so we know how to cover a large area using a grid system. Do you mind if we bring another diver along? It'll be more efficient."

"I don't mind at all," I replied, "but I would appreciate discretion. I just found out from my wife, my sister already told a friend with a local paper back home, and they ran an article. People love this nostalgic stuff. I'd prefer to keep it quiet. For now, at least."

"You met Nora at our table," AJ reminded me, "the blonde Norwegian. She's a constable with the local police."

I recalled a tall, slender young woman with a stern expression. She didn't look like any cop I'd ever seen.

"Don't worry," AJ assured me, "Nora hates the press."

I nodded. More eyes would make the search go faster and farther. I'd been torn about bringing my wife along. We were both experienced scuba divers, but someone needed to keep an eye on our restaurant.

"We'll leave our dock in West Bay at 7:30 a.m.," AJ added, rising from the bench.

"Thank you both," I replied.

Thomas jumped up enthusiastically and gave me a broad smile, "Let's find us an aeroplane."

2

I arrived at the dock fifteen minutes before I needed to. I'd woken early, had breakfast the moment the restaurant in the hotel opened, and killed the next hour fussing with my dive gear. All while constantly telling myself we were likely to find a beautiful reef full of colorful fish, and not much else. It didn't matter. The chance at a connection to my father was too much for my heart to resist. My brain and good sense couldn't keep the idea at bay.

AJ and Thomas were earlier than I was. Their dive boat, *Hazel's Odyssey*, a thirty-six-foot Newton, was tied alongside the wooden jetty where they stood chatting with Reg. He had two boats tied on the other side, with his divemasters and captains loading gear. Once Thomas saw me, he quickly took my bag, and loaded it aboard.

"Good morning," I greeted them.

"Morning," AJ replied brightly. "If you're all set, we'll go take a butcher's."

I assumed a butcher had nothing to do with our morning and this was some British term for searching, so I replied in the positive, hoping I wasn't mistaken, and we were about to set sail with a man wielding a meat cleaver.

"Morning, Reg," I said to the big man, who was eyeing me carefully. I couldn't tell if he was suspicious, sympathetic, or just ornery. I wondered if AJ had shared our mission with him.

"Mornin'," he replied and offered his hand.

We shook. His big paw swamping my hand, and I wear size large gloves.

"Wind is down. Should be nice where you're heading," he added in a deep, gruff tone. "She'll steer you right."

He nodded toward AJ who was climbing the ladder to the flybridge.

"Thanks. I'm sure she will," I replied, and stepped aboard.

I still didn't know whether Reg knew what we were up to or not, but I didn't mind if he did. He seemed like a man we'd be lucky to have on our side.

Thomas had my gear already strapped to a Nitrox tank, fins and bag stowed under the bench, and was casting off the stern line. Reg released the bow line, and we were idling away while I was still getting my bearings. These guys clearly did this every day.

Thomas gave me the boat safety briefing and then asked how much weight I needed.

"I'm diving in an old 3mm shortie, so eight pounds should be fine."

I'd dived all over the Caribbean for many years and had several hundred dives in my logbook. Still, I felt a tightness in my stomach and couldn't tell whether it was nerves or anticipation. I dropped the weights Thomas brought me into the pouches of my BCD. The buoyancy control device was the vest divers used. The tank mounted to it, and an air bladder was used to maintain neutral buoyancy at the varying depths.

Thomas put an oxygen analyzer on my tank and cracked the valve slightly open. Gas hissed slowly into the handheld unit and the number on the screen rose from 21% to 32%. I nodded when the number stabilized, and Thomas closed the valve. We repeated the exercise for three more tanks in a row. They all read the same. Putting the analyzer away, he filled out a sheet to record all the data from the tanks and had me sign, acknowledging I knew the oxygen percentage in my tanks.

The human body can only dissipate and get rid of nitrogen at a certain rate. Breathing from compressed air, equalized to the increased surrounding pressure at depth underwater, meant large quantities of nitrogen had to be dealt with. By diving with a higher oxygen content, we had less nitrogen to worry about, allowing us to stay at depth longer before our tissues became saturated. Everything became a lot more complicated at that point, requiring decompression stops before surfacing. Going into "deco" was a recreational diving no-no.

AJ took the boat out of gear, and I looked up to see what was going on. We were a few hundred yards from shore, and I knew it was at least thirty minutes south to our dive site. Thomas swung the aluminum ladder down at the stern and to my surprise, a woman in a one-piece swimsuit holding a mask and snorkel climbed aboard.

"Hey," Nora grunted as she walked by me and grabbed a towel from the window shelf below the flybridge.

Thomas tied the ladder back up and AJ pulled away, accelerating toward the deeper water. I'd forgotten the Norwegian girl was joining us. Thomas must have seen the confused look on my face.

"She was freediving on da reef," he explained.

"How deep was it there?" I asked, looking back at the various shades of blue between the shoreline and where we'd picked her up.

Thomas shrugged his shoulders. "Sixty feet or so."

Nora slipped a weight belt holding a single one-pound piece of lead from her slender waist and began drying her long blonde hair. With her tall, lean figure, she looked more like a fashion model than a freediving policewoman. She noticed me looking her way and her piercing blue eyes stared back. I felt like she was giving me a Vulcan mind-meld from across the deck. *Damn, she thinks I'm an old pervert.*

"How long can you stay down?" I quickly asked, hoping to let her know my curiosity was of an innocent nature.

"Two or three minutes," she replied flatly, as though swimming around, sixty feet underwater on a single breath, for the time it takes to boil an egg, was normal.

"She can hold da breath for more like seven minutes in shallow water," Thomas said quietly to me. "Dese two are like da fish," he added, tipping his head toward Nora, and AJ above. "Don't hardly need no air."

I smiled and finished hooking up my regulator. I realized, although I was a competent diver with plenty of experience, I'd be the weak link in the chain. I was on the boat with three professionals who practically lived on and under the water. It was both intimidating and exciting. I wanted to be in the water for every second of the search, but they'd use less gas and be able to stay down longer than I would. Finding my father's plane was more important than being there when it was spotted. If it was spotted.

Two huge floating markers bobbed in the gentle swells ahead of us. AJ had called us all up to the flybridge where she produced a piece of paper.

"I printed this last night," she explained, showing us the satellite map. "This is the flight path, directly in line with the runway at Owen Roberts."

She pointed to the shore a quarter of a mile away, where large cylindrical storage tanks marred the view. "That's the Jackson Point Fuel Terminal and the buoys are where the tanker moors. There's a pipeline on the seafloor between the two." She tapped the map, "The flight path runs just past the far side of the farthest buoy."

"They must regularly inspect the pipeline and moorings, surely?" I asked.

"Exactly," AJ agreed. "And north of us is Sunset House Dive

Resort, where divers are in the water all the time. No way anything resembling a plane, or a part of a plane has been missed there."

"So, we should start on the south side of the moorings?" I probed.

"Yes, but over there," she pointed past the storage tanks to where rugged rocks edged the coastline, with trees and shrubs farther back. "That's a public park and a small beach that's heavily used. It's a great shore dive and there's a Department of Environment dive buoy on the deeper reef."

"No way it's dere," Thomas commented.

I looked at the map in AJ's hand, then back at the ocean before us. "That doesn't leave a very big area."

"It doesn't," she replied. "Which is good and bad, I suppose."

We all looked out at the empty sea where I hoped to find a trace of my father from 1976. The lousy odds really hit home.

"We won't find anything standing up here," Nora said, and headed down the ladder to the deck.

The Cayman Islands are known for their amazing water clarity and healthy reefs. The reputation was well deserved. From the deep reef at sixty-five feet, sand flats stretched toward fingers of coral leading to the shore. To the west, the wall of the underwater mountain sloped quickly away to the depths below.

Sea fans and soft corals swayed in the subtle movement of the water, and fish flitted about all over the reef. Above us, silhouetted against the bright morning sun, was the boat and one of the huge mooring buoys. Its chains ran down to hefty anchors in the seabed, and in the distance, I could make out the regular shape of the pipeline.

We spread out across the reef, which extended around a hundred feet between the sand and the slope and ran as far as the eye could see in both directions. Starting south, we slowly finned along, and the search began. I reminded myself that anything left of the plane would have been down there for forty-six years. It wouldn't look like a manufactured part; it would have been claimed and consumed by the coral growth.

After twenty minutes, the excitement and nervous anticipation had dissipated, and the difficulty of the task set in. Everything looked the same. Gorgeous, blossoming with life, incredibly irregular, but all very similar. I found myself staring at small coral heads, seeing a uniform shape, before swimming to a new angle where it took on a completely different profile.

I'd see AJ and Nora stick their heads into crevices and small canyons, repositioning themselves with barely detectable movements of their fins. They effortlessly glided through the water and seemed just as comfortable upside down as right-side up. Above us, the boat tracked our bubbles, and after forty-five minutes, with my tank low on gas, I signaled to the other two. They returned an okay sign and AJ gave me the hand signal to ascend for our three-minute safety stop.

As I hung in the water column, allowing nitrogen to dissipate and my body's tiny air cavities time to equalize to the lower pressure, I couldn't help feeling disappointed. I hadn't expected to dive in and point to a Lockheed Vega fuselage on the seafloor, but I'd hoped for a more optimistic landscape. They were right, these waters had been dived so often, very little lay hidden anymore.

Back aboard the boat we all switched to new tanks before gathering under the shade of the flybridge. We'd stay up an hour before diving again, giving our bodies enough time to process the excess nitrogen. Thomas and AJ made sure I had water to drink and offered me fruit and snacks.

I accepted a water and stared out at the pristine ocean and tree-lined coastline to the south. The island was the quintessential picture of paradise. Perhaps it was the fact that I was here with a purpose, but it was almost a relief to finally be in Grand Cayman. Maybe the idea that he didn't die in the very waters we floated upon helped. Or perhaps it was a Band-Aid yet to be ripped off.

"You dive okay," Nora said, out of the blue.

My mouth opened, but between my wandering thoughts and the strange phrasing of her comment, I didn't know what to say.

AJ laughed. "Nora is very literal. That was a compliment," she explained with a grin. Nora just shrugged her shoulders.

"Next dive we'll move over the edge of the wall," AJ said, "You cover the last section on top, Nora and I will space ourselves apart down the slope."

"Will you be okay on gas that much deeper?" Before the words had left my lips, I realized it was a dumb question. I hadn't asked how much nitrox they had left in their tanks when we came up, but I knew it was more than I had. They both grinned.

"We'll be okay," AJ replied.

Her phone dinged and she looked at the text. She sat forward and scrolled over to something else.

"We've got some weather coming," she said, still looking at the screen. "We'll get the next dive in, but the afternoon doesn't look great."

Afternoon showers in the Caribbean were part of life in the tropics, so it had to be more than rain being forecast.

"A storm?" I asked.

AJ looked up, "Yeah. It was supposed to stay east of us but looks like we're getting the edge of it. Tomorrow afternoon should be all right again."

In my research I'd determined a storm had been around the island when my father had crashed in 1976. I guess it was only fitting I had a taste of the same weather.

3

Gray clouds were forming in the east and the wind had picked up by the time we splashed in for the second dive. We started by the tanker mooring again and with the three of us spread out we covered the rest of the reef at 60 feet. Far to my right, AJ was on the edge of the slope. On the return leg I'd be running over the same terrain she had covered, but I knew she was being cautious and keeping me at a shallower depth.

After twenty minutes we turned and moved farther west. AJ positioned me at the top of the slope as I predicted, and Nora a little deeper. I guessed AJ to be at 90 feet as we began the trek back along the sloping wall.

Protruding from the reef-covered slope were occasional coral heads, or bommies as they're called in some parts of the world. I watched the two women explore each one they encountered near their path. I tried to pay attention to my own strip of reef, but AJ had already scoured the section. The idea that the remnants of my father's plane were in deep water was taking hold, and I couldn't take my eyes from the dark blue below us.

I checked my tank pressure. It was down to 1,000 psi from the

3,000 we'd all started with. Above and just behind us, Thomas was diligently following our bubbles, tracking the disturbance they made as each cluster of exhaled gas broke the surface. We were almost back to where we'd started as I could see the first of the mooring buoys ahead. I wondered if there was any point coming out again tomorrow. Their logic had narrowed down the search area, which we'd covered already.

Talking about something being a long shot was intended to prepare you for failure. But it always left room for hope, especially when you wanted it so badly. And I badly wanted to find the wreckage of my father's Vega. For years after his disappearance, I occasionally sensed his presence. To this day, I spoke to him and shared my problems with him. But I'd been unable to touch the man in forty-six years and the thought of connecting with the plane promised the physical interaction I missed so much.

I reached the heavy lines securing the buoy and looked down the slope. I didn't see either of my dive buddies. Scanning the slope behind and below, I spotted Nora paused and staring into the deeper water. Far below her, AJ was finning below a large bommie that was covered in sea fans and soft corals. She was deep. AJ disappeared behind the outcrop, which appeared to be one large mass raised off the slope by five or six feet. Her bubbles streamed into view with each breath.

Nora looked up at me and held up a hand, signaling for me to stay put. When I looked back down, AJ was making her way back up the slope, angling toward my position. Nora joined her and AJ tapped the Shearwater Teric dive computer on her wrist while looking at me. It was a question. I replied by holding up eight fingers, indicating I had 800 psi left. She returned an okay sign and we ascended to fifteen feet for our safety stop. Once leveled off, she held up five fingers, indicating we'd spend five minutes at this depth, off-gassing as it's called. I was fine with the extra precaution, and I was sure she needed the time having been a lot deeper. I also made a mental note to order one of those fancy Teric dive computers when I got home.

As we climbed aboard *Hazel's Odyssey* and shed our gear into the tank racks, it was clear that the bad weather was fast approaching. The sun had disappeared behind a layer of hazy gray cloud, and the eastern sky looked dark and ominous. The wind was much stronger, shoved out in front of the tumultuous weather. As soon as we were out of our gear, AJ pulled the ladder up and tied it securely, then waved to Thomas on the flybridge. The diesels started, and without delay we were on our way back. With nothing to show for it beyond two very pleasant dives.

AJ beckoned Nora and me, and we gathered under the shelter of the flybridge as raindrops began to fall. She handed us both towels and we sat on the benches as the boat rode the growing swells.

"We found it," AJ said, and grinned at me.

I'm not sure what I looked like to the two women, but I know my mouth fell open and no words came out.

"It's below that outcrop?" Nora asked for me.

AJ shook her head. "No," she said, grinning even wider. "It is the coral head. Well, part of it anyway."

"You're sure it was a plane?" I asked, finally managing to speak.

AJ shrugged her shoulders, "Pretty sure. It's manmade and looks like the front of a fuselage. The back is open to the downslope. I looked inside and shone my light around. There's a rectangular opening to the cockpit. Unless I've got it backward and it's the tail."

I jumped up and grabbed my dry bag, digging out my phone.

"Did you go in?" Nora asked.

"I was going to, but a couple of lobster looked annoyed at me," AJ replied. "And the big arse green moray through the opening looked really pissed off."

I found the picture I was looking for on my phone and showed it to AJ. It was an old black and white photograph taken from the cabin of a Vega, looking forward toward the cockpit.

"That's it," AJ confirmed. "The door is quite narrow but extends from floor to ceiling. Oh, and I'm pretty sure it's upside down."

I spun my phone upside down but of course the device wanted to prove it was smarter than I was and pivoted the picture. I was about to start the perilous hunt through the settings to turn the feature off, but AJ held my hand still and tipped her head to look.

"Yup, it's upside down," she said confidently. "I can tell by the windows in the cabin, and I could see past the moray to the windshield."

"Was there any..." I started to say but stopped. How could I ask if my father's body was in the cockpit? The letter postmarked after the crash was evidence he couldn't be in there. Unless the letter was a fake. Had my mother kept it and not said anything because she knew it wasn't his handwriting? A knot formed in my stomach. My sister and I hadn't compared the letter to other documents to check the handwriting.

"I didn't see any signs of bodies," AJ said, apparently reading my mind.

"They'd have been carried away by the crabs and the sharks right after the accident," Nora said, and AJ thumped her on the arm.

I could have done without the visual, but she was correct. A shiver ran through me.

"How did they miss the wreckage when they searched?" Nora asked, undeterred.

It was another valid point. "Maybe they made a cursory look and with all the parts that washed up, determined the rest was gone," I suggested.

AJ grabbed her backpack from the window shelf and pulled out a pad of paper and a pen. She began drawing.

"The body of the plane is wedged between coral heads, and from what I could tell with a quick look, those two coral heads meet on the upside of the slope," she explained as she drew what looked like a fat upside-down *U*. "Unless the wreckage fell perfectly into the cradle formed by the coral heads, which I find unlikely, it had to have come from farther down the slope."

She drew a rough outline of the fuselage in the opening of the *U.*

"How could it ride up the slope?" I asked, "Surely gravity would take it down."

"A storm," they both answered together.

"We've probably had over a dozen hurricanes and tropical storms since the plane went down," AJ expanded. "If it was sitting down the slope, it could have been blown up the wall by the sea and happened to hit the perfect stopper."

"A storm can do that?" I asked. "That deep?"

"The Spiegel Grove is in 135 feet of water off the Florida Keys," AJ replied. "It's 510 feet long. It was sunk as an artificial reef but when they pulled the plug, it inverted as it went down. They managed to roll it on its side with air pumps and tugs, then three years later, Hurricane Dennis came along and rolled it perfectly upright."

"Damn, that's crazy," I said, shaking my head.

"The reef has grown all around what's left of the plane, so most likely it was the first big storm after the crash," AJ surmised. "From the top you can't tell what it is at all. The coral has formed a continuous roof. It was only when I saw the big opening from underneath, I knew it was the plane. There's no growth inside as no sunlight can reach it."

I sat back and tried to absorb the news. I'd spent most of my life avoiding the island where my father had died in a plane crash. With the discovery of one letter, I was now on that very island, and we'd found the remains of his plane. The Vega in which, according to his words, he didn't die. I had no idea where this trail would lead me, but I couldn't wait to call my wife Liz and tell her. My heart skipped a few beats. My next thought was to tell my mother. I'd found myself reaching for the phone to tell my mom so many things in the past few weeks. It was a gut punch every time.

"Thomas marked it on the GPS," AJ was saying, bringing me back to the moment.

"What are we looking for when we dive it again?" Nora asked, and they both turned to me.

She didn't seem to say much, but when she did, I'd noticed Nora was direct and invariably raising a good point. I hadn't thought beyond finding the wreckage.

"A note telling me what happened to my father would be handy," I replied with a smirk while I thought it over a little longer.

AJ laughed softly, but Nora kept looking at me without any change in expression. Both women were pretty, but AJ had an easy and comfortable manner about her which I'm sure made her a great dive instructor. Nora was stunning, and incredibly disarming. Not aloof or stuck up, but intense. I sensed she harbored some unresolved issues in her young mind. If I was heading into a fight, I think I'd take Reg and Nora in with me.

"If my mother's letter is real, then two men went down in that plane, and both survived," I said, piecing my thoughts together. "So, the wreckage isn't a grave, but I don't think we should strip anything out of it. In saying that, it would be nice to have something from the last plane he flew."

"If that was the last plane he flew," Nora said.

"Right," I mumbled, taken off guard by the young woman again. "I guess we'll just poke around and see what we find."

Nora nodded, seemingly appeased.

"Without disturbing the coral," AJ added as she stood up.

"Of course," I readily agreed.

AJ started toward the ladder.

"Why didn't you tell me down there?" I asked, curious rather than irritated. "You made me wait until we were back on the boat. You could have given me a signal that you'd found it. You two have signs for everything."

She paused, looking back at me with a grin. "What would you have done?"

I laughed. I would have gone straight down there, and we all knew it. Which would have been foolhardy with 800 psi in my tank. She'd told me her priority was keeping us safe. Her phone rang before I could summon a sensible answer without lying.

"Emily!" she said, cupping her hand around the phone to shield some of the noise. "How's Little Cayman?"

AJ winked at Nora, so I figured it was someone they both knew.

"You're here? Really? Bloody right we're meeting up," AJ said enthusiastically, and Nora gave her a thumbs up. Finally, the Scandinavian looked pleased about something.

4

When AJ offered to pick me up from my hotel, I'd gladly accepted. My rental car was left-hand drive, but the Cayman Islands follow their UK parent and drive on the left. It was very confusing, and I didn't trust myself driving at night. In the rain. The weather had closed in shortly after we'd made it back to the dock and had been raining ever since. By the time we pulled into a parking lot in West Bay, the sun had set, the rain had lessened in intensity, and the wind had dropped.

On the way over, AJ had explained we were meeting a young couple who had worked all over the Caribbean, and recently settled on Little Cayman to run a dive operation. She'd warned me to be prepared for Emily but hadn't explained why. Nora had just grinned. It was kind of them to drag me along, so I didn't pry any further.

Before we'd made it out of the van, a young, shapely, blonde woman came running across the wet parking lot and assaulted AJ with an enthusiastic hug.

"Isn't this brilliant!" she shouted, and AJ just laughed. "We had to pick up all this stuff for the dive place, yeah? So Booney says, let's take the boat. Of course, we pick a weekend with a bloody great big rainstorm, so we..." She broke off mid-sentence and lurched toward Nora who surprised me by allowing the exuberant young lady to embrace her. "Nora, my favorite Viking!"

Emily had a thicker English accent than AJ, and the energy of all the Spice Girls combined. She released Nora and looked at me. "Who do we have here then?" Before I could answer, my hand was being vigorously shaken.

"This is Eddie Rains," AJ said. "Eddie's chartered the boat for a few days. Eddie, this is the one and only Emily Durand."

Emily looped her arm around mine and led me across the parking lot toward an outdoor bar below a palapa. The sign read Macabuca. A tall, lean man with a grin on his face watched us approach.

"This is Booney," Emily announced as we walked up a few steps to the bar. "Otherwise known as Beanpole."

He extended a hand to me.

"Hi, I'm Boone. It's nice to meet you," he said in a calm voice with an American accent. He had a slight southern twang, mixed with another influence I couldn't pinpoint.

"Eddie Rains," I replied. "The pleasure's mine."

Boone hugged AJ and Nora in a far more sedate fashion, while Emily buzzed around the group asking a series of questions without waiting for answers. We finally took cover from more rain sprinkles under the palapa, and I found myself seated between AJ and Emily. The quiet pair sat on either end of us.

We ordered drinks and were handed menus that lay untouched as the questions continued. I wondered how Emily managed to breathe when she talked so fast, and half expected her to fall off her barstool at some point from oxygen deprivation. When she finally slowed up, Boone leaned over.

"Are you here fun diving for a few days, Eddie?"

I glanced at AJ who ever so slightly shrugged her shoulders. I took that to mean she would keep to whatever story I told. Maybe it was the excitement of the day, or perhaps the fact that AJ seemed relaxed around her friends, but I rolled with the truth.

"AJ's helping me find a wreck I've been looking for. I'm trying to keep it on the down low, so I'd appreciate you being discreet."

Emily practically vibrated with excitement, blurting, "Bloody brilliant!" before abruptly dialing down her vocal volume. "I love a juicy secret. Mum's the word," she whispered, putting a finger to her lips.

"Any luck?" Boone asked quietly.

I nodded and couldn't hold back a grin. "Yeah. Thanks to these two," I said, nodding toward AJ and Nora.

"AJ's ace at finding long-lost wrecks," Emily blurted. "If you've misplaced a U-boat, she'll find where you parked it."

She laughed at her own humor and coaxed a chuckle from AJ. I'd read about her submarine discovery on a pinnacle off the coast of Grand Cayman. It was impressive.

"This isn't as glamorous as a World War Two U-boat," I confessed. "But the plane my father flew is important to me."

My words made me think about my family, and specifically my sister. Why she'd decided to share a copy of my father's letter with a local newspaper, I didn't know. But they'd run the story of our family trying to "Discover the fate of their missing father."

Before I'd left, we'd discussed keeping it all quiet, and from my point of view I planned to continue doing that. My sister hadn't stuck to the plan, and I was too pissed off to call her and find out why. She was really close with our mom and was struggling with her passing. I could only assume she thought it would help her grief in some way. I couldn't blame her for that.

I realized AJ had been answering Emily's latest barrage of questions while I was lost in my thoughts. I was happy a distraction arrived.

"Sorry I'm late," came Thomas's voice from behind us. We all spun around. He was dripping wet.

"I told you I could pick you up, you silly bugger," AJ said.

Thomas flashed his broad smile as he greeted Boone and Emily. "It's okay, Boss. But we should talk," he said, his smile disappearing as he looked back and forth between AJ and me.

"Everything all right?" AJ asked.

"Yes, yes, but I t'ink I found out somet'ing about da plane," he said, glancing at Boone and Emily.

I stood up. My joy at finding the Vega had been interspersed with concern over where to go next. We were heading to the police station in the morning, but I didn't hold out much hope we'd learn more. The chances of reports still being around from 1976 seemed slim. If Thomas had something new, I was all ears.

The rain had stopped, and I walked with Thomas to a table under a large umbrella. AJ followed and brought a towel from the bar so we could wipe the seats dry.

"What about them?" AJ whispered, nodding toward her friends at the bar.

"If you trust them, I trust them," I whispered back.

AJ waved them over, "Bring the menus with you."

We all sat at the round table. I realized Emily had been quiet since Thomas had arrived. She might be exuberant, but she clearly read the situation and knew when to tone things down. I looked at Thomas expectantly.

"I hope you don't mind," he started, looking a little nervous. "But I mentioned about da plane to my papa."

He paused, waiting for my reaction. I shrugged my shoulders and he continued.

"My family been on da island since, well, since anyone been here. So, I have family I haven't even met scattered all about da place. My papa say he remember hearing a tale from an uncle about a plane crashing into da sea, and da pilot walking outta da water."

I noticed everyone around the table leaned in a little closer, no one more than me.

"He t'ink dis uncle still alive and live out near Bodden Town."

"Can we go and see him?" I asked, trying to contain my excitement.

"Sure," Thomas replied. "But Pap says he's in his mid-nineties, so don't know how much he'll remember dese days. He says he a bit loopy last time he see da man."

"What's his name?" AJ asked.

"Arlo. Arlo Bodden," Thomas replied.

"They named a town after him?" Emily asked.

"Not him," Thomas replied with a grin. "But like I say, we Boddens been here more dan a minute."

I sat back and took a long, deep breath. This was further evidence my father survived the crash. I prayed this old man could tell us more. If my father walked out of the Caribbean Sea, where did he go? The one thing I knew for sure was that he didn't come home to his family. My mother never remarried. Was she waiting for him to return? I never recalled her even dating another man.

As a kid I didn't think anything of it, but in my twenties when Liz and I were dating and I began thinking about marriage, I realized how lonely my mother must be. I remember asking her one day, why she'd never found someone else. She'd said, "I have the only love I'll ever need, whether your father is here with us or not. Our love is timeless." We both cried at the time and held each other. When we found the letter and I saw those same words, I cried again.

I had no idea whether my mother spent all those years holding out hope her husband would return one day, or whether she knew he was gone. My sister and I were told he had died in the plane crash, so she didn't want us hanging on to a notion we'd see him again. But she was a devoted and loving mother; that may have been her way of saving us from years of disappointment.

"When are you diving again?" Emily asked.

"Tomorrow afternoon," AJ replied. "Let the seas settle down from this blow and we'll go out after lunch."

"What are you doing?" Nora asked.

"We have to load up the boat with all the cool stuff we bought," Emily replied. "We go back on Monday, yeah?"

Nora looked at me with her bottomless blue eyes. I sensed her grin more than saw her expression change.

"You're welcome to dive with us," I said.

I guessed that was what Nora had been suggesting, and by her actual smile now, I must have been right. Her face lit up when something made her happy. I wondered again what the young woman had endured that kept her joy so deeply suppressed and hidden.

Emily bounced in her seat.

"I can't, I'm afraid," Boone replied. "I managed to get the bilge pump I needed today. I have to install it and finish loading."

Emily leaned over and rested her head against him, looking at Boone with puppy dog eyes.

"But apparently I can handle that myself, 'cause Em is going with you."

She hugged and kissed him, "You're the best, Booney."

As the fuss died down, I looked over at Thomas. "Thank you," I said. "Whether we learn something new or not, I appreciate your effort." I looked around the table. "That goes for all of you. This is a very personal trip for me. It means a lot that you'd go to such great efforts to help me."

"I hope you find some answers," AJ said softly.

"I feel more optimistic than ever," I replied, telling the truth.

AJ smiled. "Good. In the morning we'll drop by the police station, and then we'll go and find Mr. Arlo Bodden."

5

With so much on my mind, sleep evaded me. I'd tossed and turned all night and waited on the restaurant to open again. The weather had moved on and the dawn arrived to clear blue skies. AJ and Nora picked me up at 8:00 a.m. and we headed along the road behind Seven Mile Beach toward George Town. On our right, elegant hotels and condominiums lined the famous pale yellow sand beach. I could see why the island had such a wonderful reputation. My reservations about the place were slowly evaporating and I wished Liz had joined me after all.

We reached the waterfront in the narrow and busy downtown. Turning left, we weaved through a series of small back streets and arrived outside a straw-colored three-level building. We walked across the parking lot with the heat reflecting off the blacktop. The overnight rain had ramped up the humidity. It was high eighties but felt like a hundred and something.

Several officers nodded and smiled at Nora as we passed them on the way to the entrance. One man held the door for us to enter. Everyone seemed to know her. Last night, I'd googled her name, Nora Sommer, and a mass of hits came back. I'd remembered seeing the case of an American girl kidnapped on the island by this guy from Florida. The kidnapper's wife had been murdered to keep her quiet about toxic waste dumping. The guy broadcast the whole thing live across the Web. It went insanely viral. Nora had been the constable who'd saved the girl.

Nora had texted someone she said would help us, and we waited for a few minutes in the lobby. A tall, slim, Caymanian man in his fifties came down the stairwell and joined us.

"Morning Nora, AJ," he said in a polite voice, before extending a hand to me. "Detective Roy Whittaker."

"Good morning, Detective," I replied as we shook hands. "Eddie Rains. Thanks for meeting us on a Sunday morning."

"I needed to be here for a few hours anyway," he replied, leading us to a small conference room. "How can I help you?"

"It's a case from 1976," Nora explained as we all took a seat. "A plane crash off the Jackson Point Fuel Terminal. Mr. Rains's father was the pilot."

"I see, and what information are you looking for exactly?" the detective asked.

"Anything, really," I replied, "I know so little about what happened. Officially, my father died in the crash, but I have new evidence that suggests this wasn't the case. It would be helpful to see witness statements, an inventory of the wreckage recovered, literally anything."

"Excuse me for a few minutes," the detective said. "Let me see what I can find."

He left the room and once again I waited. This whole trip seemed to be one anticipation-filled test of my patience after another.

"He seems like a nice guy," I said, to fill the silence.

AJ nodded. "He is. We dive for the police when needed, so Reg and I have known him for a while."

I got the impression Nora preferred silence, so I didn't say anything more. I was dying to ask her about the kidnapping case, but I managed to restrain myself. Fortunately, Whittaker didn't take long. He returned with a laptop and placed it on the conference table.

"These days, our hard copy files are kept for five years after the case is closed, and then destroyed. But it's all scanned and digitally archived before disposal. Our system was put in place back in 2012, and the old files from before that time were scanned into the system. It was a big project that took a long time to complete."

The detective paused while he hit a few keys then looked up at me. "What was your father's name, Mr. Rains?"

"Woody Rains," I replied. "Forest Rains if he used his given name, which he never did. I bet his driver's license said Woody."

Whittaker entered the information and I waited. I really wanted to get up and pace around the room, peeking over his shoulder at the screen, but I resisted that as well.

"Here it is," he said. "Not much in the file I'm afraid."

He stared at the screen and appeared to be reading the report. This was killing me.

"No witnesses. It was just after sunset so that's not surprising. Wreckage on the shore and it mentions several photographs to catalog the parts." He clicked through the file. "Hmm, not much help. Looks like the photos had faded badly before they were scanned. It could be wreckage, or pictures of the moon, it's hard to tell."

That was disappointing but not the end of the world. We knew where the fuselage was. The no witness part was interesting. If this fellow, Arlo Bodden, did see something, he didn't come forward at the time.

Whittaker continued, "The area was dived, but it wasn't for three days after the incident. Doesn't say why but could have been weather related or the availability of divers. It mentions the cabin section was not recovered, neither was your father's body. He was assumed lost. He was listed as the only person aboard and there's correspondence in here with an airfield in Florida where he filed his flight plan."

"Did the flight plan cover his next leg?" I asked. "Was he flying directly from here to Panama?"

The detective studied the screen. "Doesn't mention Panama."

I nodded. It was a curiosity more than an important detail.

"But his flight plan wasn't for Grand Cayman either."

"What?" I was confused. The letter talked about Grand Cayman as though it were the destination, and I didn't recall my mother ever saying anything different.

"Flight plan filed was for Mexico," Whittaker explained. "Cancun on the Yucatán peninsula."

"So why did he fly here?" I asked.

"Doesn't say. And as no useful wreckage was found, and your father wasn't around to explain, they may have assumed mechanical trouble." The detective furrowed his brow as he read more on the screen to himself. "Here's something that may be of interest, although they ruled it out at the time," he said, glancing my way. "A witness came forth a week after the accident. He claimed he saw a man in the water, moments after the impact, near the floating wreckage. He told them he was on a boat, and watched the pilot disappear below the surface."

"Who was this?" I blurted.

"He gave his name as David Smith," the detective replied.

Nora scoffed and we all turned her way. "That's bullshit, right? No way that's his real name."

"People are called that, you know," AJ retorted with a slight grin. "It's used as a bluff because it's the most common name. Which means lots of people have that name."

"He could provide no ID at the time and didn't come back as arranged to complete a formal statement," Whittaker said with a pained expression. "He wasn't at the hotel he claimed to be. It was written up as an unreliable witness."

Nora stared blankly at AJ.

"Hush, Viking. You got lucky on that one," AJ said with a smirk.

"And that's it, I'm afraid, Mr. Rains," the detective concluded.

"Not much help. I'm sorry. The case was closed several weeks later when there was no trace of a survivor."

"Any description of the Smith guy?" Nora asked.

Whittaker shook his head. "Sorry."

We thanked the detective for his time and made our way back to the van. I'd been prepared for the file to be long gone, so just having the original report was more than I'd expected. Still, we were no closer to any answers, or a lead to move forward with.

"How do we track down a bloke using a false name from 1976?" AJ asked, echoing the question in my own mind.

"You don't," Nora replied as we stepped into the sweltering hot van. "But the better question is why did someone lie about seeing your father drown?"

The back door to the van opened, taking me by surprise.

"Didn't mean to startle you, Mr. Rains."

It was Thomas, loading his bicycle into the back.

AJ drove us out of town and along a road behind the fuel terminal we'd seen from the water. I guessed it had been there longer than the condos and homes which now stretched from either side of the large cylindrical tanks. We alternated between bouts of silent contemplation and animated discussion. It was all conjecture. We had nothing solid to base a theory on and a growing number of unanswered questions.

Thomas directed AJ away from the water, down a narrow road into the outskirts of the small, coastal town known as Bodden Town. Another left turn, and we were on an unpaved lane with a handful of tiny old dwellings nestled in the low trees and shrubs.

"Da yellow one over dere," Thomas said, pointing to a building smaller than most double garages back home.

AJ parked in the empty gravel driveway, and I stared at the house. Built on a concrete pad raised a foot or so above the grade, it had a front door and one window facing the street. The side I could see had another window. The place was old, a little shabby, but clean and tidy.

We let Thomas lead us to the front door, where he knocked. "Mr. Bodden, sir?" he called out.

I heard sounds of movement inside the home before the door opened. The dim interior was in stark contrast to the bright sunlight where we stood, and I couldn't see who had answered the door. I was expecting a younger relative or caregiver of some sort. The old man was reportedly well into his nineties. As my eyes adjusted, I realized I couldn't see anyone, as no one was standing there.

"Wait here a minute," Thomas said, and stepped inside.

I heard a brief exchange in a language I didn't recognize before Thomas reappeared and beckoned us inside. Well, it wasn't Doctor Who's Tardis. The interior was just as tiny as the exterior suggested, perhaps more so with light only coming from two windows. The third had a derelict looking air conditioner wedged in the lower half. The device rattled and whirred, and while the room wasn't cool by any means, it was less humid inside.

A dark-skinned old man sat in an equally ancient recliner and stared up at us. His face was heavily wrinkled and what hair he had was white-gray and wispy. He blurted something at me in the foreign language and waved a walking stick in my direction. Thomas quickly closed the front door and the room got darker still. The old man then waved his stick toward a small threadbare sofa and mumbled something else.

"Best take a seat," Thomas translated.

AJ and Nora sat down, and I squeezed my frame beside them. The room smelled slightly musty. Like an old storage barn, but everything appeared clean and put in its place.

"Mr. Bodden, sir," Thomas began, "Dis ere is my boss AJ, Miss Nora, and Mr. Rains. He's ere from America, hoping to find out some information. My Pap tells me you saw a plane crash off da coast back in da seventies, sir," Thomas continued. "Do you recall anyt'ing about dat?"

Arlo Bodden looked at Thomas with a furrowed brow. I wondered if he understood a word that had just been said and figured Thomas would switch back to whatever native tongue they'd been speaking. The old man turned toward me and waved his stick in my direction.

"Dat da flyin' man?"

"Dat's his son, sir," Thomas replied.

"He stayed wit me and Etta."

"Da pilot stayed wit you?" Thomas asked.

"Did you see the plane crash, sir?" I couldn't hold back from asking.

"Nope," Arlo replied, shaking his head.

"You didn't see the plane go down?" I asked, confused. Maybe he was senile and just muttering whatever came into his head.

"Nope," he repeated.

"But you said the pilot stayed here?" I persisted.

"Nope. Didn't," he said, and shook his head again.

I sat back on the sofa. The highs and lows of the past few weeks were wearing me down. Mainly the lows, as they seemed to be more prominent. Arlo stared at me again.

"He look same. How dat?" the old man said with another wave of his stick.

I gave Thomas a questioning look.

"I said you look like your father, Mr. Rains," Thomas said with a grin.

"I get that from people who knew him," I replied. Personally, I thought my father was far better looking than me, but most of the pictures I had of him were in Navy uniform or at the controls of a plane. He looked heroic.

"Dis is da man's son, Mr. Bodden," Thomas explained again but Arlo just frowned some more and grunted.

I took the photograph of my father from my pocket to show the old man, but Thomas subtly held up a hand, so tucked it away again. If Arlo thought I was the same man he met forty-six years ago, Thomas must have decided we were wasting our time. I couldn't argue the point.

"How long you bin in dis place?" Thomas asked.

He seemed to have moved on to polite conversation, probably to fill a little time before we left. Another hope dashed by a dead end. My mind shifted to my next move. We'd dive the wreckage and then what? I knew there was nothing in the fuselage after forty-six years to give us any clues, but I was excited to make the dive nonetheless. Maybe that was the end of the road. The newspaper my sister gave the story to would be disappointed. Sure, we found the plane, but we were no closer to finding out what befell our father.

"Forty year, suppose," Arlo replied. "Etta bin gone twenty."

"Pilot stay wit you in da old place? Wit you and Miss Etta, sir?" Thomas asked and I sat forward again.

"Did too," Arlo replied.

"But you didn't see da man's plane crash into da water, sir?"

Arlo shook his head, "It wah dark. Hear it plenty."

"Da plane crash out front your house?"

"Nope. Down a ways. I was fishin'. Etta had me catching dinner for her no-good bruddah."

"He was wit you, sir?" Thomas asked.

"Who?"

"Your bruddah-in-law."

The old man scoffed, "Dat fool don't help nuttin'. Dat why I gotta catch his dinner."

I desperately wanted to pepper the man with more questions, but Thomas was doing a much better job, so I stayed quiet. Thinking of Emily assaulting me with curiosity helped me keep my mouth shut. I also figured out they'd been speaking English all along, but with a heavy accent and local dialect. I could tell Thomas was trying to lessen his accent for my benefit.

"How long da pilot stay wit you and Miss Etta, sir?" Thomas asked.

Arlo shrugged his bony shoulders. "Just da night. He gone next day."

Thomas glanced at me and cracked a smile. I nodded back, encouraging him to continue.

"Do you recall where, sir? Where did da pilot go?"

The old man shook his head, "Etta fixed him up, and da man go."

"Can you remember anyt'ing else he say, sir?"

"Nope," Arlo replied.

Thomas paused and I could tell he was trying to think of more to ask, or a different way to phrase a question. This kind old man and his wife put my father up for a night. Between this news and the letter, I was sure he survived the crash. But where did he go?

"He say he go find da udder man," Arlo said, breaking the brief silence. "Da man wit da case."

"A second man stayed wit you?" Thomas asked.

"Nope. He walked out da water, before him," Arlo replied, waving his stick my way.

"What did this man look like?" Nora asked.

"He wet," Arlo said, looking at the blonde woman as though he hadn't noticed her before.

"He young? Old? White fellow?" Nora asked, staring right back. I sensed she was as eager as me to know more.

"He white," Arlo replied, "He tell me I don't see him, but I saw da man."

"Da pilot say who da man were?" Thomas asked, taking back over.

"Golf t'ing," he muttered.

I was sure we'd lost him to voices in his head, but Thomas gave him a moment.

Arlo's jaw moved like he was chewing on something as he thought. "Calloway! Dat's it. Say da name's Calloway, like da golf club. I only know da name 'cos I found one on da beach one time."

"He was in the crash with my father?" I asked excitedly. "They were friends?"

"Nope. He mad at da man. Say he had da gun at 'im."

"What?" we all blurted.

Arlo looked startled, "Say da man had a gun, want him fly to Little Cayman."

"But dey came here?" Thomas verified.

"Storm too bad, had to," Arlo replied.

"Did he shoot my father?" I asked, almost rising from the sofa.

"Not dat I know."

"But you said your wife fixed him up?" I was desperate for more; I couldn't hold the questions back.

"He banged up some, but Etta see him right."

"Did the other man do that?"

"Nope. I already say, Etta done fix him up," Arlo replied, looking at me as though I was an idiot. He had a point. I was getting worked up, but finally it felt like we were on the edge of finding out what happened.

"I meant the wounds he had. Did the other man assault my father?"

"Nope. Bird do dat. Damn t'ings." Arlo said. "And he crash da plane and all."

"That's why he crashed? He hit a bird?"

"Nope."

I was about to question the old man, but I was finally learning to wait a beat or two.

"Hit a bunch, he say."

"The Calloway guy left, and you didn't see him again?" Nora asked.

"Dat's right."

"What was in the case he had?" the constable continued. "Was it the pilot's?"

The Norwegian seemed more like a policewoman now, these were key questions.

Arlo shrugged his shoulders. "Don't know. Pilot didn't know either. He was wonderin' too."

We all took a deep breath. I tried to calm myself down. The accident report I'd found about the crash had been long on technical details explaining nothing, and short on conclusions. Without the fuselage and the engine, or a witness account, there were too many possibilities to form a definitive answer. Now we knew. It was a bird strike. And we did have a witness.

"The police report doesn't have a statement from you," I said, voicing my thought. "Did they take your statement?"

"Nope."

"Why didn't you say something to the police?"

"Dey didn't ask me."

6

We'd gleaned all we could from Arlo Bodden, and I thanked the man profusely before we left. He still seemed to think I was my father, with really good skin care, but at least we'd learned something. My father had survived the crash, spent the night with Arlo and his wife, then set off the next morning, chasing a stranger with a case of some sort. And a gun. Potentially heading to Little Cayman.

Emily met us at the dock in West Bay, and with delicious sandwiches in hand from a colorful shack called Heritage Kitchen, we were on the water once again. The seas weren't the flat calm of yesterday morning, but still only two-foot swells, and I couldn't wait to dive. Repeating that morning's conversations to Emily on the ride out was a good exercise for me. In the end, we still didn't know much, but the more I ran through the little we had, the more I convinced myself I had a trail to follow.

AJ left Thomas at the helm and came down to the deck as we approached the two large buoys.

"Okay, let's go over the dive plan," she said, and we sat on the benches under the flybridge to listen. "The wreck is at 120 feet, so we won't have a ton of bottom time. Watch your no-deco time carefully and let me know if your computer shows less than ten minutes. Let me know if you get below 1500 psi on tank pressure too. Either one won't mean we have to ascend immediately, but it'll give me an idea of the time we have left. It's a live boat so we'll all stay together and ascend together."

She was moving her eyes around the three of us, but I knew this was all for my benefit. They were professionals. I'd be the one bringing the group up, as I'd go through my tank first. But I appreciated her not singling me out.

"I'm going to penetrate the wreck, and I have a plan to access the cockpit. No one else try going in, okay?" This time she did look at me.

"I promise, I won't do anything squirrelly down there," I said with a smile.

Her priority was keeping the group safe, so I didn't mind her aiming that one my way.

"Nora will be helping me, so while we're doing that, Em will be in charge and staying with you, Eddie. Signal her if you need to."

Emily gave me an enthusiastic okay sign and a big grin. She was wearing the biggest pair of bright green sunglasses I'd ever seen. I couldn't help but smile in return.

"Okay, let's gear up and we'll splash one after the other, so be ready. When we get down there, if the current's too strong, I'll abort the dive. If that happens, make sure we all stay together. We don't want Thomas having to chase around the Caribbean Sea trying to find us." AJ wrapped up and looked at me, "Your dad's plane has been waiting for forty-six years, Eddie. Let's go take a look."

I could tell this was more than a charter for AJ. She'd included me in dinners, driven me all over the island, and clearly had an emotional stake in my father's story. They all did. Even Reg had shaken my hand back at the dock and wished me luck. I'd chosen Mermaid Divers from the Internet—from reviews, articles, and a gut feeling. I hadn't expected to form a close bond with these people. I nodded, as I wasn't sure I could speak.

We lined up at the swim step, steadying ourselves with a hand on the tank racks. I suddenly realized I had nothing to record this incredible occasion with.

"I don't have a camera!" I shouted.

AJ pointed to Emily. Emily patted her BCD pocket and grinned behind her lime-green mask, "I've got AJ's GoPro."

One by one we took a giant stride from the swim step and signaled we were okay and clear to Thomas. AJ wasted no time on the surface, and we descended quickly. I was pleased the storm hadn't ruined the visibility; I could easily see the reef below us.

Emily was as graceful and efficient in the water as the other two. I felt like a cumbersome human following three mermaids. Thomas had dropped us in the perfect spot, and as we reached the reef at 60-feet, I could see the large coral mound below us on the slope. There was almost no current. AJ made sure we all gave her an okay signal before dropping over the wall and gliding down another 60-feet.

As we approached the outcrop, I couldn't make out a single indicator that a plane lay beneath. For a moment I wondered if we were on the right one, or if this just looked similar. Following AJ, I dropped around the side of the coral head and stared into a dark cave. Nora turned on her flashlight and the inside of the cabin lit up. I stared in amazement.

How two men survived this crash was unbelievable. The tail section had torn away partway down the main cabin, exposing the remaining cabin section and the doorway to the cockpit. There was no sign of the high wing, and AJ was correct: the fuselage was inverted. Inside the six-foot aluminum tube was a bed of silty gray sediment, and a seat hung from the inverted cockpit floor. The narrow door to the cockpit was wedged open.

My father had somehow extricated himself from the cramped cockpit and escaped before the remains of the Vega sank. I shivered at the thought of how violent and terrifying the impact must have been. The fixed landing gear had been ripped off and the plane torn in half.

I startled and my heart raced as something moved in the cockpit. AJ nudged my arm and tapped her thumb against her fingers as though she were operating a hand puppet. It was the hand signal for an eel. I remembered she'd said there was a green moray in there yesterday. She signaled for the three of us to stay together and look around. I returned an okay sign.

As she swam away along the slope, AJ pulled a three-foot pole spear from the cummerbund of her BCD. I hadn't even noticed she'd carried it down with her. I went back to looking inside the plane and helped shine light inside for Emily to film. A few minutes later, AJ returned with a lionfish on the end of her spear. The invasive fish with its colorful fan-like fins and venomous spines had spread wildly throughout the Caribbean, causing a dangerous balance shift on the reefs. Regular culls were used to keep the numbers in check, but I guessed what AJ had planned for this one.

We all backed away from the cabin so AJ could reach in with the pole spear, holding it inside the doorway. The green moray quickly sensed the free meal and moved toward the lionfish. AJ drew the spear out, luring the moray from the Vega's cockpit. It was a big eel, eight inches thick through its midsection, with rows of needle-like teeth ready to rip flesh apart. Once the moray was clear of the cabin, AJ teased it farther away before letting it take a big bite and rip the dead fish from the spear.

AJ swam back to us and set the spear down on a small strip of sand. Then, for a moment I thought she'd lost her mind. She started taking her BCD off. We were 120 feet underwater, and she was removing the equipment that allowed her to function underwater. When Nora swam forward to assist, I finally realized her plan. She couldn't fit through the cockpit door with the tank strapped to her back.

Keeping the regulator in her mouth, AJ laid her BCD down in the cabin and a waft of fine silt billowed up. As the cloud cleared, I saw she was switching to her backup regulator, the bright yellow one known as an octopus. Her octopus had an extra-long hose to be used in emergencies, helping other divers. She slipped off her fins, placing them next to her BCD, and pulled herself into the cabin.

Emily followed AJ with the camera, and I kept back, giving her and Nora room near the jagged metal entrance where the tail had been torn away from the fuselage. Looking at what remained, I realized the plane had broken apart just forward of the cabin door, leaving eight feet of the passenger section up to the cockpit bulkhead.

AJ had a hand on either side of the doorway and peered inside, the yellow regulator hose trailing behind her. The pilot's seat filled the upper third of the opening making access to the cockpit even more cramped than I'd imagined. Seeing how little room there was for the petite woman to maneuver made me suddenly aware of how treacherous this was. We were close to the maximum depth considered recreational diving and AJ was squeezing herself into the cockpit of a wrecked airplane.

For me.

I was about to tap my tank and have her come out, when she did something extraordinary. AJ took the regulator from her mouth, placed it down, and pulled herself into the tiny cockpit.

Silt billowed and wafted from the front of the plane, and the cloud filled the cabin. I couldn't see anything. Emily nudged me and handed me the camera. I figured she was going in to retrieve her friend, but instead, she picked up the spear from the sand and swam off. Nora remained at the entrance to the cabin and appeared perfectly calm. She looked back toward me, but her eyes were focused below where I hung in the water. The green moray eel was right below me.

I had no idea what to do, but I gasped into my reg as my heart rate pegged. Morays don't see well at all, but they have an amazing sense of motion and what's around them. The silt cloud wouldn't hamper it at all. They only bite people when provoked or threatened, but I guessed rummaging around his home might qualify. As I contemplated doing something squirrelly, like prodding the eel with the camera to distract it, a lionfish showed up out of nowhere.

Emily shook the lionfish on the end of the spear and the moray looped around and gave chase as I watched a pair of lime-green fins kick away. I looked up at Nora who tapped the Shearwater Teric dive computer on her wrist and pointed at me. Shit. I hadn't even looked at my computer since AJ went inside. I winced. Nine hundred psi, I signed back sheepishly. Nora rolled her eyes. I was also at five minutes of no-deco time left. I chose not to tell her that, as I knew the first number was about to end the dive.

Nora tapped three times on the fuselage of the plane with a stainless-steel carabiner. As she did that, Emily returned and took the camera from me. Even behind her mask I could see Em was smiling. It had to kill her not being able to talk underwater. She kept filming and the silt cloud stirred as AJ reemerged. She was putting the regulator back in her mouth and carrying something. AJ handed it to me. It was a headset. The ear cushions and any other rubber or fabric had rotted away, but the rest of the headset was complete, along with the cord. My father would have worn this. He likely had it on when he crashed. I couldn't stop staring at the piece of my family's history in my hands.

Nora helped AJ into her BCD and they caught my attention, pointing a thumb toward the surface, indicating we needed to ascend. I clutched the headset. There was no way I was going to drop this precious connection to my father. We glided up the slope and I glanced at my computer. I was down to 700 psi, but my no-deco time was back over ten minutes by the time we reached the top of the reef at 60-feet. It was adjusting and telling me how long I could stay at the shallower depth.

We stayed close to each other and made our way up to 15-feet where AJ began to unclip her surface marker buoy until Nora nudged her. We all looked up and saw the hull of *Hazel's Odyssey* moving toward our position. The props stopped spinning when the boat was twenty yards away. Thomas knew where we were.

I looked down again at the headset, then up at AJ. Her eyes sparkled behind her mask. I reached over and squeezed her shoulder. She probably saw my eyes were moist, but I didn't mind.

Once we were all back aboard the boat, we took off our gear and Thomas brought over two buckets of fresh water. I dunked the headset in the one he set down by me, and gently rubbed the years of grime and silt away. I could tell everyone was full of excitement, but they remained quiet, allowing me some time to soak up the moment. I needed to say something.

"Hey guys," I said, standing up from the bench. Em sat next to me, and the other two women were on the bench opposite. Thomas stood next to AJ. "I just wanted to tell you how much what you've done the past few days means to me and my family. You've all gone above and beyond anything I could have expected."

I looked directly at AJ, "That was insane what you did down there, yet I felt safe the whole time we've been diving."

"You didn't look like you felt so safe when the moray was swimming around your fins," Nora said and gave me a big smile.

I laughed, "Okay, I peed in my wetsuit then, but Em saved the day."

Emily stood and took a bow, then pointed at AJ, "That was so bloody cool! You're a looney, but it was epic, yeah?"

AJ seemed a little embarrassed and looked down at the deck. I had a lump in my throat and tried to gather up my thoughts. It was hard to convey the depth of my appreciation. Since my mother passed, my emotions had been raw. Losing her, the letter, this trip, finding the Vega, and now holding the headset he wore; it was all too much to process.

"I have something else for you," AJ said, pulling her hand from the bucket of water beside her. She stood and walked over to me. I recognized it immediately. The Rolex Submariner given to my father by my grandfather. It was his most prized possession. A gift well outside the means of the family at the time. I recalled the size and weight of the watch when he let me put it on my tiny, eight-year-old wrist. He always wore it. Speechless, I pulled AJ into an embrace as though I was hugging my father himself.

For the next ten minutes, we passed around the watch, cleaned it, studied it, and shed a few tears. Em captured it all on film. I was done attempting a speech. They all knew. I wasn't a man brought to tears easily, and before the past few weeks I couldn't remember the last time I'd cried. Certainly not in front of anyone else.

"Do you want to dive it again?" AJ asked.

I'd forgotten it was my boat charter. We could go back down several more times if I so wished.

"You know, I don't know how we'd top that dive," I replied. "I think I'd prefer to keep that memory fresh in my mind."

"I don't think there's anything else in the cockpit," AJ told me, "and we'd probably have to lure Mr. Moray out again. Best not to mention how we did that, as we're not supposed to feed the lion-fish to the eels anymore. Trains them to follow divers around, hoping for a free meal. I doubt that fellow has ever seen a diver before, and won't again unless we dive the site, so I broke the rules this once."

"Guilty as charged, milady," Emily added.

"Let's head in," I confirmed. "This has been amazing."

AJ nodded and started for the ladder.

"What's next?" Nora asked, and AJ paused as I considered the question.

What was next? The trail was beyond vague. The mysterious man with the gun and the case was trying to get to Little Cayman, and my father left Arlo Bodden to find him. Was David Smith the same man? If so, he was on Grand Cayman a week later. It seemed clear he was lying about seeing my father in the water and wanted the world to believe Woody Rains was dead. I didn't really know what to do, but I was certain I couldn't stop now.

"I guess I'll go to Little Cayman and see if I can pick up the trail there."

"Blimey!" Em squealed. "I happen to know someone going to Little Cayman tomorrow morning."

"I couldn't impose on you…"

I was wasting my breath. Emily had the trip, where I'd stay, and most of my meals planned by the time AJ started the diesels. When she drew breath to call Boone, I went up the ladder and joined AJ on the flybridge. She had a pair of binoculars trained on the coastline.

"What's up?" I asked.

"I'm not the paranoid type, but that's a bit odd," AJ said, handing me the binoculars.

I looked at the shore, less than a quarter mile away, and slowly panned along. I stopped on a figure standing on the rocks in front of the south set of fuel storage tanks. He was a tall Caucasian, wearing a pale colored straw boater hat. Around his neck hung a pair of binoculars.

"Was he looking at us?" I asked.

"He was," AJ replied. "Dropped the binos down when he saw me looking back."

"Curious worker from the fuel terminal?" I theorized.

"Yeah," AJ said, unconvincingly. "Probably."

PART II

7

GRAND CAYMAN, MAY 10, 1976

Woody blinked away sleep, listening again for the sound that had shattered his slumber. Another vigorous burst of crowing confirmed his groggy suspicions: a rooster. The springs on the old sofa creaked as he sat up and glanced down at his wrist.

"Oh... right." He'd left the prized Rolex Submariner behind in the cockpit of the Vega.

Woody looked around the tiny house in the early morning light, wincing as he turned his head. Gingerly, he raised his fingertips to his brow, finding the stitches there. Last night, Arlo Bodden's wife, Etta, had deftly sewn him up. She'd tried to get him to go to the hospital, in case he had a concussion, but Woody had insisted he was fine.

He rose and went to the window, looking out at the dawn. Low tropical trees dotted the scraggly yard, a battered chain-link fence ringing the property. Returning to the sofa, he sat and leaned over the coffee table, examining the contents of his wallet. He'd taken out his IDs and credit cards along with ninety-seven US dollars and spread everything out to dry on a borrowed towel. A trio of traveler's checks completed his soggy assortment. He always kept a few, folded up in his wallet for emergencies, when flying overseas.

Many countries did not accept credit cards, and cash was king in the Caribbean. He pressed a fingertip to one of the checks; a tiny bit damp, but useable.

"How you feelin'?"

Woody turned to find Etta looking at him from the kitchen. "Better. Thank you again for the first aid."

"No trouble. Fix up Arlo often enough. One time, took a fish-hook outta his toe."

"Ouch."

The Caymanian laughed. "Oh, he said a lot more dan 'ouch.'" She pointed a long finger in Woody's direction. "Still t'ink you shoulda gone to da hospital."

"I'm fine, really."

"Well, if you want me to run you by da police station, you let me know."

"Police?"

Etta cocked her head at him. "Before he head out for morning fishin', Arlo told me 'bout dat man holding a gun on you in da plane. I t'ink dey call dat hijackin'."

Woody thought a moment. The only proof he'd been hijacked was his word on it. Arlo could testify to seeing the man with the gun exit the water, but he didn't strike Woody as the most reliable witness. We'd entered Caymanian airspace without a proper flight plan and crashed a pristine piece of aviation history into Grand Cayman's waters. He had no way of knowing how a police interrogation would go. And the only proof of a hijacking was gone, probably on his way to... Woody looked up at Arlo's wife. "Listen... if someone needed to get across to Little Cayman, how would they do it?"

Etta snorted. "You being a pilot, I s'pect you know de answer. You fly. Little airstrip over dere."

"Yes, I know, but... let's say you were trying to keep a low profile. Avoid airport authorities."

"You talkin' 'bout dat man with da gun."

"Yes."

"Well... dere's a few fishermen who take people across from time to time."

"Like Arlo?" Woody asked hopefully.

Etta sucked her teeth and shook her head. "With dat old boat of his? Arlo wouldn't make it halfway across. But I can take you to someone who might could help you." She turned and opened a cabinet. "First, how about some breakfast and coffee?"

Woody glanced out the car window at the one-story houses that lined the road, many painted in bright colors. Etta had driven east along the unpaved road to Bodden Town and soon approached the bay, where most of the fishermen kept their boats. "I really appreciate this," Woody said.

"No trouble," Etta replied. "Devon owes me a favor, anyhow."

"Who's Devon?"

"Me older bruddah. Devon Ebanks."

"Ebanks... that your maiden name, then?"

"It is. Hereabouts, you meet someone who isn't a Bodden, pretty good chance dey's an Ebanks. I got two bruddahs. Winston lives over on Little Cayman, and Devon lives here, in da house we grew up in." She laughed. "Arlo hates him. Always calling him lazy, but he catches more fish dan my husband most days."

Etta pulled up to an area of stubby wooden docks, scattering a variety of seabirds. She killed the sputtering engine and got out, a smile lighting her face as she spotted a young boy hauling a cooler that looked like it weighed as much as the kid did.

"C'mon," Etta said, beckoning me to follow. "Robert! Wa gwan?"

"Good morning, Auntie Etta! Just loadin' da boat."

"Your fadduh here?"

"Yes'm, he on da boat."

"Got a question for him." Etta took the cooler from the youth. "Here, I'll take dat ice for ya, and you lead da way."

They approached a sturdy-looking fishing boat; small, compared to what one might take out sport-fishing in Florida, but it appeared well kept. The name *Devon's D-Light* was on the stern. A fit-looking man in a loose-fitting tank top looked up from whatever he was working on and nodded a greeting. "Etta! Good to see you, sistuh! Where's dat good-for-nothing husband of yours?"

"He already out fishin'. Lucky for me you're still here. Devon, dis here is Woody... he got quite a story to tell."

Seven hours later, the flat, green coastline of Little Cayman came into view. Robert scrambled to the bow, eager to see the Sister Island; the boy had never been outside of Grand Cayman's waters.

"I can't tell you how much I appreciate this, Devon," Woody said. "And I'm sorry I don't have more to give you." He'd offered up eighty of the damp dollars he'd had on him, but it wasn't enough. The oil crisis of 1973 was a few years in the rearview mirror, but fuel was still expensive. Woody had promised he'd send more money at the first opportunity.

Devon shrugged, and swung the wheel slightly to starboard, angling toward the southern coast of the little island. "Like I say, I got breddren over here I been meaning to see." He laughed. "My bruddah Winston ain't even seen my boy here, yet. Good travel weather, so as good a day as any."

In minutes, a few low buildings came into view across a small expanse of turquoise water. Overhead, three brownish birds soared in the air current. Woody squinted at them, noting their blue beaks and the red feet tucked up against their tails.

Devon saw Woody looking and chuckled. "Don't worry. Dose ain't pelicans like da ones mess up your plane."

"What are they? Some kind of seagull?"

"Nah. Red-footed boobies. A lot of dem live on Little Cayman." Devon pointed ahead of them. "Now we gotta run da cut into da lagoon. Dis channel is da only way in or out. It can be a rough ride, so have a seat and hang onto somet'ing. Robert! You too!"

Robert joined Woody in the cockpit, and they held on as *Devon's D-Light* bounced over the waves and entered the tranquility of the lagoon. The instant the ride was smooth again, Robert popped back up, eyes taking in the new sights. The fishing boat approached a dock on the left side of the lagoon.

"Dis shallow water is South Hole Sound. It's da only real anchorage over here for... hmm..." Devon trailed off.

"What is it?" Woody asked.

"Well... back when you were telling da tale about your friend with da gun... I set to wonderin' who else has a good boat for da crossing. Jocko and his boat came to mind. He pointed to a small fishing boat anchored in the shallows. The name *Reel Deal* was painted on the stern in faded letters. "And dere it is."

"This Jocko... he a fisherman, too?"

"Yessuh, he is. But he been known to use his boat for udda t'ings... if you know what I mean. He come over from Jamaica a few years back."

"Do you know him well enough to say hello?"

Devon looked at Woody closely, then nodded his head toward Robert, who was getting the lines ready as they neared the dock. "I got my son wit me, Mr. Rains. If Jocko brought over a man who held a gun to your back... and dat man might be in dat boat... well, I'm afraid we are gonna be on our way to see my bruddah once we drop you off." He throttled down and steered toward the pier. "Dere's a police station just north of here, if you're interested. Well... not so much a station, as a house da policeman lives in. He got a sign on da road." He pointed off to the left of the dock. "About a half mile north of the island store over dere."

After Devon and his son said their goodbyes, a truck picked them up and they drove away, leaving Woody standing alone by the pier.

He walked out to the end and examined Jocko's boat, anchored about a hundred yards out. There was no sign of anyone aboard. Woody glanced down at the water around the dock; the bottom was easily visible, nothing but sand and seagrass, and he was fairly certain the shallow depth extended out to the *Reel Deal*. After a moment, Woody returned to shore, crossing through a sandy area with a sign announcing Blossom Village Park.

Ahead was a rough road with a row of one-story housing on the opposite side. Behind those units, Woody could see another road and a small building that looked somewhat commercial. He traversed the scraggly grass between roads, pausing as a large brownish iguana chased a smaller one across his path.

Reaching the far road which appeared to be a mixture of sand and crushed coral, Woody was greeted with the island's sole store, a small hut no bigger than a one-bedroom apartment. A sign in a window indicated it doubled as a post office. Painfully aware of his dwindling supply of currency, Woody extracted two fifty-dollar traveler's checks from his wallet and ducked into the store. Fifteen minutes later, he returned to the blazing tropical sun, his wallet stuffed with Caymanian dollars. The solitary shopkeeper had been helpful, letting him know where the police station was. Woody headed toward a nearby intersection but paused after a few strides.

I lost my plane, my livelihood. I want payback... literally. What are the chances walking into a police station is going to make me whole? You didn't do it on Grand, why do it here?

Woody about-faced to return to the shoreline, his eyes lingering on the post office sign in the general store.

The guy has a gun, Woody. Maybe... just in case...

He reentered the store and asked for a pen, paper, and an envelope. Finding a quiet corner, Woody began:

My darling Margaret...

Exiting the store, Woody squinted in the sunshine before making use of one of his other purchases, settling a wide-brimmed straw hat upon his head. Shading himself from the tropical sun was a side benefit of the real reason he'd bought it; he didn't want Calloway to recognize him, in the event the hijacker spotted him first. Woody had no way of knowing for sure that Calloway had come over on that boat, but he didn't have a lot to go on. He'd watch it for a while and try to come up with a plan.

Woody's stomach grumbled as he strolled back toward the lagoon—Etta's breakfast had been substantial, but that was eight or nine hours in the past. The pocket-size island store hadn't had much in the way of portable foodstuffs. He'd purchased a few packets of peanuts as a temporary solution, planning to enjoy those after he slaked his thirst. Woody opened a staggeringly expensive can of soda and took a grateful chug. He looked for a place to dispose of the can's pull tab, but this island was too undeveloped to have municipal trash bins. Not wanting to ruin the unspoiled splendor with littering, he backtracked to the store and guzzled the entire soda, ditching the can and tab in a small bin beside the door. Returning to the shore, Woody came to an abrupt halt in the shade of a palm tree.

Where's the boat?

Devon's fishing boat was still at the pier, but the spot where the *Reel Deal* had been anchored was deserted. Above the whisper of the lagoon's gentle surf, Woody heard the puttering of an engine off to his left. Rushing to the water's edge, he spotted Jocko's boat motoring toward the west, still inside the shallow waters of the lagoon. Woody was able to see into the open cockpit; there were two men aboard, although he couldn't make out the identity of either. He looked south toward open ocean. When Woody had arrived, Devon had mentioned the channel they'd entered through was the only way in or out. But Jocko's boat was heading away from it toward the far side of the lagoon.

Woody launched himself into action, dashing along the sandy coastline, following the boat with his eyes. The beach was mostly deserted, although up ahead he could see a few people lounging in the late afternoon sun. A hand-lettered sign proclaimed this patch of sand to be the Southern Cross Club. Up ahead, the beach ended in a clump of mangrove trees, just opposite a tiny island, probably no more than an acre in size. The *Reel Deal* passed by the little islet, then swung to port and vanished from view.

Woody bore down, running past the startled sunbathers and leaving the manicured beach for the roots of the mangroves. His newly purchased straw hat sailed from his head, but he ran on, leaving it behind. Stepping into the shallows, he maneuvered around the outcrop of trees and managed to find a hole in the branches. The lagoon's coastline angled to his left, and on the far shore he could make out a dock and three one-story buildings. They appeared to be the only structures over there, and the boat was heading directly toward them. Woody allowed himself a moment to catch his breath, thinking. The mangroves and shoreline were impassable here, but it was a fair bet that the road he'd been on earlier would run along the coast. He turned and made his way back to the Southern Cross Club, snatching up his fallen hat as he passed it.

Reaching the beach, he dashed inland. Sure enough, the rough road greeted him, and he ran along it toward the east, his lucky dog tag flopping against his boot laces. Woody had an excellent sense of direction and distance, and he figured the dock had been a little over a mile away from the club. Someone might come along and give him a ride, but he couldn't count on that—apart from the truck that had picked up Devon and his son, he hadn't seen any other vehicles. Woody dropped his pace to a jog, not wanting to arrive on site too exhausted to… to what? His military background contained some basic training in hand-to-hand combat, but as a Navy pilot, it hadn't been something he'd often practiced.

And he's got a gun, Woody reminded himself.

One thing at a time. Get to the boat. Stay out of sight.

When Woody reached the buildings, he paused beside one to catch his breath. The *Reel Deal* was tied up at the wooden dock and appeared to be empty. Boisterous voices echoed from nearby, punctuated with laughter. Woody moved to the edge of the wall he leaned against and peered around the corner. A hundred yards down the beach, a pair of men were sitting at a rickety table, beers in hand. They appeared to be locals, and judging from their clothing, Woody figured they were laborers. Fresh-cut lumber lay nearby, and the other buildings Woody could see appeared deserted. The nearest two structures were unpainted and didn't have doors or windowpanes. A resort under construction, perhaps.

The sun was low in the sky, reaching the treetops of the interior to the west. Woody stared at the boat and took a deep breath. Steeling himself, he left the cover of the building and strolled along the beach like he belonged there. Reaching the dock, he glanced back over his shoulder.

The distant workmen paid him no mind, so he mounted the dock and went straight to the boat and looked over the gunwale. After assuring himself no one was napping on the deck, he stepped aboard.

The *Reel Deal* was a bit smaller than Devon's boat but wasn't nearly as well kept. The cleats amidships were speckled with rust, and some of the lines were encrusted with barnacles. Aware that Jocko or the hijacker might return at any moment, Woody entered the shallow cockpit, eyes searching the interior. It didn't take him long.

Opening a locker on the port side of the compartment, Woody's eyes bugged out of his head. "You have got to be kidding..." he said aloud. Inside, atop an assortment of tools, lay a familiar object: the watertight case that Calloway had been so protective of.

Without hesitation, Woody grabbed the case and turned to go. As he exited the cockpit, he froze. The lapping of water against the hull had masked the sound of footfalls on the dock, and Woody found himself looking up at a familiar face.

Calloway raised his gun. "I thought you were dead."

8

PRESENT DAY

I ran the pad of my thumb over the face of my father's watch. Gone was the flawless, smooth surface I remembered; the timepiece was now pitted and encrusted from its time in the ocean. A memory bubbled up, clear as crystal. When I was very young, I'd been playing with my father, hanging off of his arm like a monkey on a tree limb. Unfortunately, during a particularly vigorous bout of swinging, I'd snagged the band and broken the clasp. I'd cried, certain my short life would soon be over, given how much I knew he loved that watch. But Dad had only smiled and handed it to me. "Here, kiddo... hang onto this for me until we get it fixed." For several weeks, I'd kept this watch beside my bed, looking at it every night.

A gentle hand on my shoulder brought me back to the present. "You all right, Eddie?"

I looked up to find Emily settling onto the bench beside me. My own reflection looked back at me from the lenses of her oversized sunglasses. She tipped them up, perching them atop her forehead as her bright green eyes scrutinized my face.

"I'm okay. Thanks." I raised the Submariner. "This brought back a few memories, is all."

Emily smiled and nodded, giving my shoulder a squeeze. We were sitting on the flybridge, AJ at the wheel. Nora and Thomas were below, breaking down some of the equipment. I looked toward the shore and saw we'd transitioned to the lighter blues of the shallows.

AJ turned her head and called out, "We're coming up on the dock now." She looked back toward shore, then abruptly cocked her head. "Em… is that your boat at the dock?"

Emily stood and dropped her sunglasses back into place. "Yeah, that's the *Lunasea* all right."

A phone rang and AJ plucked it from the holder on the dashboard and answered the call, one hand still on the wheel. The engines and wind blotted out the start of the conversation, but she abruptly dropped her wheel hand to the throttle and brought the speed down to an idle.

"Wait, wait… let me put you on speaker." AJ turned from the wheel. "It's Boone. He's asking us not to come to the dock just yet." She tapped the phone's screen. "Okay, we've stopped. Say all that again."

"I'm at your dock, and—"

"You brought the boat over from the bay?" Emily interrupted.

"Yeah, the bilge pump repair was quick. Since we're staying at AJ's just down the road, I figured we could leave for Little Cayman right from here in the morning. It'll save some back-and-forth with the supplies."

Nora mounted the flybridge. "Why have we stopped?" She saw the phone in AJ's hand. "Who are you talking to?"

Boone's voice continued, "Heya, Nora, it's Boone. I asked AJ to hold up. I'm at your dock, and when I got here, there was a guy peering into Reg's office shack. Or hut… or building, or whatever. He was yelling into a phone while he looked into every window. He saw me and asked if I was with Mermaid Divers."

"Maybe he was looking for a charter?" I suggested.

"Maybe… maybe not. I dunno, something was shifty about the

guy. I told him you were still out and were going to do a night dive. Wouldn't be back for hours."

"Boone!" Em scolded. "Did you bear false witness?"

"Maybe a little."

"This another one of your freaky hunches?" Emily asked.

"There was something off about him. When I asked the guy to leave his information for you, he clammed right up. But he wanted to know where the night dive was, which seemed kinda weird."

"What did you tell him?" AJ asked.

"House reef at the Cobalt Coast resort. Said you might dock there and have dinner first. Even gave him directions."

AJ smiled. "A wild goose chase. Nice." She turned to me. "Cobalt Coast is way up on the top of the 'fishhook' of Grand Cayman."

"But is he still there at the shop?" Nora asked.

"Yeah. He's in a gray SUV. Rental plates." Boone read off the plate number.

"What is he doing?" Nora asked, entering the plate number into a note on her smartphone.

"Just sitting there talking on his cell."

"Hey, wait a sec," I blurted. "Boone... is this a white guy? Fairly tall, wearing a funky tropical-looking hat?"

"This guy's got black hair, no hat. I think he's Cuban. Maybe Cuban-American. I went to the University of Miami, and the accent sounded familiar."

AJ shook her head. "The man with the binoculars that we saw... he couldn't get here this quickly. Not with afternoon traffic."

Nora took out her own phone and began to text. "I will have my partner, Constable Tibbetts, come pay this man a visit."

"No need," Boone said. "He's leaving. Heading back to West Bay Road."

AJ reached for the throttle. "We'll see you in a minute, Boone."

"This curry wahoo is delish!" Emily exclaimed. "Eddie, how's your oxtail?"

Emily's question caught me mid-bite, and I held up a finger as I chewed. "It's great," I managed. "Never had it before. Kind of like little chunks of pot roast."

AJ, Boone, Emily, and I were sitting at a bench beside a gaily painted shack, a yellow hand-lettered sign proclaiming it Heritage Kitchen. On a quiet stretch of coastal road, the simple restaurant didn't put on airs, serving up authentic Caymanian cuisine with a view of the ocean. The sun was about to kiss the horizon, setting the sky ablaze with oranges and pinks.

AJ checked her phone. "Nothing yet from Nora."

I nodded. The Norwegian was working the evening shift and had announced she and her partner were going to pay the Cobalt Coast a visit to look for the man Boone had seen. I wasn't sure that guy—or the man with the binoculars—had anything to do with me. But Emily had explained that her lanky boyfriend had impressive intuitive skills, and I didn't object to Nora looking for either of them.

"So, what time are we leaving for Little Cayman?" I asked.

"With the sunrise," Boone replied. "It's a six-hour trip, give or take."

"Weather looks good tomorrow morning," Emily added. "Might be able to shave a half hour off of that."

"Any idea where to start looking?" AJ asked me.

I sighed. "None. Arlo said the guy who held the gun on him wanted to get to Little Cayman… but I don't know why, or who he was. Then there's the letter with the Little Cayman postmark. Unless the post office over there has someone who was working in 1976 and is blessed with an amazing memory, that bit of information only tells me my father was over there. I have no idea where to start."

"Etta…" AJ said.

"The wife?" I shook my head. "Arlo said she died twenty years ago, remember?"

"Yes, but... families are very tight here in the Cayman Islands. Arlo may not have any siblings left alive, but maybe Etta does. Arlo mentioned a brother-in-law."

"Yes!" I perked up, thinking fast. "Is there any way your police friends could find out for me?"

"On it," AJ said, extracting her phone from a pocket and beginning a text. "Roy might still be in the office."

"Can I see your father's letter?" Boone asked. "You gave me the gist, but I wouldn't mind reading it."

"Of course," I said, retrieving and unfolding the photocopy. "Here you go."

He took the paper and read it carefully. The letter had evoked strong feelings in the others, but Boone betrayed no emotions as he absorbed the words in a methodical manner. At the end, he let out a breath and set it on the table.

"Timeless," he said.

"Powerful stuff, yeah?" Emily's green eyes were glistening as she watched him.

Boone nodded, absentmindedly tapping a finger on the paper. "Time really is the issue. A lot of it has passed. Forty... forty-six years? Lot of things have changed."

"Got that right," Emily said, stabbing a piece of fish with her fork and waving the flaky morsel at me. "Boone and I were at the Little Cayman Museum, looking at their new exhibit on Burgess Meredith, and they had loads of photos from when his son visited in 1970. Hardly anyone lived there, then."

"Wait... Burgess Meredith? The actor?"

"Yeah! Boone and I found some of his old props and costume pieces when I was acting in a movie—"

"You were in a movie?" This conversation was getting stranger by the second.

Boone cleared his throat. "Long story... and a long boat ride tomorrow, so we'll tell you all about it then. But Em's right... if I remember correctly, the little placard by those photos said there were only seventeen residents on the island in 1970. Can't imagine there were significantly more in '76. Even now, there's only about two hundred full-timers." He glanced down at the paper again. "What was the exact date of the postmark?"

I had that information burned into my mind. "May 10."

"Bingo!" AJ exclaimed. "Roy just texted. Etta was an Ebanks. Her older brother Devon passed two years ago, but her younger brother is still alive. Guess where he lives?"

"You're kidding," I said.

"Nope. Says he's in Blossom Village, Little Cayman."

"That's pretty much the address half the island has," Boone remarked. "It encompasses much of the area near the airport and the lagoon."

"It's where the post office is," Emily added.

"No street address, then?" I asked.

"Not much call for those," Boone said with a grin. "But our co-worker, Amelia, may know him. She's an Ebanks, too."

"I'm just glad we've got somewhere to start," I said. "I hadn't really thought what would come next, if I found the plane."

AJ's phone rang and she took it. "Hi, Nora. What's up?" She listened for a minute, then thanked her friend and ended the call. "She didn't find anyone suspicious at the Cobalt Coast resort," AJ said. "And no rental SUV in the parking lot with the plate number you gave us, Boone." She looked at him, as if that was the end of it.

"But...?" he prodded. When AJ raised an eyebrow, Boone continued, "Nora found *something* out, didn't she?"

AJ shook her head in amusement. "Blimey, I'm never playing poker with you."

"I'll teach you how to beat 'im," Emily jumped in. "He's got this tell..."

Boone snaked a long arm around Em's shoulder and clamped a hand over her mouth from the side. While Emily continued to speak in muffled words, he asked, "What did she find out?"

"Nora asked an employee of the dive shop if anyone unusual had been by, asking questions. A man with a Cuban-sounding accent had just been at the shop, wanting to know if Mermaid

Divers was night diving there. Nora's getting permission to look at their security camera logs... see if they caught the man when he arrived or left. And Detective Whittaker is going to check the plates with the rental car agencies in the morning. Find out who rented the car."

I wondered if this man's interest had anything to do with me. From what I'd heard, AJ had led quite an interesting life over the past few years, and perhaps she'd made enemies. On the other hand, for this man, and the individual with the binoculars... for both of them to be sniffing around right at the moment of the plane's discovery... that didn't seem like coincidence. "Maybe they're after whatever that man with the gun had," I suggested. "The case that Arlo mentioned."

"How...?" Boone began, then frowned and held up the photo-copy of my father's letter. "You said your sister printed this letter in the local paper?"

"Yes. It came out on Friday."

Boone handed me the letter. "This doesn't say anything about a case. If someone *is* looking for it... then they know it was on that plane."

9

"Morning, Eddie!" Emily called out from Reg's dock. "You sleep all right?"

I yawned. "Better than expected." The sky was suffused with a gentle glow, the sunrise still a quarter hour away. I looked with envy at the insulated mug in Emily's hand; the hotel hadn't had any coffee set up when I checked out, and I was still waking up. I looked around. There were no boats at the pier and Emily was alone with a pair of carry-ons at her feet. And a few feet up the dock... a pile of clothes and a pair of sport sandals. "Where's Boone?" I asked.

"Getting the boat," Em said, turning and pointing out to sea. "We left her on the guest mooring overnight."

I looked out from the dock and spotted the *Lunasea* bobbing in the water. A line at the bow was taut, so she was still moored. "I don't see him."

"Probably underwater. He's half-dolphin, that one."

I waited. Still no sign of Boone. "Nora's quite a freediver," I offered to pass the time.

"Yeah! Boone says she can stay down longer than he can." Emily smiled fondly, giving her head a little shake. "But Boone doesn't have a competitive bone in his body, so of course he'd say that."

At that moment, a head popped up beside the stern of the dive boat and Boone pulled himself up onto the swim platform. Dripping wet, he made his way to the *Lunasea's* flybridge and started her up. A couple pulses of the engines, and the dive boat coasted toward the mooring ball. Boone effortlessly dropped down and released the bow line from the mooring. In moments, he was back up top and headed toward the dock.

"Normally, I'd join him for the morning dip... but I'm still caffeinating." Emily took a healthy sip from the travel mug, then smiled when she caught me staring at it. She waggled the mug. "A bold Costa Rican blend that AJ keeps in stock for when Boone and I borrow her futon. Not to worry... I've got a thermos of this in a side pocket of my bag. Once we're aboard, we'll set you up."

"Bless you."

Beto Rodriguez pulled to the side of the road near the pier, just as the dive boat cast off. The Cuban frowned; Mermaid Divers wasn't supposed to open for nearly two hours. Quickly, he called his boss, who answered on the second ring.

"What is it, Beto?"

"There's a dive boat headed out already!"

"Before sunrise? A bit early to be diving."

"It's not a Mermaid Divers boat... it's the *Lunasea*. The one that tall, skinny guy was on."

"The one that sent you up to Cobalt Coast? For a night dive that wasn't happening?"

"The same."

"Who's aboard?"

Beto's employer had given him a small pair of binoculars, and he grabbed them from the passenger seat and trained them on the boat. "I see the tall guy… and there's our boy, Eddie! And… *ay, caramba*, there is a sexy little *mamacita* at the wheel!"

"Blonde? Very short?"

"*Si.*"

"She was on the Mermaid Divers boat, yesterday afternoon," his boss noted.

The dive boat began to turn, revealing its port side as it headed toward deeper water. "Bubble Chasers Diving," Beto read aloud. "I don't see any tanks."

"What is he up to…?" his employer muttered, and Beto could hear the clickety-clack of keystrokes on a laptop. "Well, well, well… that explains it. Let me know which direction they go."

Beto knew the spot that Eddie had been diving was to the south, and his boss was hopeful they'd found the missing plane. But after a moment, the dive boat swung to starboard.

"He's turning north!"

"I thought he might. Bubble Chasers Diving is a dive op on Little Cayman. Where Eddie's father wound up."

"What do you want me to do?"

"Get back to the hotel and grab Scooter, then head to the airport. You're going to Little Cayman."

"All right, we're past Rum Point," Boone said, looking to starboard at a collection of buildings on a spit of land. "Let's open her up."

"Ready for some speed, Eddie?" Emily cried from the flybridge wheel.

"You're the skipper!" I called back.

"Bloody right!" She throttled up and the gentle sea breeze on my face became a roar as the dive boat leapt forward.

In moments, we were skimming along the northern coast, headed east. The waters around us were a cobalt blue, so I knew we were in deep water, outside the fringing reefs along the north coast of Grand Cayman.

"Whoa! This dive boat's got a bit more pep than I would've expected!" I shouted.

"Yeah, she has some inner beauty hiding down below," Boone said. "Got her from a police auction. And this isn't even her top speed. We'll drop back down to cruise in a bit, but Emily likes to show off every once in a while."

"That reminds me... Emily, you were going to tell me about you being in a movie?"

"Oh, that! Well, this German director was shooting a movie here and the lead actress went missing... and I happened to look a lot like her..."

"What happened to her?" I asked.

"Hey! We've got a long trip across to Little, and you want to skip to the climax? Eddie, Eddie, Eddie... sit right back and you'll hear a tale!"

"But I'm still in that one bloody scene where I jumped in," Em concluded. "You can't see my face, but my arse looks fantastic."

"Wow." I shook my head in disbelief. The story of Emily's fleeting brush with Hollywood had proved wildly entertaining, and we were now halfway across the gap between Grand Cayman and the Sister Islands.

"And if you liked that story... Boone and I fought a crazy guy on a mountain in a hurricane—"

"That's enough story time, Em," Boone interrupted with a laugh. "Eddie... I was thinking... first thing we ought to do is chat with our partner, Amelia Ebanks. She can probably point us to Etta's brother. But we might also pop by the Little Cayman Museum. If our friend Katja is working today, she might be able to scrounge up some old *Cayman Compass* articles from 1976. See if there's anything that jumps out."

"Sounds like a plan."

It was noon when we reached the placid waters of the lagoon on the south side of Little Cayman. Emily turned to starboard and headed east. Looking down from the flybridge, I was surprised at how shallow the water was. The sandy bottom was easily visible, and an occasional stingray skated along the seagrass.

"Most of the resorts are here, in South Hole Sound," Boone explained. "It's the only sheltered spot on the island. There are a few docks on the north side, but this is where most boats come in."

"What's that little island there?" I asked, pointing at a low clump of trees and sand off our starboard bow.

"Owen Island. And to our left, that's the Little Cayman Beach Resort. Owned by the same people that run Cobalt Coast, actually. We're just around the bend ahead, in a condo complex. Suffice to say, you're welcome to stay with us. We've got a guest room."

"And Brixie loves visitors!" Emily added.

When I cocked my head, Boone answered my unasked question. "Brixton is our dog. A rescue from Belize. He's staying at my buddy Fitzroy's at the moment. Supposed to drop him back at the condo today."

In minutes, the *Lunasea* slowed and turned to port, angling toward a wooden dock. A small complex of one- and two-story condos lay in a ring around a sandy area; a few outdoor tables and chairs sat in the shade of palms and a pair of bright red flame trees. Emily deftly nuzzled the dive boat against the dock and Boone stepped across and secured the lines. I handed our bags across to him as Emily shut the boat down and joined us.

"You should call Amelia, yeah?" she suggested.

"Oh, right!" Boone took out his phone and placed a call. After a moment he said, "Hey Amelia, it's Boone. We're back! And we've got a time sensitive question for you. Gimme a call when you get this?" He hung up. "Voicemail. She might be out divemastering with another op."

"Well… you suggested we visit the museum?" I offered.

"Yes. I'll text Katja… make sure she's there. Let's grab a bite to eat, then we can head over."

The Little Cayman Museum sat atop a low rise on the south side of the main road that ran along the coast. Painted blue and white, the nondescript one-story building looked more like a home than a museum. Boone pulled into the empty gravel parking lot, and we exited the Jeep. Before going inside, Emily checked the weather app on her phone.

"Just seeing if we can leave the top down on the Jeep. Pop-up showers love to catch you unawares in the tropics. And… all clear. We'll leave her alfresco!"

Entering through the French doors, we were greeted with a blast of refreshing air-conditioning. A petite woman with a bright smile looked up from an exhibit off to one side of the entrance. "Allo, Boonemily!" The woman smashed their names together, as if they were one unit. "And you must be Eddie. Welcome to the Little Cayman Museum. I'm Katja." She spoke with what sounded like a German accent, and her hair was as blond as Emily's.

I extended my hand. "Pleased to meet you. And thank you for making time for us."

"It's what I'm here for," she replied, turning toward the back of the building and beckoning. "Follow me to the office. Boone texted me some information about your father's visit, so I pulled what we have from May to December 1976."

We walked by a number of exhibits: a British colonial governor's uniform, a number of sculptures by local artists, a small skiff, complete with oars and fishing nets. One wall was entirely taken up by a massive mural of a coral reef, composed of countless individual photos. We were approaching a nondescript white door when the last exhibit brought me up short with a double take. Inside a glass case were a purple top hat and bow tie, an umbrella, a cigarette holder, and a monocle. Surrounding these were pictures of a small light-green dwelling and snippets from newspaper articles.

"Is that...?"

Katja turned and beamed with pride. "Props and costumes from Burgess Meredith's Penguin character on the old *Batman* television show. We just finished putting the exhibit together. I presume Boone and Em told you about finding all of that, yes?"

"Yes, they did. Quite a story! And he had a house here?"

"He did, indeed; on the north coast. I believe he bought it in 1967 and didn't sell it until the early nineties. Who knows, he might have been here when your father visited. But let me show you what I've got for 1976."

We crammed into a small office where Katja had several stacks of articles laid out, along with a few full newspapers.

"Some time ago, the Cayman Islands had two competing weekly newspapers, the *Caymanian Weekly* and the *Cayman Compass*. They merged in 1974, to form the *Caymanian Compass*— although it's back to just *Cayman Compass* nowadays. We have a few full papers from 1976, but much of what's here are photocopies of articles that specifically cover Little Cayman."

We divvied up the months and began to go through them. After a few minutes, voices were audible back in the exhibit hall, so Katja excused herself to see to the visitors.

"What are we looking for, exactly?" Emily asked.

"Well... any specific mention of my father would be a home run," I said. "But I'm betting we won't get that lucky. Just keep an eye out for anything unusual."

"We'll know it when we see it," Boone remarked distantly, scanning the pages in front of him.

Ten minutes later, my eyes halted on a headline. I swallowed. "Where is Tarpon Lake?"

"It's just to the northeast of the lagoon," Boone answered. "Why?"

I pointed at the headline before me: "Deceased Grand Cayman

Fisherman Found in Little Cayman." The subheading read: "Body Discovered in Tarpon Lake."

"Blimey!" Emily whispered, rolling an office chair up beside me. Boone stood behind, looking over our shoulders, and together we pored over the article.

"Man's name was Joseph 'Jocko' Reid," I remarked, grabbing a pad of sticky notes and jotting it down.

"Cause of death," Em added, "drowning." She frowned. "In Tarpon Lake? It's like… two feet deep."

"Whoa," Boone muttered. "Last line."

I skipped ahead and read aloud: "A witness to the boat's arrival stated that Mr. Reid had one passenger with him, a Caucasian male in his thirties."

"And look at the date the witness saw the boat," Boone said.

I did, and felt a chill rise up my spine. "May 10. The same day as the postmark on my dad's letter."

10

"Tarpon Lake is landlocked and brackish," Boone said as we exited the museum. We hadn't spotted any other articles of interest, and Katja had photocopied the one about the body in the lake. "It's known for having tons of tarpon. Anytime there's a decent storm surge, more saltwater gets pushed into it." Boone reached for the driver's side door but Emily hip-checked him aside.

"Nope! My turn." She opened the door and adjusted the seat from where it had been shoved all the way back to accommodate Boone's long legs. With the efficiency of routine, Emily pushed it most of the way forward. "Eddie, up front with me!" She retrieved her enormous green sunglasses from the neckline of her tank top and slid them into place.

I sat beside Emily as Boone squeezed himself into the back, continuing his description of the area where the fisherman had been found. "Tarpon Lake is more of a pond. No more than five feet deep, and a lot shallower in most spots. Fly fishermen love it! But it can be tricky with all the mangrove roots."

"I lost a shoe in there," Emily remarked. "Bottom is all squishy sludge. I doubt that this Grand Cayman bloke was over here fishing it, though. Sounded like he was an ocean fisherman, yeah?"

I nodded. The article stated he was a fisherman from Grand Cayman, and his abandoned vessel was referred to as a "fishing boat." I looked at the photocopy again. "The big question is: was the Caucasian passenger my father? Or the man he was after?"

Boone's phone chimed and I heard rustling behind me as he turned sideways to get to his pocket. "Well, here's someone who might be able to help. Amelia's back from an afternoon dive with Reef Divers."

"See if she'll join us for dinner and drinks at Kingston Bight," Emily suggested enthusiastically. "I heard they've got the grill up tonight. And, as an added bonus..." She turned to me, raising her eyebrows behind her green sunglasses. "...it's right across the road from Tarpon Lake."

Boone's friend Fitzroy had dropped off the dog, so we swung by the condo to pick him up. Emily took the wheel again and Brixton happily scrambled onto Boone's lap in the back. The pooch was of medium build, mostly brown, with upright ears that dropped at the tips. Emily took us east along Guy Banks Road, a route that spanned the entire southern coast of Little Cayman. Occasionally, the dog startled me with a burst of exploratory snuffling from behind my ear.

"Kingston Bight's got a dock, and sometimes we take the *Lunasea*, but easier to show you Tarpon Lake if we drive, yeah?" Emily said, slowing to allow an iguana to cross the road. After another minute, we approached an intersection with a road that ran up a gentle slope to the north. As we passed it, continuing east, Boone leaned forward.

"One end of Tarpon Lake is off to our left, here. It extends along that side of the road for quite a while. Em, let's pull over at the turnoff to the bar."

"Right-o."

As we drove along, I could see tea-colored waters through occasional gaps in the tropical foliage. A half mile later, a sand road split off from the paved one we were on and Em brought the Jeep to a halt in an area of low grass to the side.

"Easy, Brix," Boone said, clipping a leash onto the dog's harness. The prospect of a walk energized the pup.

"C'mon, Eddie." Emily beckoned as she crossed the road and pushed past a stand of seagrape.

I followed. The journey was quite short, the brackish waters mere feet from the road. "Wow! Look at all of them!" Low in the sky, the sun's rays shone across the water, reflecting off the silvery flanks of numerous tarpon who were feeding on something in the mangrove roots about fifty feet from us.

"The pond is full of 'em," Boone remarked. "Most aren't very big, but you're pretty much guaranteed to land one. Or four. We could've gone to a little wooden jetty further down the road, but I doubt that existed back when your dad was here. And I wanted you to see how close this is to the road and the shore."

I looked back over my shoulder at the road. "It would be pretty easy to pull up and..." I trailed off.

Emily made a show of shivering. "Yeah. The article didn't say where in the lake the body was found... but you could dump a body anywhere along this road for a couple of miles."

We stared at the brownish waters and the tarpon splashing in the shallows, before Boone cleared his throat. "Let's get to the bar," he suggested. "I want to give Brix a proper walk on the beach."

―――――――――

The Kingston Bight Beach Bar was an open-air establishment on a little curvature in the shoreline at the eastern end of South Hole Sound. Boone took Brix down to the beach and led the dog on a high-speed walk along the water while Emily grabbed my arm and dragged me toward the bar.

"Most of the resorts have bars, but the locals have been coming here of late. Boone and I usually hang out at a place called Beach Nuts—karaoke, trivia night... and a lot of the dive-masters at the shop there are fellow Brits. But this place is growing on me!" She pointed. "They don't really have a kitchen, but I smell something scrummy on the grill! Oh, and in there..." She pointed toward a building to the left of the bar. "Pool tables! You play?"

"Not really." I actually did, but I wasn't in the mood.

"Hang on a tick," Em said, peering into a window. "Simon's in there!" She turned to me, eyes glowing. "He's a Canadian sculptor! Has an art studio on Little. You know those underwater statues in Grand Cayman? The mermaid? And the bloke with the club and shield?"

"Yeah, I think so," I said. They sounded familiar.

"Well, he made those! And Boone and I joined AJ last Christmas and helped transport his latest underwater sculpture to Grand! Although that didn't turn out too well..."

"What happened?"

"It exploded," Em said over her shoulder as she swung the French doors open. "Simon!"

Startled, a bearded man looked up from the shot he was about to take at one of the two pool tables. His face quickly transitioned to glee. "Emily!"

She went around the table and gave him a quick hug. "I didn't know you were back!"

"It was last minute!" he replied. "After the *Angels of the Deep* sculpture was destroyed, I figured that was going to be the end of it, but two nights ago I got a call from the Department of Tourism. They still want the statue! I had a meeting in George Town this morning and decided to pop over here to my studio.

"Congratulations! Simon Morris, this is Eddie Rains."

I reached across the pool table and shook the man's hand. "Pleased to meet you."

"You here to do some diving?" Simon asked. "You picked the right place for it! Bloody Bay Wall has some of the best diving on the planet."

I hesitated and Emily plunged in, saving me. "Eddie did some diving yesterday! We wrangled a ginormous green moray!"

"Where's Boone?" Simon asked.

"Getting dragged through the surf by Brixton, I expect," Em replied. "How long you planning on staying?"

"I'm not sure yet. A few days, at least. I spent the last two hours sketching. Oddly enough, that whole debacle with the original sculpture led me to come up with a superior design. I'm going to shift the mermaid, turtle, and ray around. The upward spiral will remain, but the mermaid will be more vertical, with an arched back, looking up and with arms stretched forward and curved up, welcoming the divers from above. The stingray would be in intimate contact with the mermaid's back with the wings slightly curved around her in a protective manner. This makes the whole structure much stronger. The mermaid's head would be angled back and up, and the stingray's head would follow that angle, and could be designed to almost act as a halo behind her, adding to the angel concept."

"Sounds brill!" Emily exclaimed.

"Thanks." Simon smiled somewhat shyly. "I've learned over the years that divers prefer to photograph my underwater sculptures from below, to take advantage of the sun's rays, so that view needs to remain clear and uncluttered to maximize the visual impact of the wings."

"Ace! Can't wait to see how it turns out!" Em paused as her phone chimed and she glanced at it. "It's Amelia, she's in the bar. Simon, great seeing you! Boone and I will swing by the studio sometime if that's okay."

"Absolutely, see you soon," Simon said, then leaned over to line up his shot as Emily exited the impromptu pool hall and waved at Boone who was on his way back from Brixton's walk. Together, we made our way to the bar, tropical music playing from a speaker somewhere under the roof of the open-air structure. Off to one side, a man was setting up to play a set, an electric fiddle in one hand.

"Amelia!" Emily called out.

A young woman turned on her stool and smiled. She had light brown skin and her shoulder-length black hair was braided in cornrows. "There you are, Brixton! And you brought Emily and Boone." She spoke with a light accent that might have been Caymanian or Jamaican, quite different from Arlo's. Brixton dashed to her and received a vigorous ear scratch. She looked up from the adoring pooch. "And you must be Eddie Rains."

"Hello, yes. Pleased to meet you."

She raised a Red Stripe, giving the stubby bottle a waggle. "What are you drinking?"

After beers were distributed, we adjourned to a table and deck chairs off to one side. Brixton sat beneath the table in the sand, lapping noisily at the bowl of water the bartender had given him. Up on the deck of the bar, the musician fired up his fiddle, playing something up-tempo and vaguely Irish. We listened for a moment, then Amelia thumped her beer down and leaned forward, raising her voice to compete with the amplified violin.

"Boone and Em said you're looking for information about your father's visit in 1976." When I nodded, she continued. "My mother's from Jamaica, but my father's family has been on Little for a long, long time. He grew up here, although he was going to school in Grand Cayman during much of 1976."

"Your father is an Ebanks?" I asked.

"Yes. A white Ebanks. We come in all shades," she said with a laugh. "But I understand you're looking for Etta Ebanks's brother, Winston. If we're related, I don't know where that branch of the family tree is."

"Oh." I took a sip of my beer, a local craft brew from Grand Cayman. "Do you know him?"

Amelia laughed. "Oh yes, everybody does. Winston's a character. He's over on the Brac, today."

"The... brack?"

"Cayman Brac. The Sister Island next door. He's doing some shopping, but he'll be back in the morning. We can pick him up at the airstrip and give him a ride home, and you can ask your questions then."

"Great! How about your father? Could I talk with him?"

"He and my mother are visiting her family in Jamaica," Amelia explained. "Do you want me to text him?"

"No, that's okay… wait. Yes, actually." I took out the photocopy of the article about the fisherman found in Tarpon Lake. "Can you take a photo of this and send it to him? See if he remembers anything about it?"

"Sure!" She took it, her eyes going wide as she read the headline. "Whoa. You know… one time, he took me fishing there. I remember him mentioning this. He said his parents told him about it when he got back from school in the summer." She held her phone above the paper and took a photo, then began texting.

Emily made a show of sniffing at the air. "The grill's up! Hope they've got some lobster. Or at least some…" She stopped, frowning. "Boone? Whassup?"

Boone was slowly rising from his chair, staring intently toward the adjacent buildings with the pool tables. "Hang on to Brix," he said absently. "Back in a sec."

I didn't see anything of interest in that direction, but there was something about his posture that put me on alert. As he strode purposefully away from the table, I rose and followed.

"What is it?" I asked, as I jogged up beside him.

"I could swear I saw that Cuban guy from Reg's dock yesterday," he said, not slowing as we passed the building with the pool tables and turned the corner, entering a sandy lot alongside some older buildings. A rental car was pulling away, going toward the main road, the heads of two men visible from behind. In moments, the vehicle was blocked by the building ahead of us.

"Was it him?" I asked.

"No idea," Boone said. "He had sunglasses on, and I only got a glance before he ducked back around the corner. "I can't be certain it was the same guy, but he sure as heck seemed to be watching our table when I looked his way." Boone seemed to relax, then shrugged. "Let's get back to the gals."

"*Mierda*!" Beto Rodriguez cursed. He'd been sloppy.

"Didja get made?" the driver asked, his voice a rumble. The man was crammed into the subcompact, broad shoulders overlapping the driver's seat.

"I don't know, Scooter. That tall, skinny guy looked right at me, and I think he tensed up. But I got out of sight, *rapido*."

"Do we tell the boss?"

"Are you *loco*? No!" Beto shook his head. Scooter wasn't the sharpest tool in the drawer, and perhaps he'd forgotten their employer's low tolerance for failure. That being said, Beto appreciated the Alabaman's abilities in a brawl, and his stature alone had an intimidation factor that often came in handy.

"We gotta tell 'im somethin'." Scooter drawled matter-of-factly.

"Of course. We'll tell him we found them. And their Jeep."

Before boarding the puddle jumper in Grand Cayman, Beto and Scooter had found where Bubble Chasers Divers listed their office: a condominium complex about a mile east of the Little Cayman airport. After landing and picking up the rental their boss had arranged, they'd left the airport and headed east on the main road. They'd scarcely begun the journey when a white Jeep with its top down left the parking lot of a museum and pulled onto the road ahead of them. Beto had immediately recognized the gorgeous blonde driving the car, along with the tall guy from the dock. And in the passenger seat... Eddie Rains.

They'd followed Eddie and the divemasters to the condo where they picked up a dog. Beto pulled to the side of the road and waited. Through a cluster of palm trees, he had been able to spot their boat at a dock just off the condo complex. When the Jeep left again, headed east, Beto and Scooter followed, pausing a second time when the trio exited the car to look at something on the other side of the road. Finally, they followed them to the sandy parking lot near the beach bar. After their quarry were all seated together with some Jamaican-looking chick, Beto had paid their Jeep a visit.

As they drove away from the Kingston Bight Beach Bar, Beto opened up a tracking app on his phone.

"Is it working?" Scooter asked.

"Appears to be."

"So, what now? Call him?"

Beto chewed his lip a moment. "We will... but first, while they're all at the bar... let's go take a look at their boat."

11

Winston Ebanks was a spritely old man, rail thin and wearing a pair of glasses with lenses so thick, they'd likely start a fire if left out in the sun. His dark skin was weathered and wrinkled from the one-two punch of tropical sunlight and old age. Winston waved to Amelia as he rounded the corner of the little airport building, rolling a suitcase.

"Got your text! T'ank you for da ride. Saves me draggin' dis home in da hot sun."

Amelia introduced us before taking Winston's suitcase. "Heard you went shopping," she said, putting the luggage in the back of Boone and Emily's Jeep. "This is light! You get what you went for?"

"I did indeed!" He leaned in with an impish grin. "A date with da shopkeeper, Ms. Delilah Scott." He waggled bushy eyebrows over his thick-lensed glasses. "Deeelightful Deeelilah!" He waved a dismissive hand toward the back of the Jeep. "Da shopping was an excuse. Suitcase just has some toilet paper and a few bags of crisps."

I laughed. The old man's mirth was infectious. We piled into the Jeep, and he launched into a retelling of his dinner date with the owner of a grocery store beside the Cayman Brac airport. Apparently, he'd been courting her off-and-on for months.

Winston spoke with a thick Caymanian dialect, reminiscent of Arlo's, although that was where the similarities ended; Arlo was a man whose mind was in decline, but Winston's wit was razor sharp. He kept us in stitches on the short ride to his home: a powder-blue house, small and square, on an interior road north of the airport.

After Winston freshened up, we convened in his back yard in the shade of a large allspice tree. The old man had brought a paper fan on a wooden handle and began fanning himself. "Now, whatya want to ask me?"

I looked to Amelia, who gave me a nod. "Well, Mr. Ebanks… my father was here in 1976, and I'm trying to find out what happened to him." I proceeded to lay out everything we knew, from the letter, to the discovery of the plane, to our interview with Arlo.

"Poor Arlo," Winston interrupted. "He wasn't da same after my sister passed. Doctor say he had a stroke, but I t'ink da problem in his heart, not his head." He crossed one bony leg over the other. "He didn't tell you 'bout Etta bringing your fadduh to my older bruddah, Devon?"

"What? No!" I sat forward on the plastic chair, nearly tipping it over. "He said my dad was gone in the morning."

Winston laughed. "Arlo was fishing crack of dawn, Devon told me. He didn't get along wit Arlo, so maybe Etta decided not to mention it to him. Anyway, she drive your fadduh over to my bruddah's boat, and he bring him across. But he left him at da dock. He had his young boy wit him, you see… and your fadduh say he was following a man wit a gun. Devon didn't want no trouble."

"Did he see this other man? Your brother?"

"No, but when he come into da lagoon, he see da boat da man likely come over on."

"The… umm…" I racked my brain as I dragged the article from my pocket yet again. I scanned it and quickly found the italicized name of the fishing boat. "The *Reel Deal*? Your brother saw that boat in the lagoon?"

Winston hesitated. I saw something in the man's eyes—amplified, perhaps, by the thick lenses. They wobbled and looked to the side. In my peripheral vision, I saw Boone shift his posture.

"Mr. Ebanks... do you know anything about the body that was found in Tarpon Lake?" Boone prodded.

The man's prominent Adam's apple bobbed as he swallowed, but then his demeanor abruptly changed. "Aw, hell, I'm 'bout done on dis world, might as well come clean." He paused for dramatic effect. "I'm da one who found him."

I stared, waiting for more. Winston fanned himself a moment, then continued.

"He was half in da mangroves 'bout a mile from da Kingston Bight. Da fish had been at 'im, but I recognized him from a gold tooth da man had."

"Who was he?" Amelia asked.

"Joseph Reid, but everybody call 'im 'Jocko.' Grand Cayman fisherman. But everyone who knew anyt'ing about anyt'ing knew better. Man was a smuggler on da side."

"Did you tell the police that when you brought them to the body?" I asked.

Again, Winston hesitated. Boone, whose eyes were locked onto the old man, answered for him.

"You didn't tell the police anything, did you?" Boone said in a gentle tone. It wasn't an accusation, just a simple statement of fact. "Anonymous tip?"

The man nodded slowly. "You a sharp one. Yeah. Was a pay phone by da post office. I called from dere."

"Why?" Boone asked.

Winston sighed, then rose from his chair and dropped the fan on it. "Might as well *show* you why. Be right back."

As he left, I felt a wave of relief. "If Woody came across with Devon," I said, "then the man who came over with the deceased fisherman wasn't my dad; it was the man he was after."

"And the fisherman who took the gun guy across winds up as fish food," Emily said, then blinked. "I'm sorry, that was inappropriate."

Winston returned with a shoebox and handed it to me. "Dat's why I called from da pay phone."

I opened the box. Frowned in confusion. "Shoes?" I lifted one of the beat-up Converse sneakers from inside.

"Shake it."

I did. Nothing unusual happened.

"All right den, it's in de uddah one."

When I lifted the other shoe from the box, it was clear something was in there. I pulled a wad of paper from inside and found... more paper. A small paper bag, like you might put a pastry in. Lifting that out, I looked inside and gasped. "Whoa..." I said softly.

"What is it, what is it?" Emily blurted, reaching for the bag.

I held it away from her lunge. "Careful! This looks delicate. Here..." I stood and set the lid from the shoebox on the seat of my chair, then gently slid the object onto the cardboard.

"Blimey!" Em dropped to her bare knees beside the chair, removing her sunglasses to gawk at the jewelry that lay in the lid.

The necklace was a bit more than what you'd wear for a night on the town. A delicate double strand of intricate links led to a pendant rimmed in tiny diamonds, but the focal point of the necklace was a large pink-orange gem.

"When I found da body, I was pretty sure it was Jocko, but when I checked his pockets for an ID, I found dat. It was hard times for me back den, so I took it. Damn fool. Once I got it home, I nevuh have da first idea how to sell it. And I t'ink to myself, if I even *try* to sell it... maybe I get caught and dey arrest me for da murder. So... into da shoebox."

"Is it silver?" I asked.

"Noooooo..." Emily breathed. "Platinum. But I have no idea what this gem is."

Boone chuckled. "I believe we know someone who would."

Emily looked up at him. "The treasure hunter guy we met in the Keys? Buck Reilly?"

"Yep."

Emily smirked. "You know he hit on me the whole time."

Boone laughed. "Not the *whole* time. AJ was there too. And Nora. Buck had to split his focus."

"There is safety in numbers," Em opined. "A bait ball of babes to confuse the shark."

"Maybe this Jocko guy stole this from the man with the case," I suggested. "And if so, I'm betting there was more than that inside."

"It's a pretty distinctive piece of jewelry," Boone observed. "Buck might know where it came from."

"Let's find out, shall we?" Em said, taking out her phone.

Boone raised an eyebrow. "You have his number?"

Emily's only reply was a sly grin. She took a photo of the necklace, attached it to a text, and hit send. With Little Cayman's cell service, it would take a while for the image to upload. Emily returned her overlarge sunglasses to her face, then tapped a contact on her phone and put the call on speaker. The call connected and a baritone voice answered.

"Buck Reilly."

"Pull over there on the left, just past that side road." Beto ordered, eyes locked on his smartphone.

Scooter pulled off into a sandy lot that was filled with building supplies, mostly pallets of wood and stacks of drywall panels wrapped in plastic. Many were labeled with people's names; perhaps this was where shipments were stored until a resident was ready to build.

"There's a little neighborhood off of that side road we passed," Beto said, expanding the view on his GPS map. "Just ten or eleven houses. The blip is next to one that's right through there." He pointed at thick tropical foliage just beyond several piles of lumber.

"Okay..." Scooter said, waiting for instructions.

"One of us needs to take a look. See what they're doing there." Beto didn't want to risk being spotted again, but on the other hand, Scooter was about as stealthy as a rhino. In any event, the big Alabaman decided for him.

"You go. Prob'bly a lotta bugs in there. I hate bugs."

Beto shrugged and opened a little carry-on at his feet and rummaged around. He extracted a small pair of binoculars and an SLR camera with a telephoto lens. He hung the camera over his neck by a strap and left the car, heading into the bushes and low trees.

"Well, hello, Emily," Buck said. Putting a little huskiness in his voice, he added, "Miss me?"

"You're on speaker, Bucky Boy."

Buck chuckled and cleared his throat. "Hi, Boone."

"Heya, Buck."

"So, what's up? You still in Cozumel?"

"Nope. Wanderlust got the better of us," Em said. "We're in Little Cayman."

"Great diving there, I hear."

"You hear right! Listen, Buckster, I sent you a photo... let me know when you see it?"

"Just got it... one sec." There was a pause, then Buck came back on the line, his voice excited and all business. "Where did you find this? Do you have it?"

"You recognize it?" I asked.

"Who's that?" Buck asked.

"That's our new buddy, Eddie Rains," Em supplied. "He's on a quest, you might say. His father, Woody Rains, went missing— probably in Little Cayman—back in 1976. He was tracking a man who'd hijacked his plane, and the man had a case with him. That necklace was found on the body of a fisherman who brought the hijacker over from Grand."

"Maybe the fisherman stole it off the hijacker," I interjected. "Might have had some more like it in the case."

"It might have had some sparkly friends," Buck replied, "but there wouldn't have been more like *that* necklace... it's one of a kind."

"So, you do recognize it," I prodded.

"I do," Buck replied. "That's the 'Heart of Ceylon' necklace. The gem is a padparadscha sapphire, the rarest type of sapphire. The best quality ones are mined in Sri Lanka. This one appears flawless, and a substantial number of carats. Surrounding diamonds are all about a half carat. And the necklace itself is platinum."

"Boom! Called it," Em bragged.

"The Heart of Ceylon has been 'officially' missing since 1972, when an insurance claim was paid out on it. But the rumor is, the item was stolen from a safe-deposit box in 1971. Hundreds of other safe-deposit boxes were emptied, and the robbers netted nearly three million pounds' worth of other valuables. Don't know what the exchange rate was in 1971; Nixon pulled the United States off the gold standard that year. But with inflation, in today's US dollars... the haul from the Baker Street robbery would be about... fifty-seven million bucks."

"Buck said bucks," Emily blurted. "Wait a tick... Baker Street robbery? What, like Sherlock Holmes?"

"Funny you say that. Yes. The robbery took place on Baker Street, where Holmes had his fictional home... but the actual robbery was inspired by a Sherlock Holmes story by Arthur Conan Doyle, where the burglars tunneled into a bank vault from an adjacent building."

"Wait, I think I've heard of this," I interrupted. "This real robbery... they tunneled into a bank, too, right?"

"Yes. Lloyds Bank on Baker. They rented a shop two doors down and dug their way across to the floor of the vault over the course of a month, working on the weekends when the adjacent businesses were closed. Once inside, they emptied the safe-deposit boxes."

"Did they catch them?" Amelia asked.

"They did. The lookout was talking to them on a walkie-talkie, and some amateur radio guy was listening in."

"But if they caught them, didn't they get everything back?"

"That's a whole story in itself—corrupt cops, lawsuits, government secrets. But when the dust settled, the amount of recovered property was less than a tenth of what was stolen."

"Maybe the case the hijacker was carrying had some of the other items that are missing," Boone suggested. "It was just five years after the robbery. Might take a while to sell distinctive stuff like that."

"True," Buck said. The phone was silent a moment, then: "Okay, tell you what. I've got a few things to finish up, but I'll fly down tomorrow morning."

"Ooh!" Emily squealed. "Are you going to come in your flying boat? Land in the lagoon?"

Buck laughed. "Yes, to the Grumman, no to the lagoon. The Little Cayman airstrip will do just fine."

"See you soon… 'King Buck,'" Emily said, then hung up.

I smirked. "King Buck?"

She looked at me. "It's a nickname, Eddie!" she said defensively. "I didn't give it to him." Then she got a mischievous look on her face. "Say… Mr. Ebanks? Would it be all right if I tried that on?"

The old man laughed. "Not only is it all right, but I insist! I'd offer to put it on for ya, but my arthritis won't likely cooperate with dat clasp."

"Boone, you do the honors."

"As my lady commands."

Boone carefully lifted the necklace from the shoebox lid while Emily turned her back on him and raised her ponytail with one hand. Once the Heart of Ceylon was in place, Em fired up her phone's photo app and admired herself in the selfie mode. The jewelry stood out from her lightly tanned skin, looking somewhat incongruous with her simple, spaghetti-strap tank top. Mr. Ebanks gave a low whistle.

Emily smiled. "I know, right?" She took a selfie, the phone mimicking an old-fashioned shutter sound. "Hey, Boone, I think I should send some to Buck. You know… for research."

While Boone chuckled and shook his head, Emily launched into a shifting series of glamour poses, filling the air with digital shutter clicks.

Fifty yards away, a flurry of very real camera clicks sounded amongst the dense tropical foliage. Once Beto was certain he had several good shots at extreme zoom, he slowly backed away through the brush. Turning and hustling back to the rental, he jumped inside, out of breath. Beto grabbed his bag from the floor, tearing into it.

"So… what didja see?" Scooter asked.

Beto didn't answer, extracting a folder and pulling a stack of stapled pages from within. Each page had a photo of an item of jewelry along with a detailed description. Many of the photos were of very low resolution, some with the items laid out, and some of people wearing them. He flipped through them, stopping on the fourth page; in the picture, a necklace lay on blue felt. Beto held it up for Scooter.

"This. I saw this."

12

As sunset approached, we arrived at Beach Nuts, an open-air bar on the grounds of the Little Cayman Beach Resort. We sidled up to the bar and Boone and Emily sat on either side of me. Above my head, countless chunks of driftwood planks covered the ceiling. Each was brightly painted, with names of visitors and dive ops. Boone had explained this watering hole was extremely popular with visiting divers and had a nice selection of draft beers from the Cayman Islands Brewery. At our feet, Brixton lapped noisily at a bowl of water.

Amelia had taken Winston over to her father's house to cook him a proper meal—and give him some romantic advice on courting his Brac beauty. The old man had allowed us to take the necklace, although Emily had insisted that he keep the canvas sneakers—although she called them trainers—insisting they were "in" right now. After stashing the necklace at the condo and grabbing Brix, Emily had suggested we come here for a quick bite and to strategize over a beer. We hadn't yet gotten around to the strategizing, as Emily was still busy teasing Boone.

"It's so cool that Buck is a real live treasure hunter. Like Indiana Jones, yeah?"

"Mm-hmm," Boone replied, lifting a dark beer to his lips.

"Oh, and Eddie... he's way better looking than Harrison Ford. Don't you think so, Boone?"

"*Lost Ark* Harrison Ford, or *Crystal Skull* Harrison Ford?" he asked, refusing to rise to the bait.

"I wonder if Buck'll land his flying boat in the lagoon," Em mused with a dreamy sigh.

"He said he was going to land it on the airstrip, didn't he?" I asked.

"Where's the fun in that?" Em took a sip of her Caybrew, a local lager, and swiveled on her chair. "Why don't you have a flying boat, Boone?"

Boone shrugged. "Can't fly, for one."

"Can't fly, don't have a boat with wings... don't hunt for treasure like Indiana Jones. Hmm..." Emily did her best to stifle a grin as she made a show of stroking her chin. "I may need to consider an upgrade."

Boone shook his head with a smile. "I think that jade artifact we found in Belize qualifies as treasure hunting."

"Fair point. Oh, very well. I'll give you a reprieve."

"Very generous of you." Boone turned to me. "Okay, I think she's done..." That earned Boone a punch in the arm, Emily reaching around behind me to deliver the audible blow. When I winced, Boone chuckled. "Don't worry, she does that a lot. I've got a callus there by now. Absorbs the impact."

"Okay, enough mucking about," Em said, sobering. "Buck arrives tomorrow, so hopefully we'll get some help on the necklace and what all might've been in that case the hijacker had. What else?"

"Well... I still don't have a clue what happened to my father once he got here," I said. "The body in the lake... I'm guessing the hijacker killed the fisherman."

Boone nodded. "The fishing boat that belonged to him... I wonder what happened to it? The article didn't say."

Before we left Winston's house, we'd asked him about it. The old man had told us his brother had reported it was no longer at anchor when he left. "Maybe…" I started, thinking a moment. "Maybe the hijacker killed the fisherman, then took his boat."

"Two hijackings, one by air, one by sea," Emily mused. "If he did a third by land, I think he wins a prize or something."

"We should probably call Nora," Boone suggested. "Would be good to have an official police presence on hand for when Buck gets here." A ghost of a smile rose to his lips. "And I don't think Buck would object."

"You just don't want me to have Buck all to myself," Emily said, pretending to pout. "But I'm way ahead of you. Already texted her. She'll be here on the morning flight from Grand."

"Did she ever find anything on that rental car up by AJ's dock? The guy Boone caught snooping around the dive shop?"

"Oh! Yes! Just a tick." She opened her messages and cleared her throat, then launched into an atrocious Scandinavian accent. "Ran the plate on the hire car. Was rented to a José Garcia staying at the Sunshine Suites Resort. Hotel has no record of anyone by that name renting a room, and immigration has no record of a José Garcia entering the country in the last two weeks." Emily gave a little bow and put away her phone.

"So… an alias," I said.

Emily shrugged. "Well, Mr. Whoever-he-is is back on Grand, so no worries, yeah?"

"They're still there," Beto said, returning to the car. "And I saw menus in their hands, so I think we have an hour at least."

"What's the plan? Toss the old man's place?"

Beto thought for a moment. They'd followed the Jeep on the tracker app, staying several miles behind; the island was simply too sparsely populated to risk a close tail. After it paused at a different neighborhood on the western end of the island, they'd driven past and seen the old man going into a house with the Caymanian girl. When the Jeep resumed its trek, it had returned to the condominium where the Bubble Chasers divemasters lived and where they kept their boat. Finally, they'd come here with Eddie.

"They didn't have that shoebox with them... so either the old man has it, or they put it in their condo or boat."

"You think there's anything else in that box?" Scooter asked.

"I dunno. Might be. But the necklace was the only thing they took out of it while I was watching."

"So... toss his place? Or go to the condo?"

"We've got the length of a sunset dinner," Beto mused, then made a snap decision, opening the passenger side door to get out. "We do both. Switch places, I'm driving."

Their rental was parked in the shade of a palm tree at the beach resort. Instead of circling the car to the driver's side, Beto first strode to a trio of bicycles, sitting at the side of the parking lot. Little Cayman islanders often didn't lock their doors... or chain their bicycles, apparently. He grabbed one and brought it back to the car, shoving it into the back. Beto got in and adjusted the seat.

"That's stealing," Scooter observed matter-of-factly.

Beto gave his partner a look. "Are you serious?"

The big man broke into a grin. "Gotcha."

Beto laughed as he turned onto the road and headed east toward the condo. "Good one, Scooter."

"I thought so. Why'd you take it?"

"It's your getaway car, in case you need it. We're going to split up. I will drop you at the condo. You check their place and the boat while I go to the old man's house."

"But... I don't know how to ride a bike."

"You've never ridden one?"

"Well... yeah. As a kid."

"See? There you go. You never forget."

Scooter craned his thick neck, looking in the back. "I had a Schwinn dirt bike. That thing's got gears and stuff."

"So don't use them."

In minutes Beto arrived at the sandy driveway where they'd been before. "There... I can see the dive boat at the dock. Search their condo first. First floor, that one there. They've got their dog with them at the bar, so that's a bonus. Then search the boat. I'll be back as soon as I can. If I see the tracker moving, I'll call you."

"Got it." The Alabaman exited the car, then clumsily extracted the bike from the back. "If I bust my ass on this, it's coming outta your cut."

"Fair enough."

After a satisfying meal, I followed Boone and Emily away from the lights of the bar to the beach. We paused at some hammocks suspended from a thatched roof, the surf just feet away.

"Hammocks?" Emily asked. "Or a stroll on the beach?"

"I think Brix is voting for the stroll," Boone said, the dog straining at the leash.

"I wouldn't mind working off that burger," I said. "Beach stroll sounds good. Which way?"

"East toward our place," Boone said, Brix pulling him away from Emily and me. "West turns to jagged ironshore pretty quickly."

"What is ironshore?" I asked. "Your dark beer was called that, right? Ironshore Bock?"

"Ironshore is a limestone formation," Boone explained, once he'd gotten Brix to the edge of the surf. "A lot of islands have it. It's usually very sharp, and you definitely don't want to walk barefoot on it. Millions of years of erosion and microbes chowing down on the limestone create that jagged look."

"There's even inland ironshore," Em added. "Over on Grand, there's a bunch of black ironshore in West Bay that looks so bleak, they call the area 'Hell.'"

"Oh, yeah," I said, "I've heard of that."

In moments, we were all carrying our shoes and sandals, chatting about the day's discoveries. Finally, Emily stopped. "We're halfway back, already."

Boone, up ahead with Brix, looked back. "We can get the Jeep tomorrow. Wouldn't be the first time we left it there."

After a while we reached a long dock and started up a bend in the coast. Brixton had dashed up ahead and we lost sight of Boone as he raced after the rambunctious pooch. Rounding the bend, we found him standing in the surf, staring off to the north. Brixton whined, his leash taut.

"What is it?" I asked.

"There's someone on our boat."

I squinted. "How can you tell? I can barely see it."

"You just came from the lights around Southern Cross Club. Give your eyes a chance to adjust." Without saying anything further, he started forward at a jog.

"I see a torch," Emily said, running to catch up with Boone.

"Torch?" I asked, running alongside.

"That's 'flashlight' to you, Yank."

And then I saw it, too. A momentary illumination aboard the *Lunasea*. Then it winked out.

Scooter had torn the place apart, but nowhere in that condo had he found the shoebox Beto Rodriguez had described. Disappointed, he'd headed for the dive boat. Scooter hoped to be the one to find the goods... and maybe let the boss know first, before he called Beto. He liked the Cuban okay, but sometimes he felt like the guy looked down on him. Thought he was a dumb redneck or something.

Reaching the dive boat, he looked at the writing on the side. Peering into the dark, he made out the name: *Lunasea*. "What the hell does that mean?" he muttered, before stepping across onto the boat. He began a methodical search, starting in the small hold in the bow. There was a toilet in there. What did they call those on a boat? "Oh, yeah. Head," Scooter said aloud. "I'm gonna hit the head." And he did. "Wonder where it goes when you flush," Scooter pondered. Normally, when he was searching a place, he'd check inside the toilet tank, but this one didn't have one.

Back outside, he looked inside the cubbyholes alongside the wheel, assisted with occasional uses of a small flashlight. Nothing. He turned and looked at the ladder behind him. He was about to climb it when a burst of insight struck.

"Ohhhhh... I get it. Luna. Sea. Lunacy." Scooter's journey to understanding might take a little longer, but he always got there eventually. "Heh. Good one."

His phone buzzed. A text from Beto: *Nothing here. You?*

Scooter replied in the negative, and that he was almost done himself. Beto ended with an *On my way*, and Scooter pocketed his phone and climbed the ladder. There was another wheel up here. Some other controls. Benches rimmed the deck. Not too many places to hide something. He was about to open a compartment in the dashboard when a voice called out from the dock below.

"Can we help you?"

Scooter whirled around, instinctively reaching behind to his waistband—only to remember that he'd had to leave his piece behind for the plane hop over here. Eddie Rains and the two divemasters were standing on the dock, along with the dog.

"You lost or something?" the tall, lanky divemaster asked.

Scooter tried to come up with a reason he was on their boat. "Uh..." was all that came out.

The guy was big—freakishly big. With wide shoulders, a barrel chest, and bulging arms, it was hard to tell where his neck ended and his head began. He didn't look like the man who'd been watching our diving from shore back in Grand Cayman, and he didn't look Cuban, like the individual Boone had described.

"Why don't you come down from our boat," Boone suggested.

"Oh, this is *your* boat?" the guy said with feigned surprise. "I'm sorry, I thought this belonged to my Airbnb host. I'm staying over there." He waved vaguely toward some of the other buildings. The man spoke with a thick southern drawl, his voice a rumble.

"You mean Kim and Curt?" Emily asked.

"Uh... yeah. Kim 'n' Curt. Actually, lemme text 'em real quick, then I'll be outta your hair."

"There is no Kim and Curt," Em said to me under her breath, turning away and sending a text herself.

I felt a gentle tug on my T-shirt sleeve. Boone nodded back to shore, and I followed. The three of us took up positions on the sand around the shore end of the dock. Brixton sat at Boone's feet, and while he wasn't growling, he wasn't wagging his tail either, watching the stranger step across to the dock. Emily finished her text, and I heard her mumble "Macy" to Boone. He nodded and handed her Brix's leash, stepping in front of them as the man thumped up the dock with heavy footfalls.

"Did you manage to get hold of Kim?" Boone asked the man. "Or Curt?"

The man stopped, stood thinking for a count of three, then narrowed his eyes. "There ain't no such folks, is there?"

"Nope," Boone said.

"I don't 'preciate bein' made a fool of."

"And we don't appreciate strangers poking around our boat," Emily interjected.

The man looked at each of us in turn, including the dog. Sizing us up.

"Y'all shoulda called the police."

"Who says we didn't?" Emily asked.

The man sighed, then rolled his massive shoulders. "All right then. Guess we're on the clock. Where's the necklace? And what else did that old geezer have?"

"And which geezer would that be?" Emily asked. "Are we talking about Curt? Of Kim and Curt?"

"You made them up. No, I mean the skinny old man you picked up at the airport."

"Don't know what you're talking about," I said, realizing Em was stalling for time, running verbal rings around the guy.

"We haven't been to the airport," Em added. "Been diving today. You try it yet? The reefs here are ace!"

"Nice try. We been following your Jeep since yesterday." He frowned. "Hey, where is it?"

"You looking for a Jeep? Or a necklace?" Em asked. "I'm confused."

"All right, enough of this," the big man said, stepping forward. "If the old guy don't have it, you three do." Boone was still in front of us, so the man grabbed for him... and wound up with air.

Boone simply sidestepped the lunge and dropped into some odd, shifting stance. Almost like a dance.

"What the hell are you doing, twinkle-toes?" The man grabbed for him again, and Boone actually cartwheeled to the side, snapping a kick to the guy's butt as he passed and sending the behemoth sprawling into the sand.

Brixton was snarling, straining at the leash in Emily's hands. I glanced around, looking for something to use as a weapon; unfortunately, Boone and Em kept their little patch of beach spotless.

"You're dead!" the man shouted, rising from the sand and advancing on Boone. He swung several haymaker punches through the air as Boone retreated. Suddenly, with the divemaster driven back, the man switched targets and ran at Emily, but came up short at the bared teeth and snarls of Brixton. I stepped in as well, and his eyes went from the dog to me.

"Say cheese," Emily said, raising her phone and snapping off a flash photo. The man squinted and blinked. He reached for the phone but was suddenly hurtling off to the side as Boone came in low, blindsiding him with some sort of scissoring takedown. He cried out in pain as he landed in a heap, Boone rolling away out of reach.

Discretion finally won out; when the man rose again, he suddenly turned and lumbered toward the road, grabbing a bicycle that was leaning against a tree and hopping onto it; beneath his bulk, the bike looked like something a circus clown would ride. I started to go after him, but headlights came hurtling into the sandy driveway.

Scooter wobbled on the bike and plowed into the front fender of the car, sprawling on the sand. In the distance, I could hear a siren. Far to the west, flashing lights were just visible.

"Get in! Get in!" an accented voice shouted.

"But they probably got the box," the lummox said as he staggered to his feet. "We can take 'em!"

"The police are coming!"

Limping, the big man rushed to the car and dived in. The vehicle lurched forward before the door was even closed, sand spraying from its tires. Moments later, a police car pulled in and a Caymanian woman stepped out, hand on her side where there was a pouch of some sort. Pepper spray, I guessed. In her other hand, a hefty flashlight.

"Emily! You okay?" she called, running toward us. "I got here soon as I could! Constable Thompson should be on his way direct from his house."

"We're okay, Constable Macy," Emily reassured her. "You just missed the guy. Someone picked him up and they headed east."

The policewoman started to return to her car, but Boone stopped her.

"Macy, better wait for Trey to get here. The guy we caught on our boat is huge, and he knows how to fight. And he's got another man with him."

"Are they armed?" the constable asked.

"Don't know," Boone answered. "The big guy didn't pull a weapon... but they might've had something in the car. It has rental plates, by the way. I saw it before, at the Kingston Bight. White compact car. A Honda of some sort."

"There's only a few rental cars on the whole island," Constable Macy noted. "What was this man doing on your boat?"

Boone started to reply, but Emily quickly interrupted. "Whatever he was after, he didn't find it. Went away empty-handed, near as I can tell."

"Uh… guys?" I pointed toward their condo where the glass door was halfway open.

"Oh, bollocks!" Emily shouted, running toward their home. Brixton scampered along beside her.

"Constable, this is Eddie Rains," Boone said. "He's staying with us. Eddie, this is Constable Macy, one of Little Cayman's two full-time officers."

"Pleased to meet you Mr. Rains. I'm going to radio my partner. Give him the description of the car."

Boone and I turned to follow Emily into the condo. Inside was a whirlwind of items scattered across the floor. Cabinets had been emptied and drawers removed and dumped. Pillows and the futon had been torn open, and in the bedrooms, the mattresses had been tossed aside. Inside both bathrooms, the lids from the toilet tanks had been removed, and one lay shattered on the tile floor.

"Sodding hell," Emily muttered. "There goes the security deposit."

"But he didn't find it," I said. "Not from what he was saying. Where'd you put it?"

Emily grinned, going to a closet whose contents had been emptied onto the floor. She picked up a twelve-pack of toilet paper that was missing a couple of rolls and dug down to one in the center. Rolled up and stuffed into the inner cardboard tube of the roll was the little pastry bag.

"Figured the lavatory paper was a good spot for a hidey-hole," Em said, extracting the bag and laying the necklace out on the kitchen counter.

"Maybe we should let Constable Macy take that, for safekeeping," Boone suggested.

I bit my lip. "Uhm... you sure? This Buck Reilly guy is coming to examine it. What if the police confiscate it?"

"Fair point," Emily said. "Back in the loo roll you go." She pointed to the wreckage in the room. "And why don't you two get started cleaning up the flat. I want to make a good impression for Buck."

PART III

13

LITTLE CAYMAN, MAY 10, 1976

Woody reluctantly retreated and raised one hand in the air, still clutching the case in the other. Calloway kept the gun within the frame of his body, hidden from the men ashore.

"Put the case on the seat and go to the bow, Mr. Rains. I certainly am surprised to see you."

Once Woody was a safe distance away, Calloway restowed the case and put a key in the ignition, keeping the gun aimed in the general direction of his captive. Woody looked across the dock at the two locals, laughing and enjoying their beer, oblivious to what was happening a short distance away.

"No reason to involve those two, Mr. Rains," Calloway said, noticing Woody's gaze. "In fact, there's no reason why anyone needs to be harmed if you'll do what I say."

Calloway started the engine and nodded toward the bow line securing the boat to the dock. "Throw off that line."

Woody ground his teeth. He knew the nobody getting hurt part was a lie. Once they left the dock, it was just him and Calloway—who had a gun and no doubt a preference for Woody being as dead as he'd previously assumed.

"Where's the Jocko guy? Isn't this his boat?"

"Jocko made the mistake of not doing what I told him," Calloway growled. "Now get the damn line."

Woody took his time releasing the line from the cleat and glanced beyond the building to where he knew the crushed limestone road led to Blossom Village. He wondered what fate had befallen the boat captain. *Probably the same as I have to look forward to.* Without a plan which stood even a slight chance of working, Woody resigned himself to waiting for another opportunity, and pushed the bow away from the dock.

Calloway released the stern line and motored the *Reel Deal* into the shallow lagoon, aiming for the west end and the open ocean.

"Sit down and be quiet," he ordered, and Woody obliged, parking himself on the deck with his back against the vee of the bow.

"Where are we going?"

"You've not been great at following directions from the moment I met you," Calloway grunted. "I said be quiet. Just relax and ride along. Everything will be fine."

Woody's back was aching, and he rubbed his stiff neck. He felt like he'd been in a plane crash. They motored slowly across the calm, sheltered water, and Woody noted Calloway was smart in not drawing attention to the boat. There wouldn't be much that slid by unnoticed on the tiny island, and racing across the sound would certainly draw looks from shore.

"I was only asking, as I haven't eaten anything since breakfast," Woody said, trying a benign approach at conversation. "I did have a small bag of peanuts earlier, but I'm starving."

"Tough. You can eat later."

"I have a second bag of peanuts in my pocket," Woody persisted. "All right if I eat them? Only, I didn't want to start digging around in my pocket and have you think I was up to something."

Calloway sighed and glared at Woody. "Eat your damn peanuts. Then maybe you'll shut the hell up."

Woody dug the packet out of his pocket. "Thank you." He opened the bag. "Want some?"

Calloway ignored him and pushed the throttle forward on *Reel Deal* causing Woody to throw his hands out for balance, spilling the little bag of peanuts all over the deck. *There goes my last meal.* The boat bounced and jostled over the waves meeting the entry to the sound, and Woody's back smarted as his backside repeatedly thudded against the fiberglass deck. After a few moments the jostling settled, and the bow smoothly rose and fell over the gentle ocean swells.

Woody looked over his shoulder. From his low vantage point, he couldn't tell exactly where the azure water changed to cobalt blue at the transition from shallow reef to the drop-off. It was half a mile or so if his memory served him correctly from his arrival that morning.

Deep water would be a great place to dump a body.

He turned back to face his captor. "So, what's in that case of yours?"

Calloway rolled his eyes. "You trying to tell me you didn't look?"

Woody shrugged his shoulders. "I didn't. I'd only been on the boat a minute when you showed up."

"When I showed up and caught you stealing my case."

"I wasn't stealing it," Woody hastened to claim, before thinking it over. Strictly speaking, he *had* been stealing it. "I wanted to find you. I figured that darn case seemed real important, so if I had it, pretty soon you'd come looking."

Calloway didn't appear convinced, and Woody knew his time was running out; they were making steady progress away from the island.

"Must be something pretty valuable if you're going to all this trouble," Woody probed, trying to get the man to talk. He needed discussion and movement. Stuck sitting on the deck at the bow, with Calloway behind the helm, presented no opportunity to do anything except become a victim. "I'm just curious. There's a beautiful plane at the bottom of the ocean because of that case." A thought came to Woody, and he kept talking. "You can search me. In fact, you should for your own peace of mind."

Calloway finally acknowledged him with a studied look. The man glanced back toward the island becoming smaller in their wake, briefly lost in his own thoughts. When his eyes returned to the ocean ahead, he pulled back the throttle and the *Reel Deal* dropped in the water and quickly slowed. Woody stood, held his hands out to either side, keeping his balance on the swaying boat, ready to be frisked.

Ignoring Woody, Calloway reached below the helm station and retrieved the case. He placed it on the seat and unclasped the locks securing the hinged lid to the watertight rubber seal around the rectangular base. Woody slowly shuffled across the deck to get a better look, but the barrel of the gun swung his way once more.

"Stay right there."

Woody couldn't see the contents, but the container was about the length and width of an attaché case, although much deeper. He figured it could hold a substantial amount of cash, but by the sound of things being shoved and shuffled around, there were other items in there besides paper.

"Damn it!" Calloway muttered and glared at Woody. "You took it!"

Woody stepped forward again to see, but Calloway pointed the gun in earnest at his chest and yelled, "Where is it?"

Woody had no idea what "it" was, so he certainly had no idea where "it" might be. He was beginning to wish he'd hopped the first flight home to Florida and taken his lumps from the owner of the Vega, and whatever the Federal Aviation Administration had in store for him.

"I swear," Woody began, "I never even opened the thing. Search me, you'll see. Besides, why would I take something out, then carry the case with me?"

Calloway scowled, appearing to process his options as Woody tried desperately to think of anything to save his own hide. His mind drifted to Margaret and the kids and for the second time in as many days, he was sure he wouldn't see them again. *Why didn't I write a longer letter?*

The gunman looked at the open case one more time, then returned his cold stare to Woody. His eyes narrowed and Woody knew this was it.

Thoughts raced through his brain like the fighter planes he used to fly. He could lunge, but he'd be dead before he covered the six feet between them. No, his only chance was to leap into the water, he decided, hoping Calloway would miss or only wing him. Then miss him again as he tried to swim away... and again, as he chased him in the boat.

Okay, so the odds are really lousy, but standing still has a guaranteed result.

He was about to spring for the gunwale, when the low rumble of an engine came from behind him. Calloway looked past him to the open ocean and groaned. Woody swung around to see a boat approaching at what appeared to be high speed by the wake it produced.

"Get back to the bow," Calloway ordered, and Woody did as he was told.

Not dead seemed like a solid result for the moment. Maybe the new arrival would present a better opportunity... or more likely a second nemesis, he realized, dashing his optimism.

Not dead, he quickly reminded himself.

A sleek white powerboat with red trim coasted to a stop thirty yards from the *Reel Deal,* its throaty engine burbling at idle. Behind the helm, a youthful man in a willowy white cotton shirt and a floppy sun hat secured under his chin, blew out a stream of cigarette smoke and waved.

"Would you happen to be Mr. Calloway?" he shouted; his English-accented voice barely audible above his boat's engine.

"That's me," Calloway replied, and Woody noticed the gun was now hidden from view.

The man's eyes wandered to Woody, leaning against the

gunwale at the bow. When his gaze returned to Calloway, his unasked question was answered.

"He's the pilot who flew me here. I need to make sure he gets taken care of."

The man on the speedboat stared at Calloway for a while. Woody guessed he was wondering what "taken care of" actually meant. He was certainly curious himself. A massage at the Holiday Inn on Seven Mile Beach and a first-class ticket home was unlikely to be the answer.

"My place is that way," the man said, pointing to the north of the island and grinning. "You were heading the wrong way, Mr. Calloway."

"What about my guest?" Calloway shouted, ignoring the jab.

"Bring him along, of course. I'm sure we'll find something to amuse your friend while we conduct our business."

Without further delay, the man flicked his cigarette into the ocean, opened up the throttle on the speedboat, and accelerated away in a roar of gas-sucking power and a wake which rocked the *Reel Deal*, causing Woody and Calloway to grab hold of something stable.

"What a fucking dick," Calloway muttered, before following the faster boat.

"Who is that guy?" Woody asked once they had settled in for the journey around the western tip of Little Cayman.

"He's my buyer," Calloway replied with no trace of enthusiasm.

A piece of the puzzle clicked in place for Woody. "You're selling him whatever you have in the case."

"Aren't you a fucking genius," Calloway snapped back, nervously running his hand through his hair.

"But something's missing, right?"

"Shut the hell up, flyboy. I'm trying to think."

Woody left him to his thoughts as they motored around the western end of Little Cayman and continued along the north side, staying in the shallower, calmer water. The island was incredibly flat with stands of casuarina and seagrape trees blocking any view of the interior. They traveled several miles before seeing the first signs of human existence, a few scattered cottages nestled on the ironshore coastline. A pier extended from one such cottage and the fancy white and red speedboat veered starboard toward it.

The building was similar to most homes on Little Cayman, a single-level concrete-block dwelling, raised several feet above grade, with teal siding, white trim, and a veranda overlooking the ocean. The other distinctive feature was a radio antenna of some description, attached to the side of the home and reaching well above the rooftop.

"Smarmy bastard calls this his holiday cottage," Calloway grumbled, confirming Woody's own assumption that this wasn't the man's primary residence.

Calloway pulled the boat to the other side of the pier, flipped fenders over the side, and tied them in.

"Do what I say and keep your mouth shut," Calloway said in a low voice, as he waved his hand, directing Woody to the dock. They followed The Buyer along a crushed coral pathway to the veranda. Looking remarkably out of place, two stone lions flanked the steps up to the veranda, and Woody couldn't help staring at them. It seemed like a piece of décor for a manor house had been accidently deposited out in front of the island cottage.

"I'll meet you around the back," The Buyer said, continuing to the front door.

Woody forced his gaze from the guard lions and followed a dirt trail around the building with Calloway on his heels, case in hand. They stopped when they reached a clearing behind the house. A large square area had been graded and framed with wooden boards. To the side sat a manual concrete mixer and a stack of something covered with a tarpaulin. Shovels, picks, and various other building site implements lay strewn about the place. By a back door, a wooden table with benches sat close by the dwelling in the shade.

The door opened, and The Buyer stepped out, gliding down the steps to meet them, cigarette in hand. He also had three bottles of

Red Stripe beer and an opener. He popped the tops and handed the other men a bottle each. Woody was surprised to be included, but he was parched and glad of the drink. The man looked at him and smiled.

"If you wouldn't mind sitting over there in the shade, Mister..."

"Woody. Woody Rains, sir."

"Mr. Rains. Yes, if you would be so kind," The Buyer said, pointing to the nearest trees.

"I'll be watching," Calloway growled under his breath.

Woody wandered over to the shade, sat on a concrete block he found there, and swigged the warm beer. He was glad to be out of the intense afternoon sun with sunset still hours away. He felt weary, sore, and agitated. The two men were seated at the table talking, although he couldn't hear what they were saying. Running into the woods was the best opportunity he'd had of escape since Calloway had found him on the *Reel Deal,* but after the first few trees and shrubs, the thick foliage appeared impenetrable. He decided to wait.

The Buyer was looking inside the case and quickly became more animated, standing up and gesticulating. Voices were raised, and while the two men consumed themselves in their disagreement, Woody quietly stood and picked out a route through the less dense trees toward the water.

Maybe I'd make better progress along the ironshore. After his first step, he realized the argument had ended.

"Mr. Rains," The Buyer called out, "not thinking of leaving us, are you?"

Woody stopped and sighed. He turned to see Calloway pointing his gun once again. The Buyer beckoned him over, and with little choice, Woody walked toward them.

"Grab that shovel, dear boy," The Buyer said, pointing to the tools by the cement mixer.

Woody paused. Didn't seem like a great time for gardening, he surmised with a pang of dread.

"The shovel," Calloway prompted.

Woody set his empty beer bottle down and picked up the implement. *Maybe they'll make the mistake of letting me get near them with a weapon in my hand.*

"I'm thinking of a pool in the middle of my patio," The Buyer said cheerily. "Can't grow a damn thing in this soil. Best to pour cement anywhere you want to walk, sit, or lie down. If you wouldn't mind making a start, I'd be most appreciative."

The man was lighting another cigarette and grinning. Calloway took his eyes off Woody and turned to The Buyer in surprise.

"Here?"

"Best place, I assure you."

Calloway looked at the thick woods surrounding them. "Wouldn't out there somewhere be better? Or in the deep water where I was going to take care of this?"

"Things have a habit of making their way ashore from the ocean, and you're welcome to trek out into the woods and be eaten alive by mosquitoes, but I'm staying here." The Buyer sat back down on the bench. "This delightful patio area will be filled with eight inches of concrete by next week. Personally, I think it's rather ideal."

They were using words like "things" and "this," but Woody knew they were talking about him. It wasn't a pleasant feeling.

Calloway shrugged his shoulders. "Dig," he said, waving a hand toward the middle of the marked-out patio.

With a gun on him and both men well out of striking range, Woody's weapon reverted to being good for digging and not much else. He strode to the middle of the graded dirt and slammed the blade into the ground. It penetrated a few inches, and only went a few more when he shoved down with his foot on the step. *This would be tough going.*

With thoughts of his family and, driven by the tiniest glimmer of hope which would always exist while he had breath in his lungs, Woody shoveled the dry, stony dirt… digging his own grave.

14

PRESENT DAY

The mid-morning sun beat down on us as we stood on the grass outside the two-room yellow Edward Bodden Airfield terminal and watched the twin-engine propeller plane approach from the north-west. There was a garage attached to the terminal for a fire truck, and that enclosure was nearly half as big as the terminal itself. As the plane grew closer, and larger, I realized that it was an antique, which caused me to glance around to assess whether there was anybody on duty to operate the bright red fire truck if needed.

"What kind of plane is that?" I asked.

Emily turned with a big grin, her oversized green sunglasses dancing up on her forehead as she beamed. "That's a Grumman Goose. Bloody ancient bird, but a beauty just the same."

Grumman Goose?

I wasn't much of an aviation buff, but I remembered watching a television show as a kid called *Tales of the Gold Monkey* where the lead character flew around the South Pacific in a Grumman Goose. The show had been set in the late 1930s, and that airplane had captivated me so much at the time, I remember researching it.

"Didn't Grumman stop building them in the 1940s?" I asked.

Emily's smile grew wider, and she nodded quickly. "Ten points to Eddie! I want you on my team, next Trivia Night." She then elbowed Boone. "You'd be so sexy if you had an old flying boat like that, Booney. Alas, Nora and I are left to lust after big, tall, handsome Buck Reilly instead."

Boone shrugged and did not take his eyes off the ever-growing silhouette of the oncoming plane. "I think Nora beat you to the punch on that one."

Emily's mouth turned into an open circle as she glanced from Boone to Nora, who had returned to Little Cayman earlier that morning to help pave the way with the local constable to investigate the burglaries of Boone and Emily's boat and apartment. "I'd forgotten about that, hadn't I?"

Nora's attention didn't waver from the plane. A growl from her throat was the only acknowledgement of Boone and Emily's statements. Whether it implied for them not to take the conversation further, that she was angry at this Buck Reilly, or maybe even it had been a guttural tone of lust, I wasn't sure, but from the time I'd spent with Nora, the latter option seemed totally out of character, which made it the most interesting possibility.

The ancient Grumman dropped slowly toward the single runway, and I thought the fuselage, especially the nose of the plane, had the configuration of a large sea turtle's head. It was a peculiar shape by contemporary aviation standards. White plumes of smoke silently announced that the wheels had touched down. The plane came to a stop on the apron next to the terminal, and after a few minutes, a man appeared from the opposite side of the plane.

Buck Reilly.

He checked a few details on the plane and placed chocks on both sides of the wheels, then turned toward the terminal. Buck had an air of confidence that was evident in his stride and the smile that was visible even from here as he waved to us from the other side of the fence.

Without a word, Nora strode purposefully toward the terminal, whipping open the door and entering.

"Tell me more about this guy?" I asked as I glanced back at the old plane. "He's some kind of expert on rare jewels?"

"Oh, he's a lot more than that, yeah?" Emily said before she sashayed after Nora.

Boone exhaled a long breath. "Buck used to run a company called e-Antiquity. He was a treasure hunter."

"Has he ever found anything of note?" I asked.

"Oh yeah. The tomb of the Serpent King in Guatemala, for one."

"Tomb?"

"Packed with a mountain of gold, jewels, and other valuables."

The airport was again quiet now that the engines on the old Grumman were shut down. I thought about the man's name, and as a former subscriber to National Geographic, a memory struck me.

Boone continued. "Folks started calling him—"

"King Buck," I said. "Sorry to interrupt, but now I remember reading about him, and his sudden fall from grace not long after."

"Yep." Boone shook his head sadly. "While Buck was out making important archeological discoveries, his partner bankrupted their company. Buck was humiliated and became a pariah in the biz. The guy lost everything."

"I can't believe he's here to help us—*me*—learn more about the disappearance of my father."

Boone didn't respond, so I turned to him and saw that the corner of his mouth was twisted into a rueful grin. "Not that the Heart of Ceylon had anything to do with it," he said.

"Ahh, right. That explains why Emily called him."

"Yep."

It took a few minutes longer before the front door burst open and Emily popped out first, followed by a tall, muscular man in a short-sleeved khaki shirt with epaulets on the shoulders, dark aviator glasses, shoulder-length dirty-blond hair, and short-shorts with flip-flops at the end of his long, tanned legs. Nora followed after them, and then both women flanked Buck, each holding onto one of his arms, with all three of them laughing as they approached us.

"Kind of feels like we missed something," I said.

"Get used to it," Boone said. "The girls love to flirt with Buck. Tease him a bit. Just a game really, except for maybe Nora. Not sure if anything happened between them or not."

When they reached us, the giggling stopped, and Buck thrust his hand forward. "Boone, great to see you again." Buck grabbed Boone's bicep with his other hand and squeezed it as they shook. He then turned to me. "You must be Eddie Rains. Pleasure to meet you."

His tanned face made the straight, white teeth pop, and it took me a second to grasp his outstretched hand. His grip was firm, but he didn't overdo it. "Nice to meet you, too, King Buck."

The smile faded, and he nodded toward me, pushed his sunglasses onto the top of his head, and then glanced from face to face, lingering for an extra second on Nora. Her expression was back to being as inscrutable as ever. "I haven't been to the Cayman Islands in ages. Flying in here to Little Cayman was a treat. No traffic, hardly any people and plenty of unspoiled island. Looks just like the out-islands of the Bahamas."

"Wait 'til we go to Grand," Nora said. "They can't stop building there."

"How long do we have you for, Buck?" Emily asked.

"I need to be back in Key West in a couple days. My partner, Ray Floyd, and I have a museum opening there with relics from the wreck of the *Farnese*, which contained the queen's dowry that had been lost since it sunk with the 1715 fleet off, ah, the coast of Florida."

"How exciting!" Emily held her hands together and lifted her shoulders. Boone and Nora looked at each other and stifled a laugh. Had Boone not clued me into the ladies' penchant for teasing Buck, I would have believed that Emily was pouring it on thick in gratitude for Buck flying down from Key West. I'd hug him myself if he could help us learn more about my father's disappearance.

"Can you catch me up on how you obtained the necklace?" Buck said.

Nora led us over to a picnic table in the grassy open space to the side of the terminal. Probably a spot where people watched planes land or waited for friends or packages. We all took seats around the table, and I provided the background on how my father crashed the antique DL1 Vega that he was supposed to be delivering to Panama. I showed him the picture I carried of my dad, to which he raised an eyebrow and had me continue. So, I filled him in on what we'd pieced together about the other man who had been on the plane with him.

"Great old plane," Buck said. "Wasn't it the plane Amelia Earhart flew solo across the Atlantic?"

"You know your antique aircraft," I said.

"Ironic that his plane disappeared, just like Earhart did."

"Big difference," Emily said. "AJ, Nora, Eddie, and I found Woody's plane encrusted in coral and teeming with fish. Bloody brilliant reef now."

"AJ, you said?" Buck gave a sharp glance toward Nora, whose brilliant blues eyes didn't waver a fraction.

"Eddie chartered Mermaid Divers to search for the plane, and Emily and I helped out," Nora said matter-of-factly. "Like Em said... we found it."

"Nice job." He paused and glanced toward me. "No, ah, sign of human remains on board?"

"We didn't expect to find any," I replied. "Dad sent my mom a letter, postmarked here on Little Cayman, the day after the crash. In it, he noted that a man had accompanied him on board, and that he wanted to find this mystery passenger before he would return home. But he never said why."

We took turns sharing other details to bring Buck up to speed, and he listened patiently, asking questions, nodding his head, and soaking up the information. His casual demeanor darkened at the news of the suspicious man asking questions at the dive shop, and the mysterious man we spotted on shore watching us with binoculars. His mood lightened again when Em told him of the discovery of Winston Ebanks in possession of the Heart of Ceylon.

"He took it from the body of a smuggler called Jocko Reid," Nora said. "He found the body in Tarpon Lake here on Little Cayman."

"The man traveling with my father was carrying some kind of case that we presume contained the necklace," I explained.

"Why would the killer have left the necklace with the dead man's body?" Buck asked. "And what connection did either of them have to the Baker Street robbery?"

The four of us looked at each other with a collective shrug.

Buck tented his fingers, looking out over the airstrip, "And if the case contained the necklace, might there have been more valuables in it?"

"Could have been," Nora said.

Buck smiled at her. "So, Constable Sommers, what happened to the hijacker and his precious case?"

Her eyes narrowed as if Buck had challenged her. Their gaze held for a five-count, until Nora finally spoke. "Jocko was a local fisherman and occasional small-time smuggler. If anyone had a connection to the Baker Street robbery it would have been Woody's hijacker. But that crime happened in 1971, five years before Mr. Rains crashed his plane here in the islands." She maintained a focused stare.

"Makes sense," Buck said. "But like I said when Emily called yesterday, not everything was recovered, and there's no way to know what else was not reported as stolen in the first place."

"You've already confirmed the necklace is the Heart of Ceylon," Nora said. "So how can we figure out more about its... you know... like history, but there's a fancy word in English..."

"Provenance!" Emily blurted, looking at Buck for approval. He nodded and she beamed.

A wicked smile bent the corners of Nora's lips. "There, provenance. So, Buck, are you still any good at finding missing people and treasure?"

Buck's eyes were still locked onto Nora's. A slow smile spread across his face. "Only one way to find out," he said.

"Right-o!" Emily clapped her hands. "Let's get to it, yeah?"

15

The necklace that Winston Ebanks lent us rested in Buck's palm and glistened in the sunlight from the window, shooting brilliant red beams of light off each facet. They sparkled across the wall and ceiling as if from a disco ball. We'd stopped at Emily and Boone's borrowed apartment so Buck could inspect the necklace before we advanced the search any further.

"The Heart of Ceylon." His voice had a faraway, dreamy sound to it. "It's a massive padparadscha sapphire, and based on the weight, it's easily thirty or more carats," Buck said as he raised his hand up and down with the necklace in his palm like it was a scale.

"What would something like that be worth?" I asked.

Buck shifted his gaze to each of us who were all staring back at him. Emily's mouth was even agape. "One recent comparable is the Black Star of Queensland, which is about the same size—maybe even smaller—and its value is estimated at between ten and fifty million dollars."

"Blimey!" Emily roared. "No wonder the mystery man killed people to keep his bloody case."

My mouth had fallen open, and I caught myself breathing heavily. Good Lord. I had no claim to the necklace, but who did? I shook my head to clear the cobwebs. "Are we certain this was stolen in the Baker Street robbery?"

Buck's smile spread. "It wasn't listed amongst the items that were either recovered or still missing," he said very clearly. "You'd think someone would've had it insured to the hilt, given that value."

"We'll have to report it," Nora said.

"Oh, bloody hell," Emily muttered. "Forgot for a minute that you were an officer of the law. There goes my dream house in the Seychelles. Bugger."

"Nora's right," Buck said. "But, in most jurisdictions, if it's not claimed, or there's no open case about it being missing, then finders can often be keepers."

"Wouldn't that be nice," Boone said.

"For Winston Ebanks," Nora said.

"What do you see, Beto?" Scooter asked.

From inside a thicket of mangroves, Beto had the binoculars trained on the balcony of the southernmost ground-floor unit—the one he had searched previously. "Same group of divers with Eddie Rains, and there's some new guy with them. Big *bastarda*."

"Any sign of the necklace the boss is looking for?" Scooter said.

"Neither of the women are wearing it. I need to call *El Jefe* for instructions. Here, keep an eye on them."

Scooter accepted the binoculars and first looked through the wrong side of the lenses, grunted, then turned them around. Beto shook his head and rolled his eyes as he dialed the boss's number. After two rings, the man answered.

"You have news, I trust?"

Beto took in a deep breath. *El Jefe* may be old, but he was sharp as a dagger. Beto cleared his throat. "Yes, there's another man with them now. Tall guy dressed in one of those safari shirts Indiana Jones wore in the movies—"

"And shorts, tell the boss he's wearing shorts and flip-flops," Scooter said.

Beto held his finger up to his pursed lips.

"Get a picture of the new man and send it to me. Don't let them see you, and tell your moron accomplice not to get caught again. There's no place to hide on Little Cayman, and if you get arrested, I'll have no choice but to trim loose ends. Understood?"

A frog was stuck in Beto's throat at *El Jefe*'s threat, so he swallowed a couple times before he could speak. "Understood, sir."

"Find me that damn necklace!"

A click followed and Beto lowered the phone.

"What'd he say?"

"He said to get pictures of the new guy, and if you get us caught again, we're dead *pendejos*."

Scooter lowered the binoculars and pushed a mangrove branch away so he could better see Beto's face. "That's not very nice."

"*El Jefe* is not known for being a nice man." Beto was quiet for a moment. "We need to find that necklace old man Ebanks had, and if we have to kill him and all of these other *putas* in the process, it is what it is. If we find *El Jefe*'s necklace, we'll redeem ourselves for your stupidity, and maybe get a nice bonus."

Scooter smiled. His yellow teeth had gaps between them, and his eyes appeared to be an inch too far apart, accentuating the menace in them as he pondered Beto's statement.

"That would be nice. I'm better at torturing and killing than following people."

From his backpack, Beto removed a parabolic microphone and headset, which he donned, and then pulled out the SLR with the telephoto lens.

"But first, let's hear what they're talking about, and get a picture of that new guy and send it to *El Jefe*, like he commanded."

"I have just the man in the UK who can get us more information on the Baker Street robbery," Buck said. "Harry Greenbaum, my original investor at e-Antiquity."

"Is he connected with law enforcement?" Nora said.

"He's a billionaire entrepreneur who, last I heard, owned over fifty companies. Harry's more connected than most intelligence agencies."

Buck pressed a button, and the phone began to ring. He hit another button and switched it to speakerphone. The ring was interrupted when a man answered. "Buck Reilly, so good to hear from you, dear boy."

The man's voice was jovial, and clearly, he had a fondness for Buck, even though he must have lost his investment when Buck's company went bankrupt.

"Glad to have caught you, Harry. I'm with friends in the Cayman Islands and have a favor to ask you. They're listening on the speaker."

"Cayman Islands?" Harry's voice had increased in volume. "If you have any money stashed there, it would be kind of you to repay some of my lost millions." His laugh sounded hollow, and Buck's cheeks immediately turned red.

Nora's sudden laugh turned all our heads. She appeared to get a kick out of Buck squirming.

"Funny, Harry. No stash here, I'm helping some friends investigate an old robbery that occurred in London back in 1971 that I'm hoping you may recall."

"Do tell, lad."

"It's known as the Baker Street robbery—"

"Of course, I might have known that's what you were going to say when you mentioned the year. Know it well. I had some items there that were stolen yet recovered a couple of years later. All—well—most of the thieves were believed to have been captured, but not until they'd sold some of the goods."

"I read about that online," Buck said, "but I was hoping you had more insight into any items that may still be missing."

"Something in particular you are referring to?"

"Could be… but I wanted your untainted thoughts first."

"I see." Harry paused, and Buck glanced up at Nora and winked. Her brow furrowed in response. "Are you referring to the purported items that were never noted as missing?"

"You're on the right track now, Harry."

"Some say that was all urban legend, but—am I on speaker, dear boy?"

Buck nearly dropped the phone as he pressed the button to turn the speaker off and held it up to his ear. "Not anymore." Buck listened and nodded his head as Harry spoke. "That sounds right to me." He paused again, then studied each of our eyes. "Yes, I believe one of the items is the Heart of Ceylon necklace, which my friends have recovered here on Little Cayman—"

Whatever Harry had said in response caused Buck to pull the phone away from his ear. The sound of Harry shouting something into the phone was loud, but the only word I heard clearly was "millions."

"It supposedly had been stashed in a case that a passenger had on a small plane that crashed here in 1976, but we don't know what else may have been included. That's why I called you, Harry. Can you use your considerable resources to try and learn what else may have been stolen, possibly not reported, and not yet recovered? Along with any other details that may not have been reported in the press?"

Harry's response was brief and then Buck hung up the phone. "Harry is on the case for us. Said he'd call me back quickly as he knows people who had interests in the robbery."

"Smashing," Emily said.

"The local station is nearby," Nora said. "We need to report the necklace and leave it with Constable Macy for safekeeping. We can use the computer and see if there's any more information on the dead body that Winston Ebanks found in Tarpon Lake."

"I did suggest that yesterday," Boone said.

"True, Boonester, but timing is everything," Emily said. "Now we have the context from Buckaroony and his billionaire bestie from London."

Beto ripped the headphones off his head and scrambled to his knees to position the camera.

"What happened?" Scooter said. "Did you hear something?"

"Hell, yes, I did. Get ready to roll, we need to intercept them before they get to the police station."

"What? I thought we were supposed to stay undercover, that, ah, we'd be killed if we got caught or exposed again." Scooter stood frozen, uncertainty causing his mouth to hang open. "Are you sure?"

"Shut up and get ready. They should be coming out any second now."

Still inside the apartment, Buck had been quiet for a moment, and then leaned closer to the group standing around the kitchen island. "You guys take the necklace to the police, but I'd like to go speak with the person who found it on the dead man."

"Winston lives just past the station, north of the airport," Boone said. "You can drop us at the station and keep going."

"I remember the house," I said. "I can take Buck over to see him."

"Perfect," Emily said. "I'll buzz Amelia and ask her to tell Winston we're coming."

"We're?" Boone asked.

"Well, not you, Booney. The old bloke rather fancied me. No need to be jealous. Buckster will have my back."

Boone rolled his eyes.

"Sounds like a plan," Buck said. "Let's go."

"Thought you said they were coming?" Scooter said.

"Maybe somebody had to pee, give them a minute to—there they are!"

The automatic shutter sounded like a bullet train roaring over the tracks as Beto pressed the button and recorded a couple dozen pictures of the group as they exited the apartment building and hurried to the Jeep. Beto then quickly pulled up the settings on the camera, turned on the Bluetooth, forwarded them to his phone and then fired the images off to the boss, as he'd been instructed. With that done, they scrambled back through the mangroves, stumbling and tripping in haste, as branches ripped at their limbs and slapped their faces. They finally squirted out on the other side to their waiting subcompact parked on Guy Banks Road, just up from the four-unit condo complex.

"You drive so I can call *El Jefe*," Beto said.

Scooter hurried around to the driver's side and jumped in. "Where am I going?"

"They'll be pulling out of the parking lot straight in front of us. Stay back until I get instructions, but be ready to run them off the road on my signal."

Beto then dialed the boss's number, which was answered after a single ring. "I recognize the tall man in the photos you sent," the boss said. "His name is—"

"Sorry to interrupt you, sir, but I have important information to tell you and we need instructions immediately!" Beto said.

"How dare you—what's that? What important information are you talking about—the necklace? Do they have the necklace?"

"No, I mean yes, sir, but—"

"What are you blabbering about!"

"The necklace is called the Heart of Ceylon, and it was stolen in some Bakery robbery, they say it's valued at millions of dollars. They are taking it to the police for safekeeping! It was on the body of a dead man found in Tarpon Lake back when—"

"How far away is the police station?"

By this time, the Jeep had pulled away from them at high speed.

Beto slapped Scooter on the shoulder. "Faster, you moron, they're getting away!"

"What are you idiots doing? Catch them!" the boss said. "Don't let them turn the necklace over to the police! Kill them all if you must, but get me that bloody necklace, damn it to hell."

El Jefe hung up.

Beto dropped the phone. "Faster, Scooter, run those *putas* off the road!" He then searched inside the bag for his gun, which he had not been able to bring to Little Cayman. "Damn airport security!"

Scooter stomped on the gas pedal and the rental subcompact initially bogged down at the rush of gasoline, but then lurched forward with all four cylinders whining at max RPMs. They hadn't gained on the Jeep when it reached the intersection with Spot Bay Road and turned right.

"Why are they going so fast?" Beto said. "Did they see us?"

"The police station is only a half mile up the road from here," Scooter said. "What if we get pulled over?"

Beto bit his knuckle and then slapped Scooter harder on his massive bicep. "Faster, faster, faster!"

The tiny Honda topped out at sixty miles per hour on the narrow, winding road, and while it had marginally closed the gap, the Jeep had been going too fast to catch in the short distance. The smell of burning oil circulated inside the battered subcompact. When the police station appeared ahead on the right, Beto said, "Slow down, damn it, we'll have to switch to Plan B."

Scooter let off the gas pedal and the Honda's speed slowed immediately, having been pushed well beyond its capacity. He then turned into a driveway on the left side of the road, which fed into a small, multi-building office complex. When the car stopped, Scooter, with his eyes squinted, turned to Beto. "What's Plan B?"

"When I know, I'll tell you."

16

Emily stopped the Jeep in front of the police station and Boone and Nora climbed out. She kept the engine running.

"Don't forget us," Boone said. "And slow down, will you? That Jeep's not a Formula One racer. These roads are terrible."

"Are they? Gee, I s'pose I never noticed over the past year we've been living here," Emily chided. She put the car in reverse and backed out every bit as fast as she'd pulled in. I watched Nora and Boone enter the police station. Nora clutched the pastry bag to her chest as if it were an infant.

The Jeep shot forward, and potholes bounced me around in the back seat.

"Winston's house is just a tad further up the road here," Emily said. She gave Buck a big sideways smile, but he didn't say anything. He too appeared to be hanging on for his life, given her driving.

The road was lined on both sides with thick mangroves with flashes of brown water on the right. Hot air pummeled me in the back seat, which was hardly refreshing. Emily finally slowed to a reasonable speed and pulled into Winston's small square lot with the powder-blue home that we'd visited yesterday. She turned off the engine and we climbed out; I, for one, was grateful to have my feet back on solid ground.

"What are you hoping to learn from the old man, Buck?" I asked.

"Just want to prod him for any other details he might remember that could help us figure out what happened to your father or related to the necklace he'd found."

"Out back!" a voice cracked.

Emily led us around the back of the house, and we found Winston again seated under the allspice tree, enjoying the shade and late morning breeze. "Welcome back," he said. His eyes shifted from Emily to Buck Reilly, and Winston's smile faded.

"Thanks for seeing us again," Emily said. "We asked our friend here, Mr. Buck Reilly, a world-renowned archeologist, to help us better understand the necklace you'd found as a way to help Eddie learn more about his father."

"Nice to meet you, Winston," Buck said. He removed his sunglasses and sat in a chair facing the old Caymanian, and Emily and I followed suit.

"Welcome to my humble abode. Can I get you some sweet tea?"

"Nothing for me, thanks," Buck said.

Winston checked his ancient Timex. "Don't mean to be rude, but Amelia arranged lunch for me with Ms. Delilah shortly, and I need to freshen up some first." He pumped his eyebrows.

"We won't take much of your time, sir. I just wanted to ask if there was anything else you might have remembered about when you found the deceased person in the lake."

"Jocko." Winston sat back in his chair. "Was some forty years ago now."

Buck smiled. "I just flew in this morning and had forgotten how beautiful, yet small, Little Cayman is..."

"Was you on dat old Grumman flying boat?"

"Yes sir, it's a 1946 Goose."

"She's a beauty. Thought I was dreaming of the old days when dem planes used to land here in de islands before da big airport was built on Grand."

"If my bearings are correct, Tarpon Lake isn't far from here, is it?" Buck said. "The brackish, brown-water lagoon I saw on my approach?"

"Nothing's too far from here if you willin' to walk. Fact, dat's how I happened upon old Jocko, just walking back from de old East End Lighthouse dat day. I stopped to catch some dinner and seen something glisten on da flat, brown water—water's clear, really, but da mud below make it look dirty."

Buck sat listening and waiting for Winston to continue, so I did the same.

"Knew something was outta place dere, so hiked around, and was shocked to find da body. Poor, Jocko."

"Were you alone?"

"Yes, yes, all alone." Winston took his thick glasses off for a moment and rubbed the lenses with the front of his shirt. "Scared me plenty, finding Jocko. And den, when I found dat necklace in his pocket, felt like I'd committed a crime myself." He put his glasses on and checked his watch again. I checked mine to see how much time we had. It was nearly noon.

"Did you tell anyone else about what you'd found?" Buck asked.

Winston slowly drew in a deep breath, then his head twitched at an odd angle for a moment. "Only person I ever told was my dear, departed brother, Devon. Him and his young son, Robert—well— not so young no more. Robo be in his fifties now."

"They must have been shocked to hear about Jocko."

"Oh, yeah, everybody knew Jocko was up to no good, half da time, but didn't t'ink he'd wind up as crab chum."

"And the necklace, that must have been a shocker for Devon, too, huh?"

Buck's line of questioning was shrewd, circling in closely without being judgmental or accusatory. The old man seemed relieved to finally talk about it. My stomach was queasy though, the feeling that we were closing in on what happened to my father was unsettling. Winston's laugh was dry, and he shifted in his chair. *Was he uncomfortable now?*

"Oh yeah, he thought we should sell it and buy new boats."

"Blimey, I would have!" Emily said.

"What about his son, Robert?" Buck asked.

Winston shrugged. "My bruddah and young Robert went and searched plenty around Tarpon Lake for more goodies, don't t'ink dey found nuttin' though."

Don't think?

Buck's eyes met mine, and I sensed the same thought had occurred to him.

Buck checked his watch—it was an old Rolex Submariner, just like my father's that I now wore on my wrist. "Would you mind calling Robert so we could talk to him?"

Winston's smile turned serious, and he hesitated. The necklace had been a family secret for so long, he was probably worried his nephew would be angry that Winston had shared the discovery with us, but he finally nodded once, and reached into his breast pocket and removed an ancient-looking flip-phone. "Sure, we can do dat."

Winston slowly dialed the number from memory, glanced around at us, and then held the phone up to his ear. On max volume, I could hear the ringing on the other end, even though it was pressed tight against his head. Robert must have answered because Winston cleared his throat and appeared momentarily tongue-tied.

They exchanged pleasantries, and then Winston sat back in his chair and looked at Buck, who nodded to him. "You ain't gonna believe dis, Robo, but I be sittin' here wid a world-famous treasure hunter named Buck Reilly, and also a beautiful young lady named Emily, and even more crazy, the son of da man whose plane crashed back in the seventies, just before Jocko was kilt."

Winston's eyes danced between ours while he waited for a response. Robert finally said something.

"Yeah, yeah, yeah, dese people fine and good. Eddie, dat's da man's son, trying to find out what happened to his daddy." He paused to clear his throat. "I told 'em 'bout me finding Jocko, and den da necklace, and dey gonna help us figure out what to do 'bout dat shiny old t'ing. Maybe nobody claim it, we get it back, who knows."

Winston's lips puckered as if he'd just bit into a sour lime.

"Hang on, I'll put you on speakerphone."

The first thing we heard was Robert grunt. "I'm on Grand between charters, or I'd come by." There was no joy in his voice.

"No worries, Robo, but da treasure hunter, Buck, he wanted to ask you some questions."

Buck leaned closer to Winston, who turned the phone around to face him. "Hi, Robert. All's good here, don't worry. As Winston said, our primary goal is to find out what happened to Eddie's dad, but the necklace, and the man who'd hijacked Woody's plane are all tied together, so we're hoping you might be able to share any discoveries you might have found in or around Tarpon Lake, too."

Silence again filled the line. Had he hung up?

Distortion finally crackled on the line. "What makes you t'ink I'd know anyt'ing?"

Winston put the microphone up to his lips. "Don't be stubborn, Robo. I already told 'em you and your daddy went sniffing around da lake."

A loud exhale from Robert caused more distortion. I sat forward, sensing that something important was about to be stated. "Yeah, well, we did wade all through that old swamp not long after you showed us where you'd found Jocko, dat's true."

After a pause, Winston rolled his eyes, which looked huge behind the thick glasses. "And?"

"We din't find no more fancy jewels there. Fact, we din't find nuttin'." He paused for a moment. "Least there we din't."

I spotted Buck's eyebrows lift at the last statement.

"What do you mean 'there you din't?'" Winston asked. "Did you find somet'ing elsewhere on the island?"

"Yeah, well, kind of," Robert said.

Winston turned the phone back toward himself again. "Let's not play twenty questions here, Robo. What else'd you find?"

"When me and daddy was coming along the north shore on our boat dat day, we'd seen Jocko's boat anchored up by Salt Rock Dock, near dat foreign man's house who owned most of da fishing boats back den. He hired local men as crew but kept all da profits for himself. Da man lived on Grand but had a little cottage on da north shore of Little, too."

Buck and Emily exchanged a glance. *Had something Robert said rung a bell?*

"You said the fleet owner was a foreign man?" Buck asked. "Any idea from where?"

"What I meant by foreign was dat he wasn't from here. He was British, but he was new. Being dat our islands are British Overseas Territory, wasn't no surprise, and de only reason I know he was new was 'cause my daddy said he'd bought up as many fishing boats as he could just after he'd arrived a couple years before. Man tried to buy my daddy's boat too, but one t'ing he loved was his independence."

"And you remember seeing Jocko's boat anchored there?" Buck asked.

"Was the day before Uncle Winston found Jocko dead in Tarpon Lake. Made me curious, you know, I was only eight or nine, but knew nearly every inch of Little back den, so I rode my bike— daddy kept it on da boat for me—and went to where we'd seen Jocko's boat anchored after we snooped around Tarpon Lake."

"You find anyt'ing?" Winston asked as he looked toward us and opened his eyes wide.

"Da boat was gone, which even as a kid I had a feelin' sumpin' wasn't right, seein' how Jocko was dead, so I snooped 'round dat house."

"Wasn't you scared, boy?" Winston asked.

"Wasn't nobody dere 'cept these amazin' stone lions on each side of da steps dat I'll never forget, so more curious den scared.

Anyway, out back I remember finding a fresh dirt pile 'bout da size of my granddaddy's grave. He'd just been buried the month before."

I held my breath. *A grave? Could it have been my father's?*

"Did you tell anybody?" Buck asked.

"Told my daddy. Fact, I begged him to go dere wid me since we'd seen Jocko's boat dere, and den it was gone, and den I found dat dirt pile."

"Did Devon go?" Winston asked.

Robert exhaled loudly. "Yeah, we went back, but wasn't 'til da next day, or maybe da day after dat. Daddy had work to do. And when we went, we found dat whole area behind da house covered over wid a fresh concrete patio." Robert laughed, probably at the memory. "Daddy 'bout paddled my fanny over wastin' his time, but dat dirt pile sure reminded me of Granddaddy's grave."

All four of us shared collective expressions of bewilderment. Robert had been so compelled by what he'd seen that he'd dragged Devon, his father, back to the house where Jocko's boat had been anchored, only to find it covered over with a new patio. Something definitely felt strange about that, and I could tell by the expressions on everyone else's faces that they felt that way too.

"Do either of you know anything more about the Brit who owned the fleet, or the house that Robert is referring to?" Buck asked.

Robert piped in. "My daddy used to say da man who owned da fleet was nasty. He'd pressure men like Jocko to smuggle drugs instead of goin' fishin'."

"Maybe there's a connection to the fleet owner," Buck said. He turned to Emily. "Would you mind calling Nora at the police station and asking her to look up who owned the fishing fleet back then? Maybe we could go check out his house here."

Emily produced her phone, stood, and walked to a quiet corner of the backyard.

"Do you remember anything else about the house?" Buck asked.

"Ah, not really. Wait, yeah, I do remember there was a tall metal pole attached to the house—was twice as tall as the house itself. I'd never seen nuttin' like it."

"Could it have been a radio antenna?" Buck asked.

Robert was quiet a moment, but then laughed. "Now dat you say dat, pretty sure dat's what it was. I'd never seen one at dat point, and haven't thought about it since, but yeah, dat would make sense seein' how he communicated with da fleet by radio."

Emily rejoined the group, her perpetual smile wide. "Nora's checking for the name of the fleet's owner back in the seventies. She'll call me back when she finds the information."

"Winston, do you know the location of the house that Robert is referring to?" Buck asked.

He sat back down. "Not too many houses on north shore. I was never a fisherman, so don't know da man or da house, but if dat antenna's still dere, wouldn't be hard to find."

I could tell by the introspective expression on Buck's face, and his faraway eyes, that he was contemplating something. Before I could guess what, he turned his attention back toward Winston. "Something you both should know. It seems we're not the only ones interested in this old mystery. Emily here, along with Eddie and Boone, interrupted a thief ransacking their boat just hours after they visited you last, Winston. The thief, or thieves, tore up their condo too."

Winston sat up straight and rigid. "What da hell?"

"They might be following Eddie and the group to see if they knew anything about the necklace. From what we've learned, the man who hijacked Woody's plane and forced him to crash near Grand Cayman was carrying some kind of case that must have contained the necklace, and who knows what else." Buck paused for a moment. "Turns out that necklace had been stolen in London, England, and might be worth tens of millions of dollars."

"Say what?" Winston said. His eyes were the size of hard-boiled eggs behind his glasses.

"Holy smokes," Robert said in a pained voice.

"Point is, everybody associated with it may be in danger," Buck said.

Winston struggled to stand up, so Buck clasped hands with him and pulled him forward. Winston then wandered around us in a tight circle shaking his head. "Man, man, man, man, man," he said.

Emily stood and took hold of Winston's arm. "We're not trying to scare you; we just want to keep you safe."

Buck sharing that information fast-forwarded what must have felt like ancient history, straight into the present. Winston had paled and Robert was quiet on the phone. They both must be thinking they should have let sleeping dogs lie, but it was too late now.

Buck stepped closer to Winston. "You want to take a ride with us to look for the house with the antenna?"

Winston shook his head from side to side. "Gonna be late for Ms. Delilah now, but best put all this behind us once and for all."

We took Spot Bay Road up to the North Coast Road and turned west based on Robert's recollection. Like Buck said after seeing the island from the sky, it was small and sparsely inhabited, especially along the north shore. I turned to Winston seated next to me in the back of the Jeep. "How many people lived on the island back in the seventies?" I asked.

He shrugged. "About 150 today. Back den, dey was maybe twenty or twenty-five."

Emily drove more slowly than she had earlier, and we scrutinized each home we passed. Some were down gravel roads, which she turned down without trepidation.

"We're just lost tourists trying to find our rental property," she said, rehearsing her excuse if someone confronted us for trespassing. She pointed out the window toward the water. "That's called McCoy's Dock there. Used to be a diving and fishing lodge there years ago."

"Salt Rock Dock is just up here on the right," Winston said. "Dey be selling parcels of land near dere for houses."

About a mile down North Coast Road West from Spot Bay Road, where we'd started, we came across a shell of an old house on the water's edge. The wood structure was rotten, termite-ridden, and the windows had all been broken out long ago. But a tall metal antenna, twice as high as the house, was attached to the western side of the former residence. Overgrown bushes surrounded the structure and it looked as if it had been abandoned for decades.

"Blimey," Emily said. "That Robert has quite a memory."

She parked the car and we all climbed out. An old No Trespassing sign was on the ground and partially covered with dried leaves.

Buck kicked up some more leaves and covered the sign completely, then smiled. "Don't see any reason we can't look around here."

Just then his cell phone rang.

"It's Harry Greenbaum in London," he said.

He answered the call and placed the phone on speaker as we walked.

"It's been great fun reconnecting with old friends who'd been impacted by the Baker Street robbery," Harry said.

Buck was in front of me, and behind Emily and Winston—whack! A branch smacked Buck in the chest. He shook his head but was focused on the phone in his hand. "We're snooping around an abandoned house here on Little Cayman, Harry. Can you give us the executive summary for now and I'll call you back later?"

"Dear God, my boy. Not breaking and entering, I hope."

"Can't break into a house with no doors or windows."

"Well then, the net of what I have deduced is that there were indeed several items of great value stolen that were never reported or recovered, including the Heart of Ceylon, which is valued at thirty million dollars today. The owner, who wishes to remain nameless, is willing to pay a twenty percent finder's fee if recovered, my dear boy, so well worth your time."

That stopped everyone in their tracks.

A six-million-dollar finder's fee?

Winston beamed.

Harry continued. "There was also a small painting of water lilies by Claude Monet, which would also be worth millions, in addition to a handsome collection of gold coins, all of which I presume could fetch additional rewards if recovered."

"That's amazing, Harry," Buck said, now smiling.

"Indeed, but that's not the big news."

"Okay, lay it on me—us." Buck glanced around at each of us.

"Rumor has it—and it is quite well validated—that also amongst the items are numerous photos of none other than Princess Margaret in compromising positions with a man not her husband. If these had ever seen the light of day, the Monarchy would have been—and still could be—humiliated. Some would say beyond all repair."

"Dear God," Emily said. "That is juicy. Who was dear Margot caught on film with?"

"That is where the plot thickens, my dear," Harry said. "Have you ever heard of Lord Lionel Hoskins?"

"Doesn't ring a bell," Emily said.

"He was the son of the Duke of Luton and had been known as quite the backdoor man to married women of the highest echelons. His nickname, amongst those in the know, was the Rogue Royal, although he could hardly be accorded as the sole purveyor of such activities."

"You're referring to him in the past tense, is he dead?" Buck said.

"Oh no, he's quite alive, and here's the clincher, he's been living on Grand Cayman since the mid-1970s."

"Blimey," Emily said, "that doesn't sound like a coincidence to me."

"Wow, Harry, well done," Buck said.

"Hoskins was a troublemaker of grand proportion, and there was even speculation that he was involved with the Baker Street robbery, but the police never interviewed him."

"Why's that?" Buck said.

"He vanished and his parents pulled strings to keep the authorities away from him. Perhaps even the royal family intervened due to the supposed photos, we can't be sure. He surfaced on Grand Cayman not long after."

Harry Greenbaum's information had all our mouths hanging open.

"Bloody well par for the course," Emily said.

"Indeed, madam," Harry said.

Winston checked his watch again, now woefully tardy for his lunch date with Ms. Delilah.

Buck smacked his own forearm, and when he lifted his hand, there was a smooshed mosquito and a spot of blood in his palm. "Okay, Harry, thanks for the intel, but we only have our host, Mr. Ebanks, for a little longer." He paused. "Can you see if this Hoskins still has connections to the royal family?"

"I will try, my dear boy."

Buck disconnected the phone, and we continued through the thick underbrush around the house. Around the side, we stopped to study the metal pole, and it was indeed a former antenna. Wires had been cut at the base, and through repeated use, mice, rats, snakes and lizards had enlarged the hole where the wires once fed into the house.

The concrete patio that Robert mentioned was there, but in bad shape with weeds and bushes growing up through cracks.

"Looky d'ere," Winston said. "Robo was right."

He was pointing at a pair of stone lions on each side of the steps.

"Let's go inside," Buck said.

"I be staying out here," Winston said. "Some of dese old houses be unstable."

Emily and I followed Buck in the opening that was once a back door. No finishes remained on the weather-beaten walls, but the wood subfloor had remnants of tiles and glue zig-zagging its surface. It creaked under our feet.

"We may fall right through this bloody floor," Emily said. She turned on her phone's light, and Buck and I followed suit. Together, the faint beams helped illuminate some faded graffiti—something flashed in front of our eyes.

"Aagghh!" Emily shrieked, or was it Buck, who swatted at a few birds or bats that had flushed from a hole in the ceiling.

"Cripes! Bloody squawkers," Emily said. Just then she walked through a spider web and flailed her hands in front of her face. "Right! That's it, I'm out of here," she said and hurried back out the way we'd come. Her phone started ringing as she retreated, which caused her to shriek again in surprise.

I nearly laughed, but when I turned my attention to Buck, he had his cell light focused on the ceiling where the birds had been. His expression was intense, and I wondered if he was having an archeological flashback. I raised my light toward the hole and saw that our lights had illuminated a manila-colored item above the ceiling.

Was that some kind of Caymanian insulation?

Buck started pacing around the small, three-room cottage. "See if you can find something I can stand on," he said.

I entered one of the other small rooms and found an old two-foot-long stump that someone must have carried inside to sit on. After turning it on its side, I rolled it back out into the main room, just as Buck returned, empty-handed.

"Perfect," he said. We positioned it under the hole, and he climbed on—it rocked on its uneven cut. "Hold the log steady, will you?"

Buck then grabbed hold of the edge of the hole in the ceiling. "Looks like the drywall was patched here, but not well," he said. "Or it was a hidey-hole."

He started pulling at the edges of the hole and drywall. Dust, sticks and bird shit fell all around me. I shielded my face and looked down so it wouldn't get in my eyes.

"Something else is up here," he said, grunting and spitting.

"Not baby birds, I hope." I held a hand up to shield my face from falling debris and saw that his light had again illuminated the manila item I'd noticed before and saw now that it was larger than

I'd expected. Buck then did what I don't think I'd have the guts to do. He shoved his hand up into the hole, grabbed whatever it was up there, and started pulling. More rubble rained down, causing me to again look away as debris landed on top of me.

All of a sudden, a huge chunk of ceiling broke away—

"Whoa!"

Buck lost his balance and fell, caroming off my shoulder, knocking us both to the ground. A large piece of the manila insulation hit me on the head a half second later. Up on my knees, I checked Buck. He was covered in dust and dirt. "You okay?"

I realized he was smiling, his eyes focused behind me. When I turned around, my jaw fell open. It wasn't insulation, it was an envelope that had been hidden inside the bird hole.

"Holy shit," I said.

Buck crawled forward and started giggling like a school child. "What have we here?"

My breathing was suddenly shallow. I licked my lips. "Who hides an envelope in their ceiling?"

Just then, Emily called back inside the door. "Buck? Eddie? Can you come out, please? I have important news."

Buck's giggle was infectious, and next thing I knew, we were both laughing. He grabbed the envelope and stood up. "So do we!"

17

I led the way out of the decrepit cottage, with Buck behind me carrying the bulky envelope he'd discovered hidden in the ceiling. As soon as Emily saw me, she started waving her hands and nearly jumped up and down.

"Nora called and you'll never guess who owned the fishing fleet back in the seventies, and still does today," she said.

When she spotted Buck holding the manila envelope, Emily's jaw dropped open.

"Where the hell did you find that? Is there anything inside?"

"We haven't opened it yet."

"Well get to it, yeah?" Emily blurted.

Buck placed the large envelope on the ground, and everyone hovered over him as he undid the clasp.

Winston rubbed his palms together in excitement. Maybe he was hoping there were matching earrings and bracelet to the Heart of Ceylon. Buck then unceremoniously opened the envelope wide, reached inside and pulled out a sheaf of loose, yellowed content.

"Newspaper articles?" I asked. "Why would someone hide them in the ceiling?"

Buck scanned the headlines, and then looked up with his eyes wide. "'Thieves Arrested for the Baker Street Robbery!'" he said. He handed that one to Emily who scanned it, and then looked up.

"It says the men who planned and executed the robbery were all arrested. Their names were Anthony Gavin, Benjamin Wolfe, Reg Tucker and Thomas Stephens."

"What are the odds of that being in the ceiling of the man who owned the fishing fleet?" I asked.

Buck shuffled through the stack of papers. "There are other articles cut out of *The Times, The Guardian* and *The Observer*, all tracking the Baker Street robbery case." He handed those to Emily too but kept hold of what appeared to be a legal document.

"What's that?" I asked.

Buck shuffled through the pages and then smiled. "It's a draft lease for a shop called Le Sac."

"What the hell?" Emily said.

Underneath that, Buck held up a sketch of what looked like a building with names appearing over top of three spaces. I read them aloud, "Lloyds Bank—"

"Which was the institution robbed in the Baker Street robbery," Buck interjected.

"Chicken Inn and Le Sac," I said reading the other two names. There appeared to be a plumbing line leading from Le Sac underneath Chicken Inn and then up into the Lloyds Bank. My jaw fell open. "That's a diagram for a tunnel."

"Cripes!" Emily said. She then danced in place with excitement as she lifted her sunglasses up on top of her head. "As I was saying, you'll never guess who owned the fleet, along with this house, which are all held in a corporate name of Rogue Fleet, Ltd. —"

"Lord Lionel Hoskins," Buck said.

Emily threw her hands down by her sides. "You spoiled my surprise. How the hell did you know?"

"Harry had said his nickname back in London was the Rogue Royal," Buck recalled, smiling. "It would seem he embraced that reputation in the naming of his company. And this cottage and that envelope full of details about the robbery ties Lord Hoskins to both Calloway, and perhaps your father, Eddie."

Buck's conclusion caused my heart to skip a beat. "Jocko, one of his captains, was drowned in Tarpon Lake. Robert had seen Jocko's boat anchored here—"

"And," Emily added, "we had previously connected Jocko with Calloway."

The three of us had huddled together as we each spouted off different yet related observations.

"Excuse me?" Winston's voice came from behind us.

"Harry's intel that Calloway was considered a suspect has now been confirmed, I would say, circumstantially or not," Buck said.

"Um, hey dere," Winston's voice was louder.

We turned to see him holding a gray stick up in the air. What the...?

"Um... I found dis over here in da woods. Seems dese bushes have grown through a thin layer of concrete and unearthed some... bones."

Buck stepped forward and Winston handed him the thick bone, which I now saw had large knobs on each end where the joints would have connected.

"Looks like a human femur," Buck said. "Show us where you found it."

Winston led us back a few feet into the bushes and pointed down to a depression where a thin layer of concrete had once existed but was now cracked in multiple places exposing the ends of more gray bones underneath it.

"What the hell?" Emily said. "Could it be from what Robert thought was a grave?"

The air suddenly felt thin around us, and my breathing had become shallow.

"Must be," I said.

"Yeah, but whose?" Emily said.

My stomach flopped. "Could it be my father?"

Quiet fell upon us as we stared from the pile of faded newspaper articles, over to the bushes where Winston found the bones, then back to each other.

"As an archeologist, I've dug up many an unmarked grave," Buck said. "I think we should dig a little deeper here and see what we find."

"Oh, Lord," Winston said, his hand on his heart.

"I'm game," I said.

"Creepy, but okay." Emily wriggled her fingers on her raised hands as if she were repulsed.

Buck and I pulled the shallow-rooted bushes and cleared away chunks of thin concrete from the sunken area around the exposed bones, while Emily searched the property for junk that could be used as tools to excavate. She returned with a couple of former wall studs from inside the house, and an old hubcap the size of a dinner plate she'd found in the yard. Given our limited tools, and with Buck using best archeological practices, it took us an hour to dig around the exposed bones, until we finally had revealed the remaining skeleton in the shallow grave. The flesh was long ago decomposed, and there were tatters of dark clothing clinging to the gray and brownish bones. The concrete over the hole had been deep enough to prevent animals digging it up, so aside from the growing bushes that had dislodged some bones, the skeleton was relatively intact.

"Can you recognize anything?" Emily said.

My father had been tall at six feet, two inches, and the skeleton here appeared shorter. One detail I had focused on was the shoes where the person's feet had been, which appeared to have been black leather. From my breast pocket I removed the photo of my father my mother had taken the day he'd left on his fateful journey. It was black and white, but the shoes he had on were clearly lace-up boots, and based on the light color, I assumed they had been the canvas flight boots from his time in the military. I showed the picture to the others and pointed to the shoes.

"Um, unless he'd gone shoe shopping while he was here, they don't look the same, yeah?" Emily said.

"He always wore them when he flew," I said, looking down at the photo. "He even kept one of his Navy dog tags in the laces."

"How careful do you want to be with the remains?" Buck said.

I'd been struggling with that question the entire time we had been digging but had already come to a conclusion. "I'm more concerned with the truth," I said. "If we can determine that it's my father, then I'll arrange to have his remains transferred back home for a proper burial next to my mother."

With that, Buck and I worked together using the pieces of wood to hoist up the hip portion of the skeleton. The dark fabric came easily apart, but from where a pocket must have been, a wallet and small canvas case the size of a large coin purse fell out and back into the hole. Buck bent down and plucked the wallet out. It must have once been shiny, but was now a moldy black, and appeared to be Naugahyde, or artificial leather.

Emily wrapped an arm around my shoulder. She squeezed my bicep. My breathing was shallow, and I could hardly believe how far we'd come since I'd arrived in the Cayman Islands just a few days ago.

Buck opened the wallet and held it wide. No cash. There were a couple of slots for credit cards, but they too were empty. Buck then pulled out what looked to be a form of paper identification.

"The fake leather must have protected it," he said. "It's still legible."

"What the hell's it say?" Emily asked, squeezing me tightly.

He cleared his throat. "It's a Florida Driver's License."

"We lived in Florida at that time," I said.

Buck glanced up, and his eyes narrowed. "The name is Jerome Calloway."

I realized my hand was shaking as I reached up to take it from him.

Silence befell the group as everyone took a turn examining the identification.

"Who else would have killed and buried Calloway here aside from Hoskins?" I asked. "And what about my father? Where's he?"

Emily released my arm. "And if killing Jocko was related, why would they have left the bloody necklace in his pocket?" she asked.

"All good questions," Buck said. "Grab that coin-purse-looking thing that was with the wallet and let's see what's in there."

I'd forgotten about that. There were remnants of a leather strap that had been wrapped around what was a small canvas case. The remains of the strap fell to pieces when Buck pulled at it. The canvas was musty, but undamaged. Buck slowly unfolded it as we all leaned closer. Once open, we saw a single sheet of rolled up paper inside. Buck removed it slowly—a piece fell off in his hand— and Emily took hold of the pouch on the sides so Buck could focus on withdrawing the paper. Working together, they were able to gradually pull it out.

Winston leaned in closer and held his hands together, palms up. "Lay it down here."

Buck moved slowly and draped the paper over Winston's hands. The ink on the paper was faded, and in the shade of the woods it was hard to read. Emily lifted her phone and turned on her phone's light. It was a copy of a short letter.

"Holy shit," Buck said. "It's addressed to Lord Lionel Hoskins at an address on Grand Cayman."

"Blimey," Emily said, "another link to the Rogue Royal."

"The letter is a list of items—it mentions the Heart of Ceylon," Buck said. "Goes on to list photographic negatives—and the Monet is mentioned too!"

"The end says: 'Per your request, I will meet you on Little Cayman,'" Emily read. "But the rest is illegible, aside from a dollar amount—one million dollars—and it was signed, 'Jerome Calloway.'"

"Son of a bitch," Buck said.

"There's something else in the hole," Winston said.

We all peered back down, and I saw part of a revolver that had been under where Calloway's pants had been. I got down on my knees and grabbed the revolver by its barrel and pulled it up. "Looks like a .38 caliber."

"See if any rounds have been fired," Buck said.

The bluing on the gun was coated with rust, but the latch to release the cylinder functioned and I was able to press it out. The cylinder held five cartridges, and there was a clear indent in two of the primers. "Two shots have been fired."

"Had Jocko been shot?" Buck asked.

"No." Winston's voice was a whisper. "He was drowned."

Buck carefully shifted the remains aside. He then dug a little bit deeper. "No sign of anything else," he said.

"Safe to assume whoever shot Calloway must have taken the case from him first, yeah?" Emily asked.

"And it's clear where we need to go next," Buck said.

We all turned to face him. He jabbed his index finger onto the address where the letter had been sent. "Lord Lionel Hoskins, Grand Cayman."

"What are they doing in there, Beto?" Scooter asked.

Beto glanced over at the pair of tourists standing near him and Scooter at the end of Salt Rock Dock. He was concerned that they may overhear his and Scooter's conversation. It was an elderly man and woman dressed in hiking clothes. They were staring out into the water and not paying any attention to them. The dock provided the only vantage point where Beto and Scooter could watch the house, and Beto sought to mitigate the risk of being exposed by blending in with the old people.

He frowned at his dim-witted associate and held a finger to his lips. Then, in a low whisper, said, "They been digging around over there with sticks, so maybe they found more loot from the Bakery robbery. *El Jefe* said the other *maricon* is some kind of treasure hunter. He must have figured something out."

"They're coming out!" Scooter's yell caused Beto to wince.

The group emerged from the bushes behind the house, empty-handed—at least not carrying anything visible. Beto pulled the binoculars up from where they hung on his chest and focused in on them. They initially hesitated, then glanced toward the dock—the girl pointed right at them. The rest of the group froze, studied the end of the dock, and then picked up their pace.

"Damn, they saw us." Beto realized the tall guy—Buck Reilly—was carefully carrying something out in front of him, like it was a carton of eggs. "They found something small, but I can't tell what it is."

"Must be more jewelry," Scooter said. "Let's get 'em."

Beto lowered the binoculars and saw that the tourists next to them on the dock were staring at them, their mouths pinched tight, and their eyes wide. Beto grabbed Scooter by the arm—his hand barely covered half his massive bicep—and pulled him away from the end of the dock and toward Guy Banks Road, fifty yards away. "We need to check with *El Jefe* first. He's only looking for the Heart necklace and we already seen it on that bitch's neck. Something else of value must have been buried here."

"Maybe it's something he don't know about." A slow smile bent the corners of Scooter's mouth. "If he don't know about it, we can keep it."

The moron either had a point or would get them killed for being greedy.

"We'll see."

After spotting the freakishly large thug who we'd caught on Emily and Boone's boat, with another, shorter man hiding between a pair of elderly people on the Salt Rock Dock, we'd run to the Jeep and driven like bats out of hell south on Guy Banks Road until we rounded the western end of the island, passed the airport and turned left on Spot Bay Road to return to the police station.

After explaining that we'd seen the same men following us who had rifled Boone and Emily's boat and apartment, we left Winston in Constable Macy's protection, and Boone had dropped me, Nora, Emily and Buck off at the airport.

I couldn't believe I was going to be flying in a plane, nearly as old as the Vega my father had crashed, back to Grand Cayman. But Buck had restored it to near perfection. He said his Key West-based company was called Last Resort Charter and Salvage. It sounded desperate to me, which made sense since we had been desperate when we'd called him for help.

The sound and vibration of the twin radial engines had shaken me to my bones, but I felt like a kid on my first roller coaster. That, and knowing we were closing in on some epiphany of not only what happened to my father, but also details behind why he had been hijacked in the first place.

The plan was for Boone to remain behind to keep a watchful eye on their apartment and boat *but* be ready to come to Grand if we needed help. Nora had called ahead and provided details to Detective Whittaker, who was researching Lord Lionel Hoskins to find out more about his life here in the Caymans. She had reluctantly agreed not to mention Calloway's body. At least not yet, but had confiscated the revolver, wallet, and letter we'd found in his grave.

Buck expertly flew the ancient Grumman Goose. Upon our approach, air traffic control instructed him to vector south of Owen Roberts International Airport and get in line between jetliners belonging to American and Delta airlines. The landing felt rough, but the lack of creature comforts, soundproofing and even air-conditioning made the entire brief flight feel like a scene out of a Harrison Ford movie.

Once on the ground, I rented us a van. It was the least I could do given the sacrifices and expenses my hosts had incurred on my behalf, with nothing more than goodwill, and an interest in helping me solve the mystery of my father's disappearance as their reward. Well, at least until we met Buck and he learned there was a substantial reward available if the Heart of Ceylon was returned to its rightful owner. That had visibly changed the group's motivation and risk aversion, which truth-be-told, had impacted mine as well.

Nora drove the van since she was the only one who lived on the island. "The address for Hoskins you found on the body on Little Cayman is an old one," Nora reported.

"Damn," I said.

"My contact in London says he still lives here though," Buck said.

She gave him her trademark, emotionless stare that I had come to realize was in no way pedantic, but merely her way of processing thought before speaking. "He does," she said. "In a stupidly huge house on Ironshore Drive in Governors Creek. He bought the waterfront land there in the late 1970s and then built a while later."

"Interesting timing, given when Eddie's father crashed here, Calloway's case disappeared, and both of them vanished," Buck said.

"Until today, anyway," I said. "At least for Calloway."

No GPS or map program was needed as Nora guided us north from the airport. We headed out of George Town on Esterly Tibbetts Highway, where we ran down the back side of Seven Mile Beach. We drove through multiple traffic circles until she eventually turned right at one with a sign to the yacht club. Initially heavily wooded on both sides of the narrow, winding road, we passed by another sign to the yacht club and continued into a canal-front community, catching peeks of the marina off to our right. The homes were good sized and packed closely together on the prized lots fronting the canals.

"These houses look fancy," Buck said.

"Just wait," Nora said.

We rounded another bend and larger homes on larger, mani-cured lots appeared. We turned left around an elaborate water feature and came to an abrupt stop at a security gate. "I'll handle this," Nora said.

A guard in a formal blue uniform and hat emerged, his expres-sion serious, his dark black skin as smooth as ebony. Nora lowered the window, and before he could ask, she flashed her Royal

Cayman Islands Police Service credentials to him. "Official police business."

The guard, who I estimated to be in his late thirties, scrutinized her credentials, bent down to look at her face, and then handed them back. "What address are you going to?" he asked.

"That's not your concern."

They glared at each other for a moment, but he suddenly nodded and turned back to the small security office. He had been unable to compete with Nora's icy, Nordic, blue-eyed glare. The gate lifted seconds later, and Nora drove us into the ritzy neighborhood.

Vista Drive dead-ended into Ironshore Drive where the real mansions were situated on large parcels of land, heavily landscaped, wooded, and with unimpeded views of the Caribbean Sea as their backdrops.

"Now you're talking..." Emily muttered, staring at the impressive homes.

Nora turned the van to the right. The large, multi-million-dollar custom houses on the canal side paled in comparison to the oceanfront properties across the street.

"The *drittsekken's* house is on the left. I won't slow down in case he has security cameras. It'll be better if you don't all have your noses against the window as we go by."

She continued past and I caught myself mouth breathing rapidly, amazed at the scale of the Rogue's residence.

Buck whistled. "Not bad for a guy who fled the UK in his twenties."

"I don't know what he came here with," Nora said, "but he started building the fishing fleet not long after he arrived. Since then, he's bought a bunch of land, and several banks which are basically just servers located on the island."

"Hmm, all the necessary attributes for smuggling, burying bodies, and money laundering," Buck added.

I winced at his statement, imagining my father in a similar unmarked grave to that we'd found Calloway in, but Buck's statement made sense. We continued down Ironshore Drive until it ended at a circle. The other houses were just as large as the Rogue Royal's—I couldn't bring myself to think of him as *Lord Lionel Hoskins*, it was much too respectful.

Nora hesitated in the circle for a moment, glancing back toward the mansion. "Clever location. Only one way in or out by road and surrounded by water."

"We can't just march up to the door, ring the bell and ask if he knows anything about Woody, Calloway, or Jocko," Buck said. "We need an angle to flush him out."

"We don't have enough proof for a search warrant," Nora agreed. "Even though you found Calloway at Hoskins's abandoned house on Little, we can't prove for sure he had anything to do with his death. Or with Eddie's father disappearing."

"Aside from plenty of circumstantial evidence," Buck countered. "With his history of sleeping around with married women, particularly of the British Monarchy, and given the purported photos that went missing in the Baker Street robbery, and with Calloway coming here with a copy of a letter he'd sent to Lord Hoskins saying he'd meet him on Little Cayman, I'd say we have enough clues to substantiate that his hands are plenty dirty. Let's drive slowly back up the road and see if any ideas emerge."

Nora put the van in gear and pulled forward. "Whittaker told me they've investigated him several times based on accusations from women who claimed he sexually assaulted them. He said nothing stuck. The women both withdrew their accusations, so the cases were dropped. Whittaker has a hunch he paid them off or intimidated them into backing down."

"Perhaps that's his Achilles heel," Buck said. "Beautiful women."

We drove up the short street, and Nora and I studied the homes from the right side of the van—*still seems weird to have the driver on the right side*—while Buck studied the homes on the left side of the street from the front passenger seat. As we arrived at the Rogue

Royal's house, I noticed a late-model silver Bentley in the driveway —but a sudden shout from Buck caused me to jump.

"Look over here!"

Nora pumped the brakes in front of the house directly across from the Rogue Royal's mansion. "What about it?" she asked.

"All of their storm shutters are closed tight, the weeds are out of control, and there's junk mail on the front stoop. It's obviously vacant."

"Most of these places are second homes—rentals aren't allowed," Nora said.

Buck gave her an insouciant smile. "So maybe we borrow it to observe our friend across the street."

From the back seat I could only see Nora's aquiline profile as her lips turned down and her eye squinted. "Breaking and entering? I'm an officer of the law, Buck, and I'm already on sticky ground from another case."

"I understand that, but as you noted, Lord Hoskins is likely not the most popular man in the neighborhood. Maybe the owners of this home would be willing to lend it to the Royal Cayman Islands Police Service for an undercover operation." Buck's smile was indeed charming, and I could see why Emily was blathering on about him yesterday, but Nora's inscrutable expression had not softened.

"Undercover operation?" she said. "Like what?"

"I have an idea based on what you shared about lovely Lord Piece-of-Shit."

"Such as?" she said.

"We have a party." His smile grew wider.

"A party?" Nora and I said at the same time.

"Look, we know this asshole likes the ladies, right? And to be perfectly blunt, you, Emily and AJ are very attractive women—"

"Aww, you noticed," Emily said, her cheeks turning red.

"You're all a lot more than that, too," Buck continued, "but from Lord Hoskins's perspective, he'll see beauty first and foremost." Buck paused, and aside from an initial grunt, Nora had not responded. "And I'll bet that between the three of you, we can gather several other, ah, decoys, to attend a rip-roaring, stiletto heel-wearing, low-cut dress distraction event that if invited, the horny old rogue won't be able to resist."

"Yeah, baby. Sounds bloody smashing to me," Emily said.

Nora kept a straight face, processed Buck's idea, which I too thought sounded genius, and then cleared her throat. "Distract him from what?" she finally asked.

"Eddie and I may take the opportunity to do a little innocent snooping around Hoskins's beautiful villa, as you called it."

"We can't break the—"

"*You* won't break any laws, I assure you." Buck held his hands up. "And we won't steal anything, we're just going to search for clues."

"What kind of clues?" I asked. The idea sounded interesting, but I still didn't see what he was getting at. "I can't imagine he has anything belonging to my father in there, even if he was involved in Calloway getting killed."

Buck leaned over the back of the front seat to peer at me. "You're absolutely correct, Eddie. But—" Buck held up his index finger "—if he had anything to do with the Baker Street robbery, or has photos of naked women, particularly Princess Margaret or others that could be tied to the robbery, then we'd know he got control of Calloway's case, one way or another."

Nora pressed her foot against the accelerator, and we turned left on to Vista Drive.

"Shit," she muttered. "It's a good idea... but you'd better not tell me too many details. If I know too much, I might have to arrest you."

Buck laughed out loud, turned back toward me and Emily and pumped his eyebrows.

I smiled back at him. His optimism and ideas were indeed infectious.

18

In the next twenty-four hours we were able to confirm that the Rogue Royal was at home on Ironshore Drive—he'd be expecting a quarterly pesticide visit next week—thanks to one of AJ's contacts who worked for Island Exterminating, the company that services the community. The best news, however, was that Nora had successfully researched the ownership of the vacant house across the street.

An inquiry of police records into complaints in the neighborhood, led to a discreet phone call with Mrs. Ridley McLaughlin, the owner of the home. She revealed that she and her husband were indeed estranged with Lord Hoskins and would love nothing more than to assist the police in a surveillance effort of him. At Buck's urging, Nora had not revealed the plans for the party, but they got a green light to use the home and were given sufficient family information to claim that AJ was a niece of Mrs. McLaughlin and visiting from London with a group of friends. Security would be alerted, and unless the Rogue dug deeper, a proper cover had been established.

We met for breakfast at Café del Sol, just south of Governors Creek, and were finalizing strategy and assignments for tonight's operation—that's what Buck had called it—an operation, which elicited giggles from Emily, and raised eyebrows from Nora. AJ would meet us later, as she was busy buying supplies and making preparations.

"Between me, AJ and Nora," Emily said, a twinkle of mischief in her eyes, "we have a dozen dolly birds raring for a proper rave-up to captivate the dodgy codger's attention. We'll be so dressed to the nines, all slinky and low-cut, that wanker won't be able to think straight, yeah?"

Buck smiled broadly. "That'll be a sight to see." Then his expression became serious. "Unfortunately, Eddie and I will be busy snooping through the Rogue's mansion and will miss all the fun."

"We'll have a proper afterparty, Bucky-boy. Fear not," Emily said.

Nora ignored Emily's flirtatious goading. "AJ said one of her friends is a DJ," she said.

"Long as they play proper dance music. I need a break from the classic rock that Boone moons over."

"By the way," Buck said, "I called Jesse McDermitt to see if he was anywhere nearby, in case we needed, um, more."

"Who's he?" I asked. "And more what?"

Buck looked over at the others, then his gaze settled on me. "More of whatever it takes."

"He's another Florida bloke," Em said, as if that explained things. "Saved my and Booney's arses from a deep blue goodbye a while back."

"I'm not sure exactly what it is he *really* does," Buck said. "It's common knowledge he's one of the best charter captains in the Keys—both fishing and diving—but that's definitely not enough to support his lifestyle. I heard he was some kind of old-school spook or something, a relic from the Cold War. Some say he works for DHS or one of the other alphabet soup organizations. Who knows? Anyway, his wife's recovering from something and he's staying close to home. That I do know."

"He's a proper Bond, that one," Em agreed. "Too bad he's busy. I heard that boat of his is like a warship."

"He did mention a colleague of his," Buck said offhand, "a woman named Charity Styles, who might be on or very near Grand Cayman."

I looked up. "I know that name."

"Yeah?" Em said, typing on her phone. "How so?"

I frowned, trying to remember where I'd heard the name. "It was a long time ago," I replied, rubbing the back of my neck. "She was some sort of public figure or something."

"Olympic swimmer?" Em asked, turning her phone so we could see it.

"That's it!" I exclaimed, snapping my fingers. "The 2000 Olympics in Sydney. Don't tell my wife, but I watched the games just to see her swim. Phelps stole the spotlight, but she was only twenty then, still a collegiate athlete."

Buck let out a low whistle. "I never realized it until just now, but except for the hairstyle and some slight facial differences, she could pass for your sister, Nora."

Nora leaned in and looked at the photo of the swimmer posing with a bronze medal around her neck. She only shrugged a shoulder and turned away.

"I met her once," Buck said. "A lot easier on the eyes than McDermitt. He told me he'd contact her, mention what we were doing, and that he'd pass Emily's number along to her."

"Why not yours?" I asked. "Since you know her."

"Cause *Stretch* wants me to check her out," Em said, grinning at the other ladies. "We don't want some other bird making off with our Buckaroo. I did hear some people talking about her at that party we all attended in Marathon, but I never met her. If she contacts me, I'll invite her to our big do."

"Big do?" I asked.

"A big to-do," she explained. "You know… a big party."

"Everything seems to be falling into place," Buck said. "Eddie and I will use the car AJ arranged and go get everything we need for our part. The plan is to have everyone in place and ready to go by six o'clock, right?"

Emily breathed in deeply, put her large green sunglasses back on and rolled her shoulders as if she were loosening up to start dancing. "That's the plan, Buckster. Be there or be square." Her laugh was as musical as ever.

Less than a mile away, Charity Styles was getting ready to go out for dinner, when she received a text message from her friend, confidant, and mentor, Jesse McDermitt, asking if she was busy.

She hadn't talked to the man for over a month, not since his sudden retirement in July, after his wife was shot in Key West. She'd recovered quickly, but he'd whisked her and their adopted son back to his island in the Florida Keys, returning to his reclusive ways. She and Jesse had worked for the same company— Armstrong Research—in their Mobile Expeditionary Division.

If work was the correct term.

Armstrong operated a fleet of oceanographic research vessels, which were actually a front for the company's more covert operations, working under the auspices of Homeland Security. Posing as oceanographic researchers, Armstrong personnel were practically invisible.

Charity and Jesse were undercover operatives for DHS when they'd been recruited by ARMED, but Jesse had quickly moved up to command the flagship of Jack Armstrong's fleet, *Ambrosia*, a converted superyacht. He had been slated to take command of a brand-new, nuclear-powered research vessel called *Phoenix* when the shooting happened.

Rather than text him back, she called.

"Hey," Jesse said over the phone, "I didn't figure on an instant callback."

"How's Savannah?" Charity asked, honestly concerned.

Charity and Savannah, Jesse's wife, had a history together that included four bodies at the bottom of a Bahamian blue hole.

"She's fine," he replied. "There's barely a scar now and she's back to kicking my butt on runs."

"You're running again?"

"She thinks it's *good*," he replied, sarcasm in his voice, "but I'm slamming almost eighty more pounds on each knee with every step."

"Sucks being old, does it?"

He laughed. "Better than dying young. How 'bout you? Things okay?"

"I'm all settled in again and was just getting ready to go out for a bite to eat."

She didn't want to tell him that she was envious of what he'd done and what he and Savannah had together.

"I'll get right to it," he said, never one to beat around the bush. "A friend called me a little while ago—you remember Buck Reilly?"

"The guy in Key West we took that emerald to a few years back."

"That's him," he replied. "He's with some other friends of mine in Grand Cayman and he called to ask if I was available to help with a dicey situation, involving a forty-six-year-old plane crash, missing jewels, and a royal scandal."

"He doesn't know you're retired?"

"Hell, Charity, I don't even know if I'm retired."

Charity owed Jesse a lot more than she could ever repay, and this was the first time he'd ever asked for her help. He'd asked for her assistance on several occasions, but this was different.

McDermitt was asking her for a favor.

"I have a contact with the Royal Cayman Islands Police Service," she said. "A detective. Tell me more about this *problem* your friends have gotten into."

He gave Charity a name—Emily Durand—as well as a phone number and address, which she scribbled on a note pad. It was less than a mile away, just across Governor's Creek, but at least four miles by road.

"From what Buck told me," Jesse continued, "they're there now, creating a diversion, a party, so he and another guy can sneak into some distant royal's house."

"Sounds illegal," she said.

"It does," he readily agreed. "But one of the women in the group is a Cayman constable, so maybe not. Small island police aren't equipped to take on much extra and often turn to locals with specific skills. Anyway, it sounds like they may be in a tight spot, and I'd consider it a favor if you could help them out."

He'd actually called it a favor. The man was evolving. Thanks, no doubt, to Savannah.

"Do they have food there?" she asked, looking out the back door at her boat.

He chuckled. "Call Emily before you go, it's in a gated community."

The dark coveralls that Buck and I were wearing soaked up the heat, and a trickle of sweat ran down my back as we crouched in the stand of trees between the Rogue Royal's home and the neighbor to the left, which fortunately, was also vacant. Buck had been adamant about being in place well before the party began, which based on the loud bass beat that had been pounding classic disco music for the past thirty minutes, had officially commenced. Cars slowly filled the McLaughlins' driveway, and Emily, AJ and Nora greeted every new visitor with champagne, and loud hoots and hollers that reverberated in my ears, and I assumed for blocks in all directions. Although, I don't think Nora joined in the hollering part.

Buck checked his watch. "They should be coming over any time now."

Like a Swiss timepiece, our three lady accomplices strode across the street, carrying champagne glasses, and each wearing short, sheer, low-cut dresses and high heels. Far afield from the casual clothing I'd grown accustomed to seeing them in, I hardly recognized them. Emily was singing, AJ laughing, and true to form, Nora was laser focused on Lord Hoskins's front door. Her attire and feminine form would be enough to distract most men from the intensity that burned in her pale blue eyes, and with the other two left to do the more glamorous deception. I hoped that Buck's plot would work.

They arrived at the front door and started pressing the bell repeatedly. "This is great," Buck said.

After a moment, a man answered, and even though he had to be seventy, or so, he appeared fit, and had the smile and body language of someone very comfortable in the presence of beautiful women. We were just far enough into the woods to be unable to hear the conversation, but Emily, whom I'd come to appreciate for her vivacious personality, was waving her arms, laughing and pointing across the street. AJ was stunning in the simple, yet revealing, designer frock she'd borrowed, and the colorful tattoos on her limbs were accentuated by her blown-out hair and the dramatic eye makeup she'd applied for the event.

"The old bastard's grinning ear-to-ear," Buck said. "Now he's kissing their freaking hands. What a weenie."

"He hasn't stepped outside of his house yet though," I said.

"If he takes the bait, he'll no doubt want to change and primp before heading over."

We continued to watch as the ladies poured it on thick, providing the backstory we'd carefully planned that AJ used to live here and was back to house-sit while her aunt and uncle were away, and was having a celebratory party with her many girlfriends. They expected it to be late and loud, so wanted to invite neighbors so as to not be bothersome. Plus, available men were needed to offset the deficient ratio. If Lord Hoskins was half the player we assumed him to be, it would be an invitation he could not ignore.

Emily stepped onto the stoop and kissed the Rogue on each cheek, as did AJ. Nora curtsied, which given her short dress and long legs, was every bit as captivating.

"The old prick is drooling now," Buck said.

The ladies sauntered back down the long driveway, and Lord Hoskins lingered in the open door admiring the view. From our location, his exact expression was impossible to read, but Buck's observation made sense. How and why would he refuse such a tempting offer?

An hour passed, during which time, the bright orange sun sunk back over the McLaughlin residence where the music continued to blare, additional women arrived, and torches were lit in the front yard. There, the den of iniquity beckoned like *The Garden of Earthly Delights*, which, painted by Hieronymus Bosch around 1500 was a compelling, yet twisted view of heaven and hell that felt appropriate here.

Nestled in the stagnant air of the woods, my jumpsuit was soaked with sweat. Mosquitoes swarmed in the pale light and feasted on what exposed skin Buck and I had, and all was still on the eastern front.

"I'll text AJ," Buck said. "She needs to come back by herself to encourage him."

A few minutes later, AJ walked up the drive carrying a lit torch in one hand, and a glass of champagne in the other. She was mesmerizing, the flickering light accenting her cheekbones. Her ring of the doorbell was answered quickly, and this time, Lord Hoskins did step outside. He had changed into stylish evening wear. He bowed to her, pulled the door closed, stepped off the porch, accepted the glass of champagne, took AJ's arm, and they made their way down the driveway.

"Showtime," Buck said. We both donned stockings over our heads in case there were cameras.

I followed Buck as we walked along the tree line up to the corner of the house, peered back down the drive, and then he hurried up to the front door. I awaited his signal if it was unlocked.

He arrived there, glanced around the frame, I'm guessing for any sign of an alarm, and then tried the handle. The door pushed open, and I jogged over to catch up before he signaled. My heart pounded like the bass in the disco music across the street as I followed Buck inside and closed the door behind me.

"Okay, he must have some kind of study where he keeps mementos or personal items, so let's do this quickly, and see if we can find anything that connects him to the Baker Street robbery," Buck said.

"Or my father."

I followed Buck as we delved deeper into the large home. The living room was vast and well-appointed with light-colored leather furniture, original art, and tasteful oriental rugs. We skipped the kitchen and found a gaudy dining room with a long table and large, garish chairs gilded with gold paint. The chair at the head of the table was the size of a throne, where Lord Hoskins no doubt loved to ham up his noble British heritage. We continued and found a locked door on the other side of the kitchen. We had not seen any cameras, so we pulled the stockings off our heads.

"Should we break in?" I asked.

"Nora would have our heads," Buck said. "Let's try upstairs first."

We hurried back to the front and took the plush-carpeted, curving stairway up to the second floor. The master bedroom was dead ahead, and candlelight flickered from inside. Buck held a hand up, and then raised his index finger to his lips. We continued forward slowly, then peered cautiously inside the room. There were no less than twenty candles of various sizes burning around the huge canopy bed, where leather straps dangled from the wrought iron framework that was laced with chiffon and fake flowers.

"Sick bastard thinks he's getting lucky tonight," Buck said.

I spotted a built-in camera above the bed. "And he plans to photograph it," I said.

We checked the bathroom, which had a large, two-person shower, a claw-foot tub and additional candles burning. Back in the bedroom, we hesitated. "Let's check the bedside table drawers," Buck said.

Buck went to one side and I the other. I pulled open the large, single drawer, and my eyes popped wide. "Holy crap," I said.

"What'd you find?"

I pulled a tissue from the box on top of the bedside table, reached down, grabbed hold of two large plastic dildos with the tissue protecting my hand, and raised them for Buck to see. "Perhaps Lord Hoskins has performance issues."

Buck raised a key chain from the table's drawer on the other side of the bed. "Maybe there's a key on here that will open that locked door," he said.

The rest of the floor contained four other bedrooms, all nicely decorated, and the beds were slightly dusty and did not appear to have been used any time recently. We headed back downstairs.

The third key on the chain slid into the lock on the door down the hall from the kitchen. Buck turned it counterclockwise, and the sound of the deadbolt receding made a solid click. We caught each other's eyes, and he pressed the door open—which creaked loudly as it swung. Buck found a light switch in the otherwise dark room, and when the light came on, we both stood frozen at what we'd found.

"Why did the old man tell us to come to his house?" Scooter said as Beto turned into the entrance to Hoskin's community.

"He won't be happy that we're late. Something about a neighbor having a party that was suspicious," he said. "Bunch of beautiful women coming on to him and asking him to join them across the street. We were supposed to be there before he left, but he said he'd leave the door open when I told him we were close by."

"He wants us to go to the party?" Scooter's smile reminded Beto of Frankenstein's monster, when he had first spotted Lady Frankenstein.

"No, Scooter, to wait in his house in case something happens."

Scooter grunted and slumped lower in the passenger seat. "We never get to have any fun." His southern accent made his whining even more intolerable.

Beto stopped at the security gate, where the uniformed guard stepped outside and approached their vehicle. Beto lowered the window of the shiny SUV they'd picked up at Grand Cayman airport. "We're here to see Lord Lionel Hoskins."

The guard carried a clipboard, which he consulted. "Your name?"

"Beto Rodriguez."

The guard ran his finger down a short list, hesitated, and then looked up. "You're all set. I'll raise the gate."

Beto watched the guard reenter his booth. "Make it quick, *maricon*, *El Jefe* was very angry we were late."

The walls inside the locked room were covered with photographs of naked women, several engaged in sexual activities, and none from glossy men's magazines. No, these were not the favorite centerfolds that the Rogue Royal had pinched from his collection of lurid magazines; they appeared to have been taken from hidden cameras, and in many instances, given the vacant expressions in some of the women's eyes, of victims who'd been drugged.

"Holy shit," Buck said.

We stood in the middle and studied each wall, end to end, aghast at the sheer number of photos, each of a different woman. Some of the images were visibly dated, just based on the yellowed patina and graininess of the image, but others appeared more recent. I spotted something familiar and stepped forward to point to a picture of an attractive black woman whose arms were bound, and she was slumped over performing fellatio on a man who, based on the angle, must be the person who took the photo.

"Those are the same shackles from the bedroom upstairs."

"Sick bastard," Buck said. "Lord Hoskins is a deviant of the highest magnitude. There's probably evidence here to support prosecution in the cases that Nora said had been withdrawn here on Grand Cayman." He paused. "But I don't see anything that might be related to the Baker Street robbery."

In the back of the room was another door. Buck tried the handle, and it too was locked. He tried every key, and none worked. "Crap," he said.

I checked my father's Rolex Submariner. We'd been in the house for twenty minutes. "Now what?"

Buck glanced around the room, but not finding whatever he was looking for, turned to me with a wry smile. "Sorry, Nora."

With that, he lowered his shoulder and crashed hard into the locked door. The frame partially splintered, and while it sagged inward, the door had remained closed. On his second attempt, however, a shriek of wood occurred as the door tore open. Inside, we found another dark room. I found the light switch, and once the room was lit, we again stood in shock.

"Is that a Monet *Water Lily*?" I asked.

"Sure as hell is. And look over there." He pointed to the wall behind me.

I turned and found more framed photos, these definitely older, and of a face I recognized. "Is that Princess Margaret?"

"I'm no Anglophile," Buck said. "But it sure as hell looks like it. And I'm guessing the man she is sitting on top of is none other than a younger Lionel Hoskins."

"Look what she's wearing."

Dangling around Princess Margaret's throat was the necklace we'd found—the Heart of Ceylon.

"According to Harry's intel, those pictures and the painting are all from the Baker Street robbery," Buck said.

No sooner had he finished his sentence, then we heard a voice.

"Hello?"

"Oh shit," Buck said. "Someone's here! Turn the lights off and close the door that opens to the kitchen."

"Hello, Boss, are you here, sir?" a man with a Hispanic accent said.

I pushed the door closed and it again creaked loudly. "Damn it!"

Buck stood next to me in the dark. "Someone's looking for Lord Hoskins." His voice was a whisper.

We heard footsteps outside in the kitchen, which sounded like multiple people. "Boss, you in there?" The voice was just outside the door.

"What do we do?" I asked.

"If we wait here, they'll find us." Buck paused. "Maybe better to rush them by surprise and run for it."

My breathing was shallow, and I could hear my heart pounding in my ears. Being stuck in the dark room was so claustrophobic, I couldn't take it. "Okay, let's do it."

Buck stepped in front of me, took hold of the handle and with his fingers counted to three. He then swung the door open, and I was on his heels as we rushed into the bright kitchen—straight into a mountain of a man.

"What the hell?" another, much smaller man said, and jumped out of the way. "Get 'em, Scooter!"

The giant called Scooter stepped up face-to-face with Buck. "What the hell are you doing here?" His southern drawl was thick.

Buck didn't hesitate to lower his shoulder and plow into the man who was just as tall as he was but outweighed him significantly. The man grabbed Buck in a bear hug, and they caromed off walls, spun in a circle, and crashed into stools at the kitchen counter which sent them flying.

Each man fought to land punches from their death grip.

The other man and I watched with open mouths, until he produced a small gun and aimed it at me, thus further freezing me in place. I now recognized them as the men we'd seen on Little

Cayman. The big man was the one who'd trashed Emily and Boone's condo.

A noise sounded from the front of the house—it was the door slamming closed.

"Hello? What in the Queen's name is going on here?"

Everyone froze, and the beast of a human released Buck from the bear hug and stepped back. Lord Hoskins walked into the room. Anger had chiseled his face into a mask not unlike Zeus ready to hurl lightning bolts at his enemies. I'd thought earlier that he'd looked fit but based on his laser-focused eyes and agile movements, he came off like a man half his age.

"Speaking of the Queen, nice pics of you and the princess back there," Buck said.

The Rogue's yellowed teeth appeared and reminded me of a hyena. "Those pictures have provided me a very nice stipend for the last fifty years." His voice had the gravelly grit of a man who had smoked a pack or two every day for most of his life.

Buck's eyes narrowed. "Blackmail, huh?"

"Such a vulgar term. I like to think of it as compensation for agreeing not to return to merry old England."

Someone walked slowly up behind Lord Lionel and my eyes bulged wide.

It was Nora.

She ambled forward, slightly stooped, her eyes far away, with her arms hanging at her sides.

Had she been drugged? What about the others?

Buck spotted her at the same time, and recognition lit in his eyes. He hesitated for a second as he studied her in the hallway, and then spun on his toe and launched an uppercut that caught the big man squarely under the chin. The large man crashed like a felled oak, bouncing his head on the side of the counter on the way down.

"Shoot him!" Lord Hoskins ordered.

A second later, the other man pointed his arm toward Buck, a loud snap sounded, and a pair of wires extended from the small gun and hit Buck in the chest—he instantly shook like a fish on a spear. He'd been tased.

Fifty thousand volts of electricity tore violently through his body, his limbs went limp, and he collapsed on top of the man he'd knocked out.

I stood frozen, unable to move, speak, or seek to help Buck.

"Who the hell are you men?" Lord Hoskins asked me.

"Ahh—"

"We caught them coming out of this room here," the smaller man we'd also seen on Little said. He pointed to the door we'd burst out of.

Lord Hoskins pushed past us, turned on the light, and must have seen the shambles of the second door in the room. He removed a Walther PPK from under his pressed linen shirt and glanced down at Buck still lying flat on the floor.

"You're the treasure hunter from Beto's pictures," Lord Hoskins said. "Buck Reilly."

I took a deep breath and exhaled it fast. "And I'm Eddie Rains. My father's plane was hijacked by Jerome Calloway, who had come here in 1976 to sell you valuables stolen in the Baker Street robbery."

The old man's eyes narrowed, and the wrinkles on his temples deepened.

"All I want to know is what happened to my father," I said.

"How unfortunate for you. Weren't you happy enough to find his sunken plane?"

At the recollection of Calloway's shallow grave, a burst of anxiety poured through my veins, and I flinched. Lord Hoskins raised his gun to my face. "There are zip cuffs in the second cabinet to the left of the sink, Beto. Get them and secure these men. There is a roll of duct tape there, too. Cover their mouths and ready the van behind the house." Lord Hoskins turned back to me and smiled. "Lovely night for a boat ride, wouldn't you say, Mr. Rains?"

19

The small man called Beto was driving the van, with Hoskins in the passenger seat, and me cuffed in the back seat jammed against the left side door. The huge man they called Scooter was next to me. He had a fresh gap in his teeth from Buck's uppercut that had knocked him out, and his eyes remained glassy.

Nora, in a zombie-state, was to his right, and Buck was wedged into the luggage compartment amidst a bag of camera equipment and tripods. We pulled out of the driveway, and I saw smoke billowing from the McLaughlins' home across the street.

"Tell me, Mr. Rains, what led your group of vigilantes to me?" Lord Hoskins asked.

I tried to speak but my mouth was still covered with duct tape. When I didn't respond, he turned around sharply to see why. He waved to Scooter. "Remove the tape."

"Yes, sir." Scooter grabbed the edge of the tape closest to him and pulled it as if he were starting a small outboard motor. My head whipped to the side and pain shot through my neck.

I caught a last glance of the McLaughlins' home where AJ, Emily, Nora and their friends had held the party as a diversion. "Is the house on fire?"

"Mmm. All those torches. They really are a hazard, aren't they?" Lord Hoskins said.

"You're going to burn the house down out of revenge against the McLaughlins?"

"That's part of it, but with so many witnesses there, what choice have you left me?"

My jaw began to shudder. "You'll kill everyone!"

"I'd returned home for a can of petrol for an accelerant and found you and Mr. Reilly instead. But it does seem to be catching nicely, doesn't it?"

Just then a motorcycle sped toward us and caused Beto to swerve the van. "*Mierda*! Damn fool," he hissed.

The motorcyclist, dressed in tight-fitting full black leather and a black helmet, was barely visible in the darkness, but the shape was definitely female. I prayed that she would see the smoke and call for help.

"Back to my question, Mr. Rains," Lord Hoskins said. "What do you know, and what were your intentions?"

I cleared my throat. I decided not to mention Buck's friend, Harry Greenbaum, who had provided us detailed insights on the Rogue Royal, so he wouldn't be in danger. And, if we all disappeared, at least he'd know what we'd been doing and could alert the authorities.

That thought sickened me, but guarded cooperation seemed like the best course of action here. "Jerome Calloway hijacked my father's plane and it crashed just off Grand Cayman."

"I know all that," Lord Hoskins said. "I watched from shore as you searched for and apparently found the remains of the wrecked plane."

"We also found Calloway's body buried at a house on the north shore of Little Cayman—your house, Lord Rogue Fleet, Limited."

"Haven't you been busy?"

"In Calloway's pocket was a copy of the letter he'd sent to you which listed several items, a request for one million dollars, and said he was coming to see you—which is why he'd hijacked my father."

Hoskins turned in his seat to face me. "When Calloway came to my cottage and presented the case, the Heart of Ceylon was missing. He became enraged, as did I, and when he turned his vitriol toward me, I simply overpowered him." The Rogue paused. "Self-defense, and all that, you know? So, where is that letter now?"

"Um, ah, our friend Emily has it with her," I lied.

"In the McLaughlins' house?" The Rogue grinned. "Ashes to ashes."

How could he have subdued our entire group?

"What happened to everyone at the party?" I asked.

He turned partially toward me again, and I could see his evil smile. I knew instantly that he was the kind of man who felt himself mentally superior to everyone else. A lifetime of successful manipulation had made him arrogant, albeit careful. He had countered our trap with one of his own, which was far more deadly.

"Flunitrazepam is the scientific name, also known as Rohypnol. On the street they're simply called roofies. Double dose in the champagne bottles, glasses for everyone, followed by a toast to welcome them to the neighborhood." The Rogue was as smug as they came. "Did Ms. AJ really think I hadn't noticed her on Grand before? Those tattoos are quite memorable, but not nearly as much as her lovely face and remarkable body. Plus, who could have missed the news of her discovering that U-boat previously? Additionally, my men had photographed you all on multiple occasions over the past few days. So lovely. Such a shame she and her little friend couldn't join Nora and myself this evening."

I tried to digest the malevolence that was so evident in his warped mind.

"Are you really so cold blooded that you're going to burn the house down with everyone still inside?"

A loud crash came from the back of the van. Buck was kicking at the side of the vehicle, and by the sound of glass breaking and metal crunching, also at the bag that held the camera equipment.

He must have regained consciousness and heard the conversation.

"Tase him again, won't you please, Scooter?" Lord Hoskins said.

Beto handed Scooter the small gun over the seat.

The beast next to me giggled, reached forward and took the Taser, lifted his arm over the seat, and without even looking, zapped poor Buck again. The wires from the Taser hung over the seat, and Scooter tugged on it with a twisted smile on his face. The smell of electricity and ozone gas accompanied new convulsions as the current must have pulsed through his body.

Buck fell silent.

The Rogue leaned back to face me again. "How did that old wretch, Winston Ebanks obtain the Heart of Ceylon, and where is it now?"

A tinge of hope tickled my spine. Perhaps we had some leverage against getting killed. Even though my hands were numb from lack of circulation due to the zip cuffs, I balled my fists behind my back and gritted my teeth for a moment to muster determination.

"What happened to my father?"

The Rogue studied my eyes, his beady like a rat's. "Quid pro quo. I tell you what you want to know, and then you reciprocate. Deal?"

If I could only pound that pedantic smile off the bastard's face. I nodded deeply.

"I'll even go first. When Calloway attempted to double-cross me, your father assisted in repelling him."

"My father helped *you*?"

"He was quite upset about being hijacked, losing the plane, and the way Calloway had treated him."

My stomach flopped over at the memory of the musty hole that contained Calloway's bones. The smirk on Hoskins's face made me realize he was probably lying. Another question gnawed at me. "If Calloway attacked you, why didn't you call the police rather than burying him in your backyard?"

The Rogue's eyes bunched up from what was now a full-fledged smile.

"I didn't bury him, Mr. Rains; your father did."

His statement caused a sudden lightning strike of flashes in my head.

My father buried Calloway.

Lord Hoskins continued, but it took a moment for me to focus sufficiently enough to hear his words. "Jerome Calloway was a known accomplice in the Baker Street robbery, and if the authorities found him here in the Caymans, it would have been too bloody close to home for me—especially if he was interred *at* my home. Dumping his body at sea would have been preferred, but if it somehow floated to shore, there again, too many coincidences. You see, Mr. Rains, my... leverage over the royal family could only be expected to go so far." He paused for a moment, his smile disappeared, and he turned back to face the road.

I suddenly clenched my fists tightly and tried to pull my arms free from the zip cuffs. The Rogue turned back around and watched me, the shit-eating grin never leaving his face. I shook with rage.

"Now, enough from me, it's your turn. Where did you find my missing necklace?"

I exhaled a sharp breath and mustered my remaining defiance. "One of your captains, Jocko, was found dead in Tarpon Lake," I said.

"Of course, Jocko had been assigned to watch Calloway."

"Winston found Jocko's floating body and checked his pockets. Your man had apparently stolen the necklace from Calloway."

"That ungrateful wretch. Got what he deserved then." The Rogue peered back at me. "More importantly, where's the necklace now?"

It may be my last laugh, but I'd enjoy the moment. "In a safe place."

The roll of his eyes I got in return was not what I'd expected.

"I see," he said. "A man of no integrity as well. Well, I'm sure,

Ms. Nora will be fully cooperative..." He smiled again. "In more ways than one."

We'd been driving for what felt like an eternity and had passed through George Town, then scattered pockets of small communities until we reached Bodden Town. On the far side, where businesses and homes thinned once again, the van finally pulled off the road on the right and up to a gate. The Rogue climbed out, removed the padlock that held it closed, and climbed back inside the vehicle. The crushed coral driveway ran between two single-level buildings to the shoreline where two private piers extended into the reef-protected Bodden Bay. Both sides of the piers were packed tight with fishing boats, using every available inch of space. Nora had informed us earlier that the Rogue had owned a large fishing fleet ever since the seventies, which I presumed we were now looking at.

"Go to west dock," the Rogue instructed. "The *Peach* is the oldest of the fleet, so will be the least missed."

"What are you going to do to us?" I asked.

"Reapply the tape, won't you, Scooter?"

Scooter had been ogling Nora, even touching her bare thigh, as her head lolled on his shoulder, her consciousness lost in a drug-induced semi-coma that left her vulnerable in so many ways. She began to moan quietly. Was she coming out of it? From what I had seen of her, and had learned about her past, she was a true survivor, but once drugged, there wasn't much she could do.

"Scooter!"

The beast sat up straight, his eyes now forward. "Yes?"

"Put the bloody tape back on Mr. Rains's mouth. Now!"

Scooter scrambled—his sudden movement jammed me into the side of the door, the angle caused a shooting pain up my awkwardly placed arms, thanks to the zip cuff. He ripped a six-inch length of tape from the roll and slapped it loudly on my face as if to ensure that the Rogue had heard it.

The van stopped in the middle of the small marina. The Rogue and Beto climbed out and opened the passenger doors in back. Beto pulled me out, and since I couldn't grab the door for support, I fell to the ground amidst trash and debris. Spying a large shard of clear glass, I rolled to my right, leaned around and blindly grabbed it on the first try. I clutched it tightly, hoping it would not be visible in the darkness. Beto pulled me to my feet in time for me to see the Rogue squirt some liquid into Nora's mouth.

"Sleep for now, my dear, our time will come soon," he said, and then closed her door. "Get the big one and drag him to the *Peach*."

Scooter literally ran around to the back of the vehicle. Opening the doors, he dragged Buck to the edge of the cargo area and let him fall to the ground. Buck landed with a thud and didn't move.

"Let's go," Beto kicked me in the rear end. He then took hold of my arm and led me to the decrepit-looking pier.

I clutched the glass and kept my hands together. *Please, Lord, don't let them see it.*

Ahead was an ancient, weather-beaten, wood fishing boat. Its paint was peeling, the metal structures visible above deck were all rusty and the name *PEACH* on its bow was barely legible. My body began to shake uncontrollably as I knew I was about to board my coffin.

The Rogue had said he would have preferred to have dumped Calloway's body at sea, but if found, his connection to the Baker Street robbery would have been too close of a geographic connection to him. No such luck for me and Buck.

Tears ran down my cheeks and mucus dripped from my nose. I snorted—unable to breathe due to the tape that covered my mouth. I used what air I had in my lungs to blow hard from my nose—snot shot out onto Beto's chest as he stood smiling at me like a sadist.

"Eww, *pendejo!*" He punched my chest, but I hardly felt it.

Scooter came out from behind the van carrying Buck over his shoulder like a roll of carpet. The Rogue appeared from around the front of the vehicle.

"Put them in the forward hold," he ordered. "Perfect opportunity for an insurance claim, don't you think? Scuttle that old tub out past the southern ledge."

Beto's brow furrowed. "How are we supposed to get back?"

"In the dinghy, you fool." Lord Hoskins shook his head. "When you return, sleep in the office, I'll fetch you in the morning."

"You're not going to wait?" Beto said.

That earned a vicious glance. "The woman here was starting to come to, which means the others will be soon as well. I need to get back and dispose of them if the fire hasn't." He pointed a ramrod-straight arm and finger toward the *Peach.* "Now go!"

Beto forced me aboard by kicking me repeatedly in the ass. He opened a hatch and pushed me down the hole and I landed awkwardly. Pain shot through my shoulder and knee, which had taken the brunt of the fall. My solace was that I'd kept hold of the broken glass, but it felt wet now, which I realized was because the shard had cut my hand in the fall.

The scant moonlight disappeared, eclipsed by Scooter holding Buck over the hatch. I squirmed out of the way, just as a loud groan accompanied Buck hitting the deck. He rolled to his right, closer to me, and I saw his eyes flutter open momentarily. Mine popped wide when he suddenly winked at me, then closed his eyes once more.

Had the effects of being tased the second time already worn off?

The hatch was closed over our heads, and the sound of a rusty latch screeched a moment later. The engine turned over several times before catching, and the *Peach* was moving, albeit slowly. The two dusty portholes on either side of the superstructure provided some moonlight to faintly illuminate the cabin, which was in worse shape than the hull had appeared. The Rogue was not only prepared to kill us but had chosen this boat to scuttle us in, to get an insurance claim as well. Freaking sociopath.

Before long, the engine RPMs increased, and we were jostled around as the boat picked up speed in open water. The Cayman Islands were great if you were a diver because the reefs were all close to shore, but unfortunately for us, so was the deepwater drop-off. In fact, the depth dropped to over a thousand feet less than a quarter mile from the southern coast of the island.

"You okay?" Buck's voice startled me.

"Yeah, you?"

"That dipshit Scooter missed me with the Taser. I faked the convulsions and kicked the shit out of Lord Asshole's bag. Hopefully I destroyed his cameras so he can't take pictures of Nora."

"I grabbed a piece of glass off the ground when they threw me out of the van," I said.

Buck's white teeth glistened in the moonlight. "Good man."

We rolled toward each other and then got in seated positions with our backs pressed together. My hands and wrists ached badly from the restraint, and it felt as if my fingers were swollen to the size of sausages. I had to adjust my entire body to get my hands in position to reach Buck's wrists, and once I did, I probed until I felt the exposed plastic.

"I'll try not to cut you," I said.

"Don't worry about that, we need to get free and out of this old tub before they send it to the bottom."

My hands were now bloody from the cut, and sweaty from the combination of fear and the hot, fetid conditions below deck. I had to twist my torso from side to side to get the piece of glass moving with enough momentum to cut the plastic shackle—I dropped the shard of glass.

Damn it.

I had to scoot forward and lean back lower to try and find, then retrieve, the glass. I grabbed it; my fingers even more numb from using my hands with the circulation so constricted. I scooted back into position, and again started rotating at the hips, relying on my middle-aged abs and core strength to apply sufficient pressure for this work—the glass again slipped from my hand.

"God damn it!"

"Keep your voice down," Buck said.

Just then the sound of the engines changed in pitch, and the sensation of forward movement reducing speed was evident. We were now being rocked around by the seas, making it even more difficult for me to relocate the piece of glass.

"Let me try," Buck said.

He found the shard quickly, and again pressed his back hard against mine. I couldn't see what he was doing, but based on the shaking, it felt like the rotation method I had tried.

"If they're where they plan to scuttle us, they may come check us first, so we have to hurry," he said.

Buck was able to concentrate his efforts precisely on the side of my wrist, and he sliced away at it steadily. A wet sensation added to the moisture in my palms, and I realized it was more blood, now from my arm.

The boat's engine suddenly shut off.

"Come on, baby." Buck's words came in a harsh whisper. "Cut the damn thing."

I felt a sudden snap and my hands fell to my sides. "You did it," I said.

"Now cut mine, quick!"

CLANK-CLANK-CLANK!

The sound of something crashing against the hatch caused me to freeze and look up.

"*Adios*, assholes!" Beto's Cuban accent was clear.

"Hurry up!" Buck said. He hunched forward to provide me with the best angle possible, but the dark cabin made it impossible to see what I was doing.

My hands were covered in blood—I again fumbled the glass shard.

"Come on!" I said.

I wiped my hands on my shirt to clean off the blood.

The sound of a small outboard motor starting up cut through the silence. The dinghy that Lord Hoskins had mentioned.

I heard rushing water. Were we caught up in the current? Would we be dragged out to sea? I suddenly felt water on the cabin's deck. I slapped my hand on the deck and water splashed.

"Are we sinking?" I asked.

"My ass is wet! They must have cut the hoses into the thru-hull. We're running out of time here, Eddie!"

I leaned forward and sawed back and forth at the plastic strap—

now it was Buck's blood that appeared dark against his pale skin. My hands tingled at the renewed circulation, but my fingers were still swollen.

The sound of the outboard motor moved around the port side of the boat. "They're leaving us out here to drown!" I said.

"Keep cutting, Eddie, it's almost done."

I leaned back down and again started sawing away—

BOOM! BOOM! BOOM! BOOM!

Gunshots blasted, which made me jump, and geysers of water started shooting inside the cabin from the port waterline, adding to the rapidly rising level of water in the cabin.

Snap! Buck's restraint broke free, just as the sound of the outboard roared away, the two men in the dinghy laughing.

He jumped up, shaking his hands to accelerate the blood flow, then climbed the few steps to the hatch, and pushed at it, but it didn't budge.

"We're locked in!" he said.

He tried to batter his shoulder against the wood hatch, but the angle going up the stairs didn't provide sufficient leverage. "Look for anything we can use to break this hatch open!" he said.

He jumped back into the darkness and the unmistakable sound of water sloshing around under his feet redlined my anxiety. I felt around blindly in the near darkness. The sound of Buck in the bow, pounding on the deck above our heads, reverberated inside the small chamber.

The boat began to list to the port side and more water started pouring in from holes the gun had blasted above the waterline.

"What are we going to do?" I yelled.

Buck didn't reply.

PART IV

20

LITTLE CAYMAN, MAY 10, 1976

Sweat poured from every inch of Woody's body and dirt clung to his flesh and clothing. The Buyer and Calloway sat at the table in the shade, drinking more Red Stripe. He hadn't been offered a second bottle and been denied water when he'd asked.

Woody wasn't sure how many lives he had available, but he knew he'd used up several in the past two days. It was a miracle either man had survived the plane crash, and earlier that afternoon, The Buyer had interrupted his certain execution. Or postponed it at least.

If the men didn't come near enough for him to attack them with the shovel, his last-ditch plan had been to run like hell. But now he was exhausted from digging and wasn't sure he could manage to walk very far, let alone run.

He'd been taking his time as he couldn't think of any upside to hurrying, and his captors appeared happy to chat and drink their beer, The Buyer smoking one cigarette after the other. He'd hoped their earlier disagreement would come to something more, but they were acting like old chums now. Woody wondered what it was that was missing from the case. If he knew, maybe he could figure out a way to use it to his advantage. Although, he was sure there weren't any words in the world that could save him. He'd been reduced to a desperate shovel swing at this point.

He let out a long breath and looked down at the hole he'd dug in The Buyer's backyard. Lost in thought, he'd made remarkable progress, much better than he'd planned. He was sure he could lay his six-foot, two-inch frame down in the grave with six or eight inches of room for dirt above him. Not that he planned on voluntarily modeling it for them.

Calloway stood up and sauntered over, stopping several yards away. Woody quickly stepped from the hole, nonchalantly closing the gap between them by a few feet. He was still just out of reach, but Woody noticed Calloway didn't have the gun in his hand. *Tucked in the back of his waistband?* The time it would take him to retrieve the firearm should be about the time Woody needed to reach him.

It was now or never.

"That's a fine hole you've dug, Mr. Rains," Calloway said with a hint of amusement.

Woody looked down at his grave while he took a firm grip on the handle shaft of the shovel, hoping his averted eyes would give Calloway a false sense of security. Summoning all his remaining strength, Woody glanced up to sight his target as his arm brought the shovel around in a wide, powerful arc.

"You son of a..." Calloway began to shout.

A loud crack echoed around the backyard, drowning out Calloway's words, as Woody's shovel hit nothing. He staggered off balance. Something had smacked him in the face, blinding him, and he clawed at a gooey mess running down his cheek. If he was hit, he didn't feel any pain, but he'd heard shock could do that to a man. Dropping the shovel, he rubbed his eyes with his filthy hands, trading grit for whatever crap was oozing out of his head. Finally, he blinked away enough crud to see the backyard. The Buyer stood a few yards away with a gun in his hand. Calloway's gun.

Slumped half in the grave was the body of the hijacker, the back of his head a bloody mess.

"Couldn't think of a good way of telling you to dig that hole for two. Figured Calloway might get a tad upset," The Buyer said casually. "But go ahead and keep digging now, old chap."

Woody looked at the man. "I guess you don't care about the missing stuff then," he heard himself saying.

The Buyer squinted at him. "You know where the necklace is?"

"Of course," he lied. "I have it."

Woody couldn't believe he was bumbling his way through this, and more so that it appeared to be working.

"Where?"

"I'm hardly going to tell you that, am I?"

"Suppose not," the man said, eyeing him thoughtfully. "You'll be wanting to make a deal, I suspect?"

Woody shuddered as he wiped Calloway's blood and brain matter from his face, hoping the hard bits were little stones from his hands and not splinters of skull. "Not sure your deals are to be relied upon, Mister...?"

"Hoskins. Lord Hoskins."

Woody noticed his voice took on a more pompous tone with the word *Lord*, adding to his already highbrow English accent.

"So, what is it you want?" Hoskins asked.

"Not getting shot would be my first condition," Woody quickly answered. "And I must insist that's a nonnegotiable point."

Hoskins laughed. "Understandable. You have my word."

Woody looked at the corpse at his feet then back at the Englishman. "I'm guessing he had your word too."

"Indeed. But he stole from me." Hoskins's brow knitted for a moment. "Well, actually as it turns out, it appears you stole from me, and this poor chap was telling the truth after all. Although he didn't suspect you, he thought that Jocko fellow must have pinched it."

Woody held up a hand. "Just to clear up a detail, Mr. Hoskins..."

"*Lord* Hoskins."

"Sorry, Lord Hoskins," Woody responded, correcting himself. He wasn't sure exactly what a "Lord" was or how you became one, but he was sure the Queen of England would yank the moniker if she knew what the bastard was up to. "My point, sir, is that I took it from Calloway, not you. I was completely unaware of your existence when I snuck the necklace from him. I only took it because he'd held a gun on me and forced me to divert my flight. I grabbed it while he took a leak in the back of the plane."

Woody's stomach clenched as he suddenly realized he wasn't certain the man had said necklace. *Maybe it was bracelet, or something else altogether*. The more he thought it over, the more unsure he became, but Hoskins hadn't batted an eyelid, so he held his breath and hoped.

"Fair point, my good fellow. I shall not hold it against you."

Woody sucked in a deep breath. "I appreciate that. Now, how about you put the gun away?"

Hoskins looked at the gun in his hand, then grinned at Woody. "Dear chap, you know the whereabouts of my necklace, and I hold your life in my hands." He waved the gun to emphasize his point. "What stops you trying to knock me off if I don't have this?"

"*My* word?" Woody replied, knowing he was a God-loving man who held honesty above most else… but in this case he'd make an exception and hope his maker would understand. Besides, he'd already told one lie, so he was committed now. Of course, God might argue that it always started that way, but Woody would cross that bridge when he stood before the Pearly Gates.

The point was moot, as Lord Hoskins wasn't about to believe him anyway. "Very noble of you Mr. Rains. In fact, that is a good suggestion."

To my complete surprise, he threw the gun in the bottom of the hole. I stared at it for a long moment, and just as I was about to jump in and grab it, Lord Hoskins reached under his shirt and removed a Walther PPK.

"With the murder weapon now disposed of, it's good that I keep this insurance policy on me at all times."

Woody nodded. *It had been worth a shot.*

Hoskins looked at his wristwatch. "Don't just stand there, my good man, kick him in the hole and get him covered up. Toss the extra dirt over to the side somewhere. The locals are supposed to be here tomorrow to pour cement, and I need to get back to Grand." He paused and stared at Woody. "After we retrieve my necklace, of course."

"In that case, I'll be going to Grand with you," Woody said. "Happens to be where your necklace is."

Lord Hoskins frowned for a moment before his face relaxed into a smile. "Then best you hurry up so we can push off. We'll already be arriving near dark."

The crossing took close to four hours. The open ocean was relatively calm, and Hoskins boasted how his Magnum Maltese could make it in half the time, but only if a gas station popped up in the middle of the Caribbean Sea. Much to the lord's displeasure, he was forced to throttle back, ensuring they'd reach their destination.

The two men traveled in silence for much of the trip. The throaty engine made conversation almost impossible unless they stood right next to each other, which neither man was willing to do. Woody tried to sleep and recover his energy for whatever lay ahead. *And what did lie ahead?* He was only certain of one thing… there wasn't any necklace waiting for them on Grand, so he'd better come up with a plan before their arrival.

Hoskins kept the gun tucked in the front waistband of his pants and made Woody stay in the passenger seat opposite his own. The man methodically scanned between the sea ahead, the compass on the dash, and Woody, leaving no opportunities for a surprise attack. Hoskins seemed to have an endless supply of cigarettes which he was determined to burn through faster than Keith Richards. Deciding he'd wait until they were closer to land, Woody returned his attention to sleeping.

The world jolted and bounced, making thudding noises and a roaring sound which seemed to surround him. Woody blinked his eyes and struggled to focus. For a moment he was completely disoriented and thought he was in a darkened room, but he couldn't be... *rooms don't move.* As he jerked fully awake, he realized he'd been crashed out for a while, and the sun had almost set ahead of them.

"What did we hit?" he asked.

"Gets a bit lumpy through the cut in the reef." Hoskins shouted back.

Woody could see the low profile of the island ahead, but they were still a long way from land.

"This some kind of lagoon?"

"The North Sound, dear boy," Hoskins explained. "Reef runs from point to point behind us. Still three or four miles to the marina in Governors Creek," he said, steering the boat slightly to starboard, following a new compass heading.

Woody grunted a response. He needed another ten hours of sleep to feel human again. His neck and back had not been improved by grave digging, nor flopping around in the seat as he'd snoozed during the crossing. He also needed to pee. However, none of that mattered a damn if he didn't figure out a way to disarm and overpower his Lordship.

"This would be a good time to tell me where we're heading, Mr. Rains. I have a car at the marina, I just need to know a destination."

"I'll direct you once we get to your car, don't worry about that," Woody replied, summoning a tone of confidence.

He sat back and rubbed his tired legs, hoping they'd magically regain their strength, and noticed Hoskins was less concerned about gas now they were nearing home. He pushed the throttles forward, skimming across the flat, calm water of the sound. The low trees, shrubs and mangroves were getting larger as they neared shore, and Woody began sizing up whether he could shove the man over the side of the boat.

The problem was the wraparound windshield which tapered down to meet the gunwale just behind the helm chair. It was tall enough that he'd need to lift the man off the deck to get his mass over the Perspex. Lord Hoskins wasn't a big man and Woody likely outweighed him by a good margin, but he was sure the Englishman would put up a fight... and pull the gun.

Looking ahead, Woody struggled to make out where exactly they were going; it all appeared to be thick foliage lining the coast. To the northwest he could see a few buildings, with more southwest of their position. He was beginning to wonder what Hoskins was up to when he spotted a pair of wooden posts with channel markers.

Woody Rains had flown jet fighters in the war and was neither afraid, nor shy about engaging the enemy, and this situation was no different. He'd told himself his hesitation had been the lack of good opportunity, but deep down he knew there was never going to be a perfect time to strike. He'd received basic training in hand-to-hand combat, but the little he knew seemed to elude his mind every time he considered making a move. Seeing the channel markers and watching the man light his umpteenth cigarette, cast all his planning and strategy aside. Something triggered in Woody's mind, and he knew the time had to be now.

With adrenaline surging, Woody leapt from his seat, took one step toward Hoskins, and swung his right fist, solidly connecting with the man's jaw. The boat veered suddenly to the left as a sharp pain surged through his knuckles, and at the same time he felt a jab in his side. Woody heard a loud crack as Hoskins collapsed into the helm, shoving the throttle forward. The engine roared and the bow bucked, then the boat straightened again, throwing the two men rearward into the second-row bench seat.

Woody scrambled to his feet first, fighting for balance on the speeding boat. Hoskins was a step behind, pushing himself up from the bench, and Woody swiftly pounced. He lurched at the man, leading with a punch which connected with Hoskins's nose. Woody felt bone and cartilage crunch as his momentum drove him into his opponent, his shoulder hitting the Englishman's chest. The force sent them both against the starboard gunwale where Woody clutched at anything within his reach to stop himself tumbling into the water. As he did, he felt Hoskins's body disappear over the side.

Quickly shifting his attention back to the boat, Woody could make out land ahead, silhouetted by the setting sun, slightly to the right. Their struggle had veered the boat to the left, which he knew meant the Magnum was no longer aimed for the channel. Grabbing the back of the helm chair, Woody dragged himself forward. The powerful engine drowned out any other sounds, but Woody felt the sudden jolt as the prop drove into the sandy bottom, acting like an anchor and throwing him forward, bouncing between the two chairs and slamming into the bulkhead.

The bow dropped, momentarily rocking the prop from the sand, but before Woody had time to pick himself up, the boat jarred, and he was slammed back against the bulkhead and companionway door. Sounds of screeching, gouging, and shredding fiberglass matched the engine's roar, as branches tore the outside of the boat to shreds. Above him the windshield exploded, sending pieces of Perspex flying.

Crushed against the bulkhead, Woody felt his body ride up as the runaway Magnum violently ground to a stop, succumbing to the grip of the woods. The engine spluttered, stalled, and all fell silent beyond the whistling sound in Woody's battered head.

He lay on the deck and tried to breathe. All the air had been forced from his lungs, but Woody couldn't believe he'd survived another wreck. Slowly picking himself up, his movement caused the boat to creak and groan and he steadied himself with a hand on the battered helm chair. Looking toward the water, Woody gasped at the trail of devastation left in the wake of the crash, the backdrop lit in tangerine hues from the sunset hitting the eastern clouds.

A perfect path running fifty feet from the sound to where the boat came to rest had been smashed through the small trees and shrubs. Beyond it, he could just make out the channel markers they'd been heading toward, now a good mile to the north.

Woody turned and stared deeper into the woods. Beyond the battered bow, all he could see was dense, impenetrable foliage. His only way out would be via the water. As his adrenaline rush subsided, Woody's aches and pains returned, with a new set adding to the collection. He felt a stinging pain in his side and looked down.

Surprised to find his shirt covered in blood, he raised the sodden fabric and wondered what had caused the gash in his side. It would need stitches. Woody let go of his shirt, urging himself into action. First and foremost, he needed to get to the authorities and explain everything. After that he could get patched up, and tomorrow he'd take them to Calloway's grave on Little Cayman.

He opened the companionway door and reached inside, finding the case. The contents would be the evidence which would tie his story together, from the plane hijacking, to whatever happened to the Jocko guy, Calloway's murder, and finally the wrecked boat in the pristine lagoon.

With renewed determination, Woody scrambled over the bench seat and the engine cover, dropping to the bed of flattened vegetation below.

"I never stopped to notice what a gorgeous spot this is," came Hoskins's pompous voice.

Woody looked up to see the Englishman's gun once more pointed at his chest. Blood streaked the man's face from his broken nose but otherwise he appeared none the worse for wear considering he'd been thrown from a speeding boat. How he'd hung on to the gun, Woody had no idea.

"If I'm not mistaken, this whole stretch is for sale," he continued as though they were casually chatting in a café. "I must give my estate agent a bell and make some inquiries."

Woody touched his side and recalled the loud crack as the two men had wrestled at the helm chair. It must have been Hoskins's bullet that'd grazed him. He added the near miss to his growing tally of narrow escapes from the past few days. A list he sensed had received its last entry.

"You never had the necklace, did you, old sport?" Lord Hoskins asked, but his tone suggested it was rhetorical. The man had figured out the ruse... and Woody knew his luck had finally run out.

21

PRESENT DAY

Buck cursed and pushed harder against the deck hatch, straining with every fiber of his being, as I watched helplessly. There was nothing in the cabin of any use for forcing the hatch open, and room enough for only one of us.

Suddenly, there was a splintering sound and Buck grunted as he fell backward.

"What happened?" I asked urgently.

"Damned step broke," he replied, struggling to get up. "I got the hatch undogged, but that ape put something heavier than me on top of it."

The water was collecting in the left rear part of the cabin, as the bow began to rise higher, and the boat continued to roll. There was a sudden shifting of something heavy up above us, then a sliding sound, and a heavy thud.

Buck quickly mounted the stairs again, stepping past the broken one and threw his weight almost horizontally at the hatch, the boat nearly on its side. The hatch flew open and almost as quickly, water started pouring in.

"Hurry!" Buck shouted, scrambling through the opening. "The

release of this air pocket is going to make her go down faster than a Tijuana prostitute."

I was right behind him, literally diving sideways through the overhead hatch and into the dark water.

"C'mon!" Buck yelled, as he swam hard to get away from the boat. "When it goes, it'll suck everything on the surface down with it."

I struck out, kicking my feet and flailing my arms as hard as I could. Behind me, I heard a horrendous splash and turned to see the boat roll completely over. Then the bow came up out of the water and it silently submerged, a stream of detritus being blown out of the hatch.

"Buck!" I shouted.

"Right here behind you," he called back. "I found a cooler."

I turned around and saw the large white object, but everywhere else was just blackness. When I swam over, I finally saw him hanging onto a large plastic cooler, probably a fish box. Unlike the boat, it looked fairly new.

"That dumbass put a heavy tool chest on top of the hatch," Buck said, draping an arm over the cooler and grabbing my shirt. "It must have slid off as the boat rolled."

I did the same with my right arm, grabbing Buck's vest, then pointed with my left. "Look! We're only about a quarter mile from shore. The ride seemed longer."

"It was longer," Buck said. "I don't suppose you know what the tide is right now, do you?"

"The tide?" I asked, hearing surf crashing for the first time. "Oh, shit. We have to get across the reef."

"The boat went around it," Buck said, paddling harder to turn us in the direction of the current. "Hopefully, we can find a way back through it. I don't like the sound of breaking waves on a coral reef."

We started kicking and paddling with our free hands, as the current carried us along the coast, hopefully in the right direction.

There were a few lights on shore, so help was just a short distance away. But first we had to get there.

"How far does the reef go?" I asked.

"No idea," Buck replied. "Hopefully, *it* runs out before the island does."

When Charity rolled her new Ducati Monster 1200 to a stop in front of the address she'd been given, she could see smoke coming out of two windows in the front. In one fluid motion, she killed the engine, put the kickstand down, got off, and flicked the dark visor of her full-face helmet up.

Her blue eyes surveyed the scene as only those of a covert assassin would, taking everything in instantly—possible hiding places, points of egress, or any other concealed dangers.

It was the right place—the number was on a post at the top of the driveway.

She ran to the door, her boot heels thudding softly on the concrete. The door was locked. She looked around, then drew a small handgun from under her tight leather jacket. She then pulled a suppressor from the other inside pocket and threaded it onto the barrel. Guns weren't permitted on the island, but she was glad that she'd retrieved the very narrow and concealable Diamondback DB9 from its hiding place on her boat. Charity rarely went anywhere unarmed, even if that meant violating local law.

She aimed carefully at the deadbolt, and with one shot, the bolt snapped and the door flew open. Charity's gun led the way as she entered the house. The air was thick with smoke, so she flipped the visor back down. It wasn't airtight, but the helmet's fresh air intakes did have small filter cartridges in them. They worked best when air was forced through them and out around her neck, so she kept her breathing shallow.

She quickly found the source of the fire, some sort of fabric stuffed into the oven in the kitchen. It was ablaze, flames reaching out and tickling the ceiling above the stove. It would only be a few minutes before the ceiling caught and then the fire would soon spread quickly.

Wearing leather riding gloves, Charity reached in and yanked whatever it was out of the oven, letting it burn on the marble floor, as she reached over the stove and turned the oven off.

The flames quickly diminished, having no heat source to keep them going, and Charity recognized the charred mess as a seat cushion—something usually made of a flame retardant material. But in a four-hundred-degree oven, flame was inevitable.

Whoever had stuffed it in the oven had been in the house only minutes before.

Her mind flashed to the van that had almost hit her as she came up the road. It was being driven by a Hispanic-looking man with an older man in the front passenger seat. The back windows were tinted, so Charity had no idea if there were others in the van.

Were the people she was supposed to meet in the van? she wondered, as she looked back into the living room.

Two bodies lay on the couch, which was missing a cushion.

Charity threw open a window and door in the kitchen, then headed for the front of the house to open more. The continuous breeze on the island would get the smoke out quickly.

She opened the windows on either side of the couch, on which two young women's bodies were arranged. Their legs and arms were askew, as if they'd been dumped there, one against the other, then shoved into a heap to pull the cushion out. Each woman was dressed in clubbing attire, one missing a high heel.

She looked around and saw two more women similarly dressed, piled onto a plush chair, one on top of the other. The one on top retched and coughed.

Charity hurried over and checked the second woman's pulse, whose lap the first was sitting on. They were both alive. None of the four had any visible injuries.

She grabbed the smaller blonde by the arm, draping it around her shoulders and getting her into a sitting position. Then Charity reached between the woman's legs, and heaved her up into a fire-man's carry, and hurried to the door.

"Stop where you are!" a voice boomed, as Charity exited the house.

There were flashing lights from two RCIPS police cars blocking the drive, and a man in front of her, holding out a badge.

Charity flipped her visor up, so he could see her face. "There are at least three more people inside, Roy!"

"Whatta we do?" Scooter whined once more.

As big as the Alabaman was and given his total lack of morals and often sadistic nature, he acted like a seven-year-old a lot of the time.

"Shut up and hold the boat steady," Beto said, trying to look through the binoculars.

They'd seen the flashing lights on the road as they'd headed toward the dock and instead pulled up to a smaller pier about a hundred yards away, driving the little boat into the darkness under the boards.

There were two cop cars and a van at the Rogue's marina. Beto and Scooter had hunkered down while a bunch of cops snooped around the boats. And now, a new arrival: someone dressed from head to toe in shiny, black clothes. They stopped at the end of the pier where the *Peach* had been docked and looked all around and out toward the reef.

"Can they see us?" Scooter asked, holding the little boat steady against the dock over their heads. "I don't like this little boat, Beto. I ain't a good swimmer."

"No, I don't think they see us," Beto replied. "But something weird's goin' on over there."

"What, Beto?"

"The cops are making someone dressed all in black take their clothes off."

Scooter bumped him, trying to move for a better view and Beto almost dropped the binoculars over the side. He shoved the brute back and readjusted the binoculars.

"Hold us steady, *pendejo!*" he whispered harshly.

The person in black had their back turned, facing all the cops, one of them an older man in plain clothes. The orange lights above the pier gave Beto a good view of each person, and the one in black was talking to them, as she removed her jacket. Beneath it, she wore a flimsy yellow tank top.

"Holy crap," Scooter said. "I think it's a woman."

"Hold us still!" Beto whisper shouted. "I can see that. You just be ready to start the engine. I gotta call the boss."

Lord Hoskins answered after the phone rang several times. "What's the meaning of this interruption?"

"We're close to the fishing pier," Beto whispered. "There's cops everywhere."

"They were at my house, as well," Lord Hoskins said, matter-of-factly. "Did you sink the boat?"

"Yeah, they're gone," Beto said. "But we can't go back to the pier."

There was a rustling sound and Beto thought he heard a woman's moan. His mind flashed back to the tall blonde Lord Hoskins had brought back from the house across the street. Then he heard the boss's voice, muffled, as if he didn't have the phone up to his mouth. "Sorry, my darling. I'm afraid we'll have to continue this at a later date."

There were more grunts and moans, then *El Jefe* came back on. "What's going on there?"

"It's weird, man," Beto said. "The cops just made a woman strip and get in the water."

"That makes no sense at all. However, it does appear the police might be on to me. Where are you? I'll collect you, then we can take Miss Nora to my yacht."

"I think you oughta cut your losses, Boss," Beto said, searching the water for the very shapely woman.

"I don't take advice from a common criminal. Where are you?"

Suddenly, there was a splash, and something long and white shot up out of the water, grabbed Scooter, and kicked the boat backward, causing Beto to drop the phone into the boat.

In an instant, Scooter was gone.

Beto's eyes had seen it happen, but his mind couldn't process what they'd seen. A nearly naked woman, wearing only a little tank top and panties had leapt out of the water and taken Scooter under. It was the woman from the pier, but that was a hundred yards away.

And Scooter was almost three times her size.

I ain't a good swimmer, the Alabaman's voice echoed in his mind.

"Beto!" came a tinny voice from the phone on the deck, causing him to jump. "What is going on? Where are you?"

His eyes wide with fear at what might come out of the water, Beto leaned slightly over the edge just in time to see Scooter float to the surface, face down, just a couple of feet away.

Beto screamed and scrambled backward in fear, a move that proved his undoing, as he was grabbed from behind and dragged under the black water.

Buck was on the right side of the big cooler, closer to the dangerous coral heads. We'd found we could make greater headway, gripping each other's shirt sleeve over the cooler and turning sideways in a modified side stroke. So, I was in no position to see anything except black water, a blacker sky, and thousands of stars. It was a cloudless night and the moon had gone down about the time the boat did. If I ended up as fish chum, pounded into the jagged coral by the waves, or got swept out to sea and devoured by sea monsters, at least the view would be nice.

"I see a break in the reef!" Buck shouted, his hand tugging on my shirt sleeve.

The words were no more out of his mouth when I heard a high

buzzing sound behind us. I chanced a look back and saw a dinghy racing toward us.

"We have company!" I shouted. "I think it's those two guys coming back."

We stopped swimming and turned toward the dinghy now coming right at us.

"Go under," Buck said. "Back-to-back, under the cooler. Maybe that's all they can see."

"Get on the other side of it first," I said. "We'll wait until they're closer."

We moved around the cooler, barely holding onto it. I doubted the wisdom of hiding underwater, remembering the clarity of the previous day's dives. That was until I looked down. I couldn't see my hand a few inches below the surface. I also recalled that in the darkness, I'd only been able to see the cooler and not Buck.

There was a chance.

"They're getting closer," Buck said

The good thing was that I hadn't seen any kind of flashlight or anything, so maybe they would just see a cooler and go away.

I could hear the approaching outboard but not see it. The engine slowed to an idle and the dinghy burbled closer still.

"Now," Buck whispered and submerged.

I waited only a second then went down to join him. We put our backs to one another, our hands under the four corners of the big cooler to hold us in place.

Underwater, it sounded like the outboard was right on top of us —a scary enough sound to a diver, never mind the guns the two men had.

Suddenly, the sound of the engine stopped.

For the longest time, all I could hear was the pounding of my blood in my own temples. This was insane. They obviously knew we were there. I was certain they were just sitting up there aiming their guns and waiting for us to surface. Then we would be the proverbial fish in a barrel.

After what seemed like ten minutes, but was probably less than two, with my chest burning, I began to convulse.

My conscious mind knew it was just my body wanting to rid itself of the excess carbon dioxide and nitrogen building in my lungs. There's enough oxygen in a single breath of air to keep a person alive for up to fifteen minutes. It was what made movie scenes so fake, when the strangling victim died in just a minute.

I was surprised when Buck abruptly pushed the cooler aside before I could. I was ready. We both surfaced, gasping and looking up at the dinghy, waiting to be blasted apart.

By the light of the stars, I saw a woman wearing a wet camisole top, smiling down at us. She was beautiful. Her hair was wet and plastered to her scalp, framing an exquisite face. There was a small black thing wrapped around one of her ears.

I thought I'd drowned and was being greeted by a heavenly angel.

Then I remembered the face in the photograph Emily had shown us.

"Hello, Buck," Charity Styles said, smiling.

22

We'd sat on the dinghy's hard deck, close together, as low as we could get, as the former Olympic swimmer had steered the little boat at top speed, bouncing from wave to wave, as if she were no stranger to small boats.

Once inside the reef, the chop diminished, and shouting over the engine and wind noise, Charity had explained how she and Detective Whittaker had gotten Emily and AJ out of the house, along with two other women. AJ had awakened long enough to tell them that Nora had been abducted by Hoskins. A subsequent search of his home had revealed signs of a huge fight and a room that she said could only be described as a sex dungeon or hedonistic shrine.

Charity explained that Whittaker had ordered every police officer on the island on the case, and they'd fanned out to every location where Lord Lionel Hoskins had holdings, and that she'd followed Whittaker on her motorcycle to the Rogue's marina.

"But how did you find us?" I shouted, leaning against her thigh.

"I just followed the phosphorescent trail the dinghy left in the water," she shouted back. "The hired muscle that brought it in didn't need it anymore."

I couldn't get my head around how this woman—athletic as she may have been—could take on two men, one of whom was at least twice her size.

As we pulled up to the dock, I saw Detective Whittaker waiting with two men in custody, hands zip-tied and sitting on the dock at his feet. It was the two men who'd tried to send us to the bottom a thousand feet down.

Most of the officers turned away, as Charity climbed quickly to the dock wearing next to nothing, and moved toward their cars. Whittaker handed her a towel, then offered me a hand.

"It is good to see you both," the detective said, ignoring the nearly naked woman drying off beside him. He glanced down at the two men at his feet. "The big one almost drowned. Had Agent Styles not resuscitated him, we wouldn't have been able to ask him any questions. Not that either of these men have answered any. Did they happen to say anything in front of you, about where Lord Hoskins might have taken Nora."

"Nothing," Buck said. "But if you'll turn your back for a minute or two, I bet I can find out."

"You can't beat it out of a handcuffed prisoner," Charity said, pulling a pair of leather pants up over her hips. "That's against the law."

"I'm afraid that's not how we do things in the Cayman Islands," Roy said. "Agent Styles is correct."

"It wouldn't take me long," Buck said, as Charity sat down and pulled her boots on, lacing them quickly.

"The police will get the answers, Buck," I cautioned the man. "They'll find Nora."

"Money can buy a lot," Buck said. "Including a quick exit off the island."

"He's right, Roy," Charity said, getting to her feet and stomping her boots. "I think it'd be wise to alert the airport and all dockmasters on the island."

Whittaker looked at her for a moment, then glanced at his prisoners, before walking toward the foot of the pier. "I'll get them working on it," he called back over his shoulder.

"Okay, on your feet then, big boy," Charity said, standing, and taking the giant man by the hair and tugging him forward.

The behemoth almost toppled but he planted a foot and nearly pulled Charity off balance, as he tugged back, his shoulder and neck muscles flexing in defiance.

He screwed his face up at Charity and snarled, "Take these cuffs off, Agent Bitch, and we'll see who pulls the hair."

"Get on your feet, you ape!" Charity hissed, flecks of spit flying, as she released her hold.

The big man pushed himself up, his upper body bulging, as if he might snap the cuffs.

"Stuff something in the other guy's mouth, Buck," Charity said, pulling her hair back over her ears. "And Eddie... unleash the beast. Let's see what he's got against a woman who can fight back."

"I can't do that," I said, as Buck stuffed a wet handkerchief in the smaller man's mouth. "Are you crazy?" I asked, staring at the woman who I'd once secretly idolized. "That guy will kill you!"

She grinned at me and winked. "Cut him loose."

Grudgingly, I used my pocketknife and removed just one of the flex ties. The man's arms popped out like they were spring loaded and I stepped away. I had no idea what Charity was going to do. But Roy and the other cops would be back quickly.

"Hey, big man," Charity said, standing with her feet wide, motioning the much bigger man toward her. "What's your name, anyway."

He turned and faced her, wet hair hanging over his eyes. "Scooter."

"Seriously?" Charity asked, holding her hands to her ribs and laughing.

Whittaker had called her Agent Styles, so I assumed she was also some sort of police officer, but poking a bear is seldom a good way to get information.

"I think you should rethink what you're doing," I warned her.

"So far, Detective Whittaker can charge him with kidnapping and attempted murder."

Her eyes flashed to mine. "Let me handle this, Eddie."

Then she turned back toward the man who called himself Scooter, as she slowly moved around him, a good ten feet out of reach.

"Like what you see, *Scooter*?" she asked, her voice mocking him in a sultry Southern drawl, as she again motioned him toward her. "Yum, yum, get ya some."

He unexpectedly lunged, arms going wide like a net to entangle her.

Charity moved with lightning speed, ducking under the man's arms and hammering his left ribcage with solid left and right blows.

Scooter roared and spun around, sweeping a powerful backhand at her head, only to take a stinging whip kick to the same ribs, as her body ducked under the blow.

He clutched his side, as the air was forced from his lungs, and without replanting her foot, Charity snapped her leg back and executed a second kick, this one higher, which caught Scooter in the side of the head, toppling him to his knees.

She danced back, whipping the hair from her eyes. "Had enough there, Scooter?" She laughed again, hands on her hips, and leaning toward him so low that her camisole fell open, giving him ample view. "Because, you know, I'm not even warmed up yet."

Detective Whittaker hurried back, but stopped next to me, seeing that the man was subdued.

At least for now.

"Who is she?" I whispered, truly puzzled.

"Special Agent Charity Styles," Roy replied. "With your own Department of Homeland Security. She spotted these two hiding under a pier and swam underwater to get them out of their boat. She would have gotten to you sooner, except for having to revive this big fellow."

The big man heard the exchange and dropped his head slightly.

I could tell that he knew he was defeated. Even if he could somehow overpower this athletic warrior, he was surrounded by police officers.

"Pay attention, Scooter," Charity said, her voice low and commanding. "I can break every bone in your body and not even work up a good sweat. I was trained by Mossad in Krav Maga, and the only way you'll ever lay a hand on me is if I *make* you do it, and then I'd just ride you like a stallion until you were totally used up, spent, and worthless."

He started to get up, planting one foot in front of himself and clutching his ribs. For a moment, I was worried for her.

"No, no, no," Charity scolded him, while smiling and wagging a finger. "Get up if you want more pain. Or... you may stay on your knees when you address me."

He lifted his head slowly, pain evident in his eyes. Then he moved his foot back into place, so he was resting on his knees.

"I'm sorry," he whispered.

"What was that?" Charity said. "*Where* did you say Lord Fauntleroy took Nora?"

The muzzled smaller man emitted a series of muffled shouts through the gag.

"I think he took her to the construction site," Scooter said, like he was an adolescent boy trying to gain the favor of the pretty, substitute teacher.

"I didn't even think of that," Roy said, motioning to two of his men.

They stepped forward and quickly refastened Scooter's hand-cuffs as Charity stepped around them and joined us.

"How did he get out of the restraints?" Whittaker demanded.

"I've never seen such strength," Charity said, winking at Buck. "He broke them, so I had to subdue him."

"Didn't think of what?" I asked, finding myself staring at Charity. "That was incredible."

"My men have searched every piece of property Lord Hoskins

owns," Roy said. "But ownership doesn't occur until construction and inspections are finished."

He turned away, his fingers on the keyboard of his phone.

"I thought you said we couldn't beat it out of him?" Buck said, smiling at Charity with something between admiration and lust in his eyes.

"No," she replied, picking up her leather jacket and shrugging into it. "I said *you* couldn't beat it out of him. No real man would ever bow to another man, even if he is better. But all men will bow to a powerful woman."

She turned and went to Whittaker, who showed her his phone, then she spun on her heel and started marching away. She put a hand to her ear and started talking, as if someone was with her.

The thing wrapped around her ear, I thought, looking after her. *Some sort of communications device? Who was she talking to?*

"Hey," I called out. "Where are you going."

"I can get there faster alone," she called back over her shoulder, as she put on a helmet and threw a leg across one very serious-looking motorcycle.

"Tibbetts, follow her," Roy ordered one of the officers, who sprinted to get to his car. "And try to keep up!" he shouted after the man.

"Can we go with him?" Buck asked urgently.

Roy looked at the two of us, then nodded. "Stay out of the way."

We both sprinted and got in the police car with Constable Tibbetts, as Charity roared off into the darkness.

Buck looked over the seat and grinned. "I wish I'd known what a badass she was when we first met. My initial impression was timid wallflower or McDermitt's arm candy."

"Wallflower?" I muttered, looking back at Scooter, as Tibbetts took off after Charity. "Boy, were you way off."

Nora's head was swimming. The lights around her were blinding and they seemed to be moving—bright red, blue, and yellow lights, and even brighter white ones, all swirling and flying back and forth. She suddenly realized they weren't moving at all—she was tossing her head from side to side. She stopped and focused on a fan slowly turning on the ceiling, directly above her face.

She was lying on a bed in a small room. Her hands and feet were bound, and she couldn't move, not that her body was responding to much anyway. She felt nauseous as she tried to focus.

The last thing she remembered clearly was Lord Hoskins toasting his new neighbors, as AJ and Emily danced in the living room with two friends of AJ's.

Nora rarely drank, but to keep up appearances, she'd smiled and sipped the bubbly. She'd felt the effects of the drug almost immediately, as the other four women drank the champagne.

A few faint echoes of a memory stirred at the edge of her consciousness—walking across the street with the old man, seeing Buck and Eddie, then Hoskins forcing something in her mouth.

After that, she remembered nothing until she woke up in a van with lights spinning through the interior—lights from emergency vehicles. Hoskins had waited, watching the lights through the windshield with the engine running. She remembered trying to move and he'd backhanded her face. Then he'd put the drug in her mouth again and started backing the van up.

She'd awakened on the bed, as Hoskins had been attaching the last of her restraints.

He'd climbed on top of her as she'd awakened, pawing at her dress. She'd tried to struggle against him—bucking her hips in an attempt to throw him off her.

Then he'd hit her again.

"Phone," she murmured, remembering. Her tongue felt thick and swollen and her lips cracked.

She remembered looking up at him as he reached down to undo

his pants and a phone had suddenly started ringing. He'd grunted as he reached over the side of the bed to grab it, still on top of her.

She also remembered hearing a consistent click and whirring sound going off every few seconds. She'd been moderately coherent when he'd talked to someone on the phone but couldn't remember what'd been said.

Then he'd put something in her mouth again, leaning forward and whispering in her ear to go to sleep. She remembered thrashing for a moment, then blackness.

Nora opened her eyes again and forced herself to focus on the center of the fan. She heard the clicking again and recognized the sound as a camera. It was mounted on a short pole coming down from the ceiling, off to the side of the bed, and pointing at her.

The shutter clicked again, and the camera made a fake whirring sound—a digital camera with a timer.

She convulsed, the taste of bile rising up in her throat.

Suddenly, she heard the sound of an engine. It came roaring to a stop just outside. A moment later, there was another different vehicle and more lights started flashing, competing with what she now realized were stage lights mounted all around the bed.

The bed was the stage—Nora's stage.

The bile rose higher in her throat.

23

Constable Tibbetts drove like a maniac, trying to keep up with the woman on the powerful motorcycle. Sitting in the back seat, I caught an occasional glimpse of the red taillight, but little else, as we raced out of Bodden Town then turned right.

Finally, Tibbetts turned into a large construction site, following a dust cloud. I looked back and saw two more police cars approaching on the main road, as the constable slid the car to a stop next to Charity's motorcycle.

"She already goin' in," he grunted, throwing the door open, and heaving himself out of the driver's seat. "You two stay put, ya hear."

We were parked in front of a large temporary construction office. Huge concrete slabs occupied acres of land and several at the far end had block walls below wood-framed second and third floors. The van Hoskins had left the marina in was nowhere in sight.

"C'mon," Buck said, slinging the front door open as Tibbetts entered the building after Charity.

I was about to argue that we'd been told to stay put, when I heard a woman's shout from inside. I scrambled out of the back seat and Buck and I both mounted the three steps in a single stride. We entered what appeared to be a front business office, with a table and chairs, an architect's desk, and several filing cabinets. I chased after Buck as he ran down a hallway.

When we reached the back room, we both stopped. Tibbetts was just inside, eyes wide, mouth agape. The room seemed to be set up for temporary quarters, maybe for a night watchman, or an overnight worker.

Except for the bright lights shining down on the bed.

I stepped past Buck, as Nora rose unsteadily from the bed. A camera mounted to the ceiling clicked and whirred as Nora and Charity faced one another.

"I think I'm seeing double," Buck muttered. "They could be twins."

He was right. Nora was in bare feet and Charity had boots on, but that only put her the thickness of her boot heels taller. They both had long legs and slim, athletic bodies, high cheekbones, blond hair, and blue eyes. The resemblance was uncanny.

Detective Whittaker came into the room and went straight over to Nora.

We followed.

"Are you hurt?" Roy asked his constable. His voice was like that of a doting father, soft and caring.

Nora and Charity turned their heads at the same time to look at him. The move was reminiscent of Patty Duke playing two parts in a fake mirror at the opening of the show.

"A little woozy," she replied. "Give me one minute with that *drittsekk* and I will be fine."

I didn't know what a *drittsekk* was, but if she meant Hoskins, I wouldn't want to be in his shoes when Nora caught up to him.

She turned back to Charity. "Who are you?"

"Charity Styles," she replied. "I'm a longtime sailing friend of Roy's."

Nora started to take a step and nearly collapsed. Buck and

Charity were quick to catch her and help steady her as she started to hobble away from the bright lights.

I heard a clicking sound, and Nora stopped and turned around. "The camera."

A silenced pistol appeared in Charity's hand, aiming at the device hanging from the ceiling.

"No!" Whittaker shouted. "That's evidence."

Nora turned, and I could almost see the laser intensity of her gaze. She was definitely coming around.

Charity looked at Roy with the same intense gaze. "Nobody. Not even forensic techs are going to see those pictures, Roy," Charity said, moving toward the bed. "I can remove the SD card without touching the camera. Any prints on it will be your evidence, but not the pictures."

Roy looked at Nora, his face a mask of anguish over what I'm sure he was imagining was on that card. Photos of Lord Hoskins tying an unconscious Constable Nora Sommers to the bed. I knew that would be compelling evidence.

Roy's face fell under Nora's gaze.

"Hold her," Buck said.

Nora was standing okay on her own, but I slipped an arm around her anyway, in case she lost her balance. Her face slowly turned toward me. She had crusted blood on her cheek from a split lip and her eyes were slightly bloodshot, but they were intensely focused. Her jaw was firmly set and her body stiff. I got the feeling I was about to be hurt.

"I can stand on my own, Eddie," she said.

I withdrew my arm but remained close to her, as Charity removed her riding gloves and stepped up onto the bed. The camera wasn't directly above the middle, but hung from a rod, about three or four feet out from the edge of the bed.

Charity couldn't reach it.

She looked down at Buck. "Remember *Dirty Dancing*?"

His eyes opened wide and without waiting for an answer or giving him a warning, she fell forward. Buck's hands were fast, and he caught her just above the hips, as she sailed out over him like a ballet dancer.

"Steady now," she said, balanced like a wooden plank. "Take a half step back."

Buck stepped back and wobbled a little as he brought his feet together but quickly stabilized and looked up at Charity. He adjusted his position so she didn't have to move her arms, which would throw off her stability. She was balanced perfectly, abs flexed like steel plates. Buck held her rigid body at an angle, her hands almost touching the ceiling.

Charity used just her fingernails, which I noticed were painted blood red, and delicately removed the SD card from the camera. She looked down at Buck. "You can put me down now."

He lowered her slowly, just like in the movie, and she allowed herself to slide down his torso until her feet touched the floor, their faces inches apart.

She smiled and patted him on the shoulder. "Thanks for the lift, sailor." Then she turned and walked back toward us, Buck's eyes trailing after her.

She stopped in front of Nora, searching her eyes. "Did he—?"

"No," Nora replied, cutting her off before she finished the question.

Charity extended her hand, the SD card in her palm. Nora took it, then spun around, her face as enigmatic as ever.

"Where is he?" she demanded of Whittaker.

"We are looking for him," Roy said. "Every constable on the island is." He nodded toward Charity. "Even America's Homeland Security is helping. We must get you to hospital."

"I don't need a doctor," Nora said. "I need—"

"To go to hospital," Roy said, softly but firmly. "They will give you something to flush the drug out of your system. You can get cleaned up and put your uniform on. Only then may you help find and apprehend Lord Hoskins."

We all started outside, but Nora paused in the outer office. She went over to a break area, where there was a refrigerator, a sink and a small microwave oven. She opened the microwave, put the SD card inside, then closed it, and turned the unit on high, setting it for ten minutes.

The microwave started to hum, as they usually did, then there was a crackling sound, and I could see bright sparks through the glass door. In seconds, a small fire erupted as Nora turned on her heel and left the building.

Tibbetts was assigned to take Nora to the Cayman Islands Hospital in George Town. Roy told her that it was where AJ, Emily, and the other two women were being treated to flush the drug from their system, and that Buck and I should go with her.

I think he just wanted us civilians out of his hair and putting all of us at the hospital, along with Nora, a police constable, would accomplish that.

"What kind of drug was it?" Nora asked her partner, as Buck and I got in the back behind her and Constable Tibbetts.

The older cop put the car in gear, then glanced over at her. "I do not know. We haven't heard anyt'ing from da tox lab yet."

A light shone through the back window of the police car, and I turned to see that Charity was following us.

"Roofies," Buck said. "He put it in the champagne bottle to knock you all out."

She looked back over the seat at us, and her eyes locked with mine. "I remember seeing you at his house."

"His men caught us," I said. "They put us on a fishing boat and sank it."

"But you escaped?"

"Yeah," Buck said. "Then Agent Styles found us floating on a cooler."

When we arrived at the hospital, we were expected. Tibbetts left us with a nurse, so he could rejoin the search, and the nurse escorted the four of us to a room, where she knocked softly on the door. It opened and Emily stood just inside.

"Nora!" the tiny Brit screamed and rushed to hug the taller woman.

AJ was there also, sitting in a chair with her legs crossed and tucked under her. She sprang up and rushed to Nora. "Are you okay?" she asked.

"*Ja*," Nora replied, as the nurse guided her to a bed.

"Let me be the judge of that," the nurse said, fitting a blood-pressure cuff over Nora's upper arm. In a minute, the nurse had Nora's vital signs and then told her to lie on the bed, so she could clean the injury to her lip. "It doesn't look like you'll need any sutures, but the doctor will be here in just a moment."

When the nurse left, Nora sat up in bed and looked around at all of us, finally stopping on Charity. She studied the woman for a moment, then said simply, "Thank you."

"Um, yeah," Emily began, stepping toward Charity. "Just who are you, anyway?"

"Special Agent Charity Styles, United States Homeland Security," Buck said. "Never much cared for Feds, but this one, well, she's got potential." He smiled then swept an arm toward the two women. "Meet AJ Bailey and Emily Durand. They're divemasters here in the Cayman Islands."

"You rang me up," Emily said.

Charity nodded. "When I arrived at the house, smoke was coming out of cracks around the windows. I broke in and was carrying you out when Roy arrived."

"You showed all those blokes my bum!"

Charity smiled at her. "At least it wasn't charred."

Em plucked her lime-green sunglasses from a table and put them on. "Did they find the bugger, Agent Styles?"

Charity shrugged. "I'm not a part of the inner circle here," she replied, reaching into the inside of her jacket. She produced a cell phone and turned to Nora. "Roy said to give you this when the doctor released you."

"Which… he hasn't," Nora said, taking the phone.

"You look good enough to me."

"Speaking of looks," Buck said, moving toward the two tall blondes. "Have you two had a good look at each other?"

Charity and Nora glanced at one another for a moment, then Nora shrugged and went to work on her phone. "I don't see it."

The leather clad DHS agent turned to Buck. "See what?"

"You two look exactly alike!" he almost shouted in exasperation.

Charity glanced around the room, turning away from Buck and winking at us. "Who two?"

"You and Nora!"

"Nah, you're bonkers, mate," Em said, obviously playing along at poor Buck's expense. "I mean, they both have blond hair and a bit of mystery about 'em, yeah? But so do I, Bucky Boy."

Nora sat up on the bed. "Roy found him," she said, slinging her long legs over the side. "He's sending Jacob back to pick me up."

"Did he say where his Lordship is?" Charity asked.

"About eight kilometers north of here," AJ said. "At Cayman Islands Yacht Club."

Nora glanced over at AJ. "How did you know?"

"He whispered in my and Em's ears," AJ said, shuddering. "Just before I passed out, he was piling her on my lap and feeling us both up..." She paused and looked around. "I couldn't move or scream out or anything. He said he wanted to take us there. It's where he keeps his boat, *Aphrodite*."

Charity turned toward me. "From the bits and pieces, I've picked up, this Lord *Drittsekk* is a wealthy English royal who might have something to do with your father's disappearance. Is that right?"

AJ snorted a laugh. "You do know that *drittsekk* means asshole in Norwegian, right?"

"Fitting," Charity replied, then turned back to me. "My dad died when I was still a kid, Eddie. If I can help, let me. Tell me what happened."

I gave Charity a super-condensed version of what we'd learned —how my dad had been hijacked all those years ago, ditching his plane, which we'd found, and how he'd managed to make it to shore, and how we'd found the body of the hijacker.

"Then you should have a front-row seat when they take him

down," Charity said with a smile. "Ever rode on the back of a motorcycle?"

"I've ridden a few," I said in surprise. "But never on the back."

She gave me a wicked smile. "You might grow to like it. Just hang on and move with me."

24

Together, we snuck out of the hospital just as Constable Tibbetts pulled up where he'd dropped us just a half hour earlier. Buck held the door open for the three women, shaking his head as each one got in. Then he glanced over at us. Or more precisely—at Charity.

"'Water, water, every where, ne any drop to drink,'" he muttered, squeezing in beside Emily.

"Over here," Charity said, turning away.

"What'd he mean by that?" I asked, trotting after her as the police car took off.

"From the poem, *The Rime of the Ancient Mariner*," she said, pulling a helmet off the mirror of her motorcycle and thrusting it at me. "The mariner is lamenting about being becalmed for days, surrounded by beautiful, cool, clear water that he can't have a single drop of."

I put the helmet on and opened the visor. It was a little snug. "You don't have two?" I asked.

She slung a leg over the bike, put the kickstand up, and started the engine in a single fluid motion. "No need," she shouted over the rumble. "Get on."

I got on the motorcycle. It was that or be left behind. Perched above and behind her, my butt resting on a tiny little pad that couldn't pass for a seat by any stretch of the imagination, I was apprehensive to say the least.

She reached back and grabbed both my arms, pulling them around her. "Don't be shy," she ordered, putting the bike in gear. "Hold onto me tight. Keep your body plastered to mine, your head centered, and don't bash the back of my head with that brain bucket."

In an instant, before I could even think about a reply, we were off. Charity leaned into the turn exiting the hospital, with nothing more than a cursory glance for traffic. The front tire came off the ground for an instant when she shifted to second gear and again when she hit third.

I held onto her for dear life, as the engine revved higher and we flashed past buildings, resorts, and the occasional car. I estimated our speed at eighty miles per hour when we flew through the first intersection. The sudden rise in the road's surface sent us airborne. The bike came down smoothly and Charity twisted the throttle again.

In less than a mile, we caught up with Tibbetts's police car and Charity didn't slow down. At a speed that was probably higher than a hundred miles per hour, she passed him in the bicycle lane, as we raced northward.

After about four miles, which were the fastest and longest four miles of my life, she slowed and made a series of turns. I spotted the police cars and their white van, as well as the van the Rogue had taken me and Buck to the marina in.

Charity pulled the bike in behind the police van, right next to a boat advertising "Nick's Private Charters." I got off feeling stiff and my legs were shaking. Detective Whittaker was talking to several constables, while holding his phone to his ear.

"Some grip you got there," Charity said, swinging a leg over, then heading around the side of the van. "Hurry," she added. "I need it now."

"Like that wasn't enough of a hurry?" I asked, still a bit shaken, but trotting after her.

Then as if speaking to someone else, she said. "Yeah, that's it. The Greek goddess of love." She paused a moment and said, "Echo one. Got it."

I remembered the device in her ear and assumed she was talking to someone else, as we walked toward Roy and the others. Tibbetts pulled in beside us and everyone got out of his car.

"We know the boat is here in the marina," Roy said to Nora and Tibbetts, then glanced with an annoyed expression at the rest of us. "We're still trying to locate the night dockmaster to find out which dock it is parked in."

"Slip one," Charity said. "On E dock."

Echo one, I thought, recalling what she'd just said. Echo stood for the letter E in the phonetic alphabet, something I knew military people and police used. The Rogue's boat was in slip E-1. Charity had access to intelligence the local constabulary didn't.

"You are certain?" Roy asked.

"It's a Pershing 9x named *Aphrodite*," she replied. "It has twin MTU high-performance diesels that can push it to forty-two knots. If we don't catch him here, I hope you have something faster."

Roy arched an eyebrow. "Do you know where E dock is?"

Charity pointed over his shoulder along the very wide main dock. "That's *Aphrodite* right there. And her engines are running."

Roy looked where she was pointing. "The big one on the end?"

Charity nodded. "What's your plan, Detective?"

Roy looked over at the marina office, a two-story block structure sitting across the drive. I noticed there was a fire escape that went all the way up to the roof.

"Up there," he said to one of his men, who was armed with a rifle.

The man took off toward the building.

"I have an idea," Charity said. "A way to get answers that you can't, or that might take forever to get out of him."

"What's that?" Roy asked.

"Let us go in," Charity said. "Nora and I are both trained police officers. He might be less resistant to talking to four women than a bunch of uniforms."

He looked over at Nora, who was just standing there, staring at the expensive yacht at the foot of the pier. If her eyes could fire missiles, the yacht would be a smoldering wreck.

"Did they get the drugs flushed out of you?"

Though I knew better, Nora faced her boss and merely nodded.

"Not you two," he said pointing his finger back and forth to the two UK divemasters. "It could be dangerous."

Both women looked at him indignantly but before either could say anything, Charity said, "We'll need them. He doesn't know me, and he kidnapped Nora. AJ and Emily will add to his distraction and confusion. We know he's at least a degenerate, and probably a rapist."

"Eddie and I will go with you," Buck said. "Nora would never ignore the fact he kidnapped her, unless she needs him for some reason. We can pretend to be blackmailers or something like that— offer him an escape in exchange for a few trinkets from his treasure chest."

"Whoa, wait," I said. "I'm not a cop or anything."

Emily stepped closer to me. "I'm not either. But you want to be there when Nora slaps the bracelets on the tosser, yeah?"

"It'll work," Buck said to Roy. "I know guys like this."

"I might have a better idea, yeah?" Em offered. "Tell him you found something in your dad's plane that he didn't know was there."

"Like what?" I asked.

"Yeah, yeah!" Buck said. "Like fifty pounds of gold bars. That could easily be hidden inside a plane. It wouldn't take up any more room than a Thermos bottle or small toolbox." He pulled his pack off and dug down into the bottom. "I even have something here that'll sweeten the pot."

Roy looked along the dock toward the yacht, then turned to his small group of men. "One at a time, head out along the side of the dock and stay out of sight behind the bushes. We'll see if they can get him to talk."

The rest of the constables moved out, staying low and moving quickly, leapfrogging one another to reach positions near the yacht.

Pulling up a number on his phone, Roy stabbed the screen with his finger.

"She's fine, Pam," he said to whoever answered his call. "I need you to keep this line open and start recording."

He listened for a moment then said, "No, we don't need a warrant to record my own phone call to the communications center." Then he turned to me and put his phone in my shirt pocket. "If you can get him to talk about the murder of Calloway, your father, or kidnapping Nora, we've got him. But you have to be fairly close. My men will be all around you and a marksman will have the boat in his sights at all times."

"What do we do?" AJ asked.

"Go for a stroll," Charity said, shrugging out of her leather jacket, and tossing it on the trunk of the police car. Then she turned and smiled at Whittaker. "All men will bow to a powerful woman, Roy. But they'll sell their soul to four."

She took one of Buck's arms and nodded at Nora.

The Norwegian's face cracked slightly with a smile. Really just one corner of her mouth turned upward slightly, but I'd come to learn that was a smile nonetheless. She took Buck's other arm and the three started down the dock.

Suddenly, Em and AJ had both my arms pulling me along. We caught up to the other trio, then walked alongside them, six abreast on the wide dock.

"Yoo-hoo," Charity sang out in a loud voice. "Oh, Lord Hoskins? Where are you?"

After getting his emergency stash box aboard, Lord Hoskins started going through the procedure to ready *Aphrodite* for leaving the dock. Unlike a smaller boat, which you could just start the engine, throw off a couple of lines, and go, *Aphrodite* usually had a crew of at least two, just to get away from the marina smoothly, and nearly twenty minutes of preparation.

Hoskins skipped much of the checklist. He wasn't about to climb down into the engine room to do all the checks the engineer usually did. *Aphrodite* ran fine just a week ago when she was last used and should perform the same this time.

It did take an inordinate amount of time to untie all the lines after he finally got the engines running. He was on the bow, about to throw the first of the bow lines off, when he heard a woman's voice calling his name.

For decades, Lord Hoskins had used his charms on women, bending them to do things they normally wouldn't. He'd never met one who could resist his charms and the allure of his money, and many had sought him out. But this voice didn't sound like one of those.

Going to the rail, Hoskins peered out over the boats next to him in the direction the voice had come. To his surprise, he saw four women and two men walking toward the stern of his boat, the men with a woman on each arm.

One of them was Nora.

She was walking arm in arm with the treasure hunter, Buck Reilly, along with another woman he'd never seen before. His eyes opened wider.

She looked just like Nora.

Hoskins was momentarily mesmerized by the sight of the four beauties, long legs flashing with each step. The three women from the burning party house were still wearing the revealing dresses they'd had on earlier. The fourth woman was dressed in skintight leather pants and a flimsy top with thin straps.

Then he recognized the *other* man whom Beto had said was dead along *with* Buck Reilly. He had one of the female divemasters on each arm. The two idiots couldn't even accomplish sinking a boat right.

The sight of the four women together again should have given Lord Hoskins pause. The divemasters and both men should all be dead. Their being alive and at his boat, was most unfortunate, and he should have recognized the danger.

Instead of bolting, he looked around the marina grounds as an idea began to formulate in his mind. He could see nothing out of the ordinary and was intrigued by this strange, yet lovely visit.

The sight of the scantily dressed women excited Hoskins and his first thoughts didn't immediately leap to how he could get out of the situation, but instead he remembered the camera equipment discreetly set up in the forward VIP quarters and its massive bed.

What they were doing there on the dock, he didn't know. But if he could lure them into the boat's cockpit, he had a firearm hidden there. It would be nothing to force them all up to the flybridge. The engines were running, and they were more than powerful enough to rip the last two dock cleats out or snap the lines.

A slow smile spread across his face at the prospect. Once out to sea, he could shoot the two men and throw the bodies overboard.

Then the *real* party could begin.

25

I could see movement on the foredeck. A shadowy figure was slowly moving aft along the side of the yacht. When he stepped into a pool of light, I saw he was wearing the same pale sort of straw hat I'd seen the man with binoculars wearing while we were diving Dad's plane.

Ahead of us, two constables were hiding behind a large box, out of sight of the yacht. I knew there were two more somewhere close, plus the man with the rifle on the roof of the marina offices.

"I see you freed yourself, Nora," Lord Hoskins said, strolling along the deck as if her being kidnapped, brutalized, and nearly raped were all in a day's work for a Cayman Islands constable.

All of us stopped at the back of the yacht and Nora replied, "If you hadn't slipped the drug in our drinks, we would have been able to tell you what we *really* invited you over for."

He stopped midstride. "What drugs?"

"Come on," Buck said, taking a step forward. "You told me and Eddie here what you put in their drinks. What was it you called it? Funky spam, or something? She's talking about the roofies."

"So, you had an ulterior motive for inviting me?" he asked. His tone made it clear he considered it distasteful to talk to mere commoners.

"You didn't really think these beautiful young women had any kind of romantic interest in an old man like yourself, did you?" Buck asked in a taunting tone.

"And I suppose these lovely ladies were going to enlighten me as to what that was while you two were breaking into my house?"

"They were only after your keys," Charity said. "I'm afraid my friends were going to steal your boat if you didn't help them willingly."

"And just who are you, my dear?"

"Gabriella Fleming," Charity replied. "My friends call me Gabby."

"So, tell me, Gabby," Hoskins said, taking another step toward the cockpit. "Aside from *Aphrodite* being the most magnificent vessel on the island, why did you want to steal her?"

"What else does one use a boat for, your Lordship?" Emily asked, laying it on thick. "To leave this bloody island with what we found on Eddie's father's airplane."

"And this particular boat," Charity added, "has twin MTUs and several thousand horsepower, which is exactly what we needed."

Lord Hoskins took the first step down and stopped. "There was nothing on that plane aside from what a courier was bringing to me. Your father was just a delivery driver."

Buck took another step forward as his hand dipped into his pants pocket. "Something like this is easy to stash," he said, holding his hand out, palm up.

I glanced over and almost allowed my jaw to drop open. Buck held a shiny gold bar in his hand, not much bigger than a postage stamp.

"What is that?"

"One troy ounce of 99.99 percent pure gold," Buck replied. "Woody had a small toolbox loaded with these when he went down. Don't you just love how gold remains so bright and shiny even after decades underwater. Why, I've found gold buried under the rubble and decay of three centuries of jungle rot and it always takes my breath away." Buck smiled. "Woody had fifty pounds of it. I'll give you one pound to take us to Mexico. You can keep whatever trinkets you have in that case. We're not interested in that."

I stepped up beside Buck, not sure where the gold bar in his backpack came from, but sensing the Rogue was interested. "I've searched for him and his plane for years, all over Mexico, hoping to find this gold. All this time, it's been just inside the reef here on Grand Cayman. Fifty pounds of it."

Even at this distance and in the low light of the dock lights, I could see his eyes widen and pupils constrict. He was nibbling at the bait.

"Because of where Eddie's father got those little things," AJ said, "and because they were found in territorial waters, the Caymanian government has an equal claim as the original owner. We might get a finder's fee, but split six ways, that would be next to nothing."

The Rogue smiled broadly at me. "Are you trying to tell me your father was a smuggler? Or was he just a common thief?" He took another step down and smiled. "Or perhaps both. It makes one wonder just how far the apple falls from the tree."

I'd been insulted by the best as a kid, and never let it get to me. I was playing a part here, and I'd be damned if I'd let him goad me into revealing our true intentions.

"There was nothing common about Woody Rains," I said flatly. "He was going to deliver that plane to Panama, but it was just a cover for the theft of the gold. He'd planned to send for me and my mom, and then we were going to settle in Panama. Your man Calloway ruined that."

"Then your father was a fool besides being a common thief," Hoskins said. "With that much gold aboard, it was asinine to accept a last-minute passenger. But I must say, your story intrigues me. Would you care to come aboard, and we can discuss it?"

Zing! I could almost hear the line spooling off the reel.

"Your engines are running," Emily said.

"Just a routine warm up, my dear," Hoskins lied. "We start them regularly, whether *Aphrodite* leaves the dock or not." Then his gaze cut to Nora. "Tell me, Constable Sommers, in what capacity are you here?"

Nora's expression was like ice, totally unreadable. "For the gold. It's always been about the gold."

"That seems contrary to the oath you took," he said, provoking her.

"Do you have any idea how little a constable earns?" she said.

"I don't know if you've noticed," AJ said, "but none of us are *from* here and the one thing we all have in common is an allegiance only to ourselves and a desire to leave."

"Oh, I'd still love to kick your ass," Nora said.

Emily patted Nora on the back. "Remember what we talked about, yeah? That would only slow our escape from this bloody rock in the middle of nowhere."

Charity stepped up beside me and Buck. "Just a minute, Lord Buckethead. How do we know you won't try another fast one, like you did at the house?"

He smiled at her. "Your insolence aside, I rather fancy you, Gabby." Then his face turned cold. "To answer your question, you don't. However, there are two men against one here, and the one is not as young as he once was."

"But you're as good once as you ever were?" she asked, cocking her head slightly. "You left out the four of us women."

"Oh, I can handle four women," he said, lecherously, as he moved across the expansive cockpit. "Won't you come aboard, and we can discuss how best to solve this predicament? You appear rather conspicuous standing out there on the dock."

There was a boarding staircase, mounted to the dock. Charity took the three steps up and stood at the opening in the boat's rail. "Permission to come aboard?"

"Please," Hoskins replied, sweeping an arm toward an expansive seating area. "How delightful to meet someone with a modicum of nautical etiquette. There is room here for everyone. Come aboard."

Buck was up the steps quickly, and followed Charity, stepping over to the cockpit.

Nora was right behind them, and I waited until AJ and Emily ascended the steps and joined the others. I would have to be the one to get him to open up, since it was my father who'd been hijacked by Calloway.

"I have to know something," I said, as the seven of us sat down around the table. I noticed a slight bulge at Charity's waist, barely visible. "Why'd he do it? Why did Calloway hijack my dad's plane? That's the thing I don't get the most. Was it random? Was he just in the wrong place at the wrong time?"

"I'm afraid that would be something you would have to ask him, my boy," Hoskins said, leaning back in his seat at the end of the table. He draped an arm over the back. "That happened before I met him and your father."

Met him? He was there! I had to play it cool here. The Rogue had just dealt me the card I needed for an inside straight.

"He didn't say anything to you about it?" I asked.

"When your father arrived at my home with Jerome Calloway, it was not of his own volition, but as Calloway's prisoner. How he came to be that way, I didn't ask, and neither of them volunteered such information. Now, about this gold?"

"It's in the boot," Emily said. "Buckaroo only brought the one, on account of your past history, yeah?"

"You must have talked about something," I pressed. "We've already learned a lot about *what* happened, I just want to know why."

"When a storm comes, do you ask why?" Hoskins asked. "Things happen that we have no control over and when they do, we needn't bother asking why, but only what can be done about it. When it rains, your first thought isn't why, but where to seek shelter."

In my mind, I could picture my father there at Hoskins's now-abandoned house with him and Jerome Calloway. It suddenly dawned on me. Hoskins wasn't a collector—it was him in the pictures with Princess Margaret—he just wanted back what he'd owned. Calloway had come to *return* the lord's belongings, I felt sure of that now. The receipt for the store the robbers had used on Baker Street. If the rumors of Hoskins's involvement in the robbery were true, then Calloway had somehow gotten the contents of Hoskins's own box, which had been caught up in the heist. Maybe it had even been intentional on his part.

Finally, it all made perfect sense to me. Those pictures had been the Rogue's leverage over the royal family since before I was born. Not that Princess Margaret's reputation was at stake; according to Emily she was very promiscuous, but it was the fact that Hoskins, regardless of how distantly, was a relative of the princess—an in-law. Under old canon law, issued by leaders of the church, there were certain people who another person, not related by blood, may not marry. A widow was forbidden from marrying her late husband's brother, her brother-in-law. Princess Margaret's escapades had been scandalous enough, but to be involved with a relative? And the sister of the Queen, no less?

Hoskins had been outcast because of his amorous antics, and like the Remittance Man in Mark Twain's *Following the Equator*, the royals had paid him off to keep silent. Even after the pictures and jewels were stolen, Hoskins had continued his blackmail, the royal family none the wiser about the loss.

He got his belongings back and even displayed them in the secret room for his own self-amusement. But he didn't have the necklace.

The three of them, Hoskins, Calloway, and the man he'd hijacked, had been together, alive, behind the Rogue's home on Little Cayman. One was a royal outcast, one was a thief, and one was my dad. Only Calloway had been buried there.

I looked across the table at him. "What did the two of you talk about, while Calloway forced my father to dig his own grave?"

A slight tic in a tiny muscle in his right cheekbone told me I'd nailed it.

"That was over forty years ago, old boy. I'm afraid anything we might have said has been lost from my memory."

When I was younger, I played cards every Friday night with a few friends. We rotated whose house we played at, but it was always at the home of one of the core group of four of us, and whoever we could round up to make it six. Some said I was lucky, others thought I was a card shark. I just knew when to fold and I could tell when someone was bluffing.

Hoskins was lying.

"Calloway was pissed because he thought my dad had stolen the Heart of Ceylon," I said. "And I imagine you were pretty upset about it, too. What did that necklace mean to you?"

He looked around at the others for a moment, then locked eyes with me. "It belonged to Margaret. She was going to leave the pompous 'Earl of Snowdon' and we were to go away together. He learned of our plans and forced her to give me the necklace. I was told to take it, disappear, and keep quiet about the whole affair. I was still a young lad. Oh-ho, the things that woman could do."

Glancing around at the others, they seemed almost shocked. Well, except Nora and Charity, who looked like two sides of the same coin, both seeming to have expected this revelation.

"You were in love with her," Emily said. "Really, truly in love, yeah? That's why you didn't sell the necklace to make a new start."

Hoskins looked at her, his face now stoic and unreadable. "Quite. She was twenty years older than I, but not in the ways that mattered." His eyes drifted for a moment, then they snapped back into sharp focus. "However, I quickly got over her, and his offering of the Heart had given me an idea. It was his camera equipment we used you know—Antony Charles Robert Armstrong-Jones, First Earl of Snowdon, the pretentious fool. Since then, the royal family I *should* have been a part of back in jolly old England has been paying for me to live a life of luxury here in the Caymans, as long as I remained quiet."

"So, you do remember talking to Calloway about the Heart of Ceylon while my father was digging the hole that was supposed to be *his* grave but ended up being Calloway's."

I said it as a statement, now even more certain that my father had struck a deal or something, and hadn't been buried near Calloway.

"You are very observant," Hoskins said. "Yes, I was quite upset at the loss of the necklace. When your father finished his task, he attempted to strike Calloway with the shovel. I could have used a man like him, all heart, that one. But he was too slow, so I shot Calloway with his own gun. Very careless of him to leave it on the table."

He'd said it. He'd confessed to the murder of Jerome Calloway.

"I'd planned to shoot them both," Hoskins said offhandedly, as if only he knew who had the upper hand. "But your father said he knew where the necklace was." Hoskins leaned a bit farther to his right, seemingly relaxed. "Now, since I have given you that information, I think it is time for quid pro quo, don't you think? Where did the gold come from?"

"It was part of a theft of nearly three hundred pounds of gold from Cuba in 1975," Buck replied. "The Kremlin paid Castro in gold to finance their part in the war in Angola. Fidel never reported the loss to Brezhnev for fear of losing face with his only ally."

Hoskins looked at Buck, then back at me. "And your father was a part of this theft?"

It took all I had not to swallow or react. To allow someone to call my father a thief was no easy task, and saying it myself, even though I knew it to be untrue, left a lump in my throat.

"They flew it out in my dad's plane," I said. "He landed on the side of a mountain south of Havana to pick his team up, then flew under Cuban radar all the way back to Florida."

"And the gold is here, in the car park?" Hoskins asked.

"Quid pro quo," Charity said, finally speaking up. "Where is Eddie's father?"

He looked at her and smiled. "I thought you were in a hurry to get off the island?"

"It's close enough we can grab it in a few minutes," AJ said. "And yeah, we are in a bloody hurry here. But it's important for Eddie to know what happened."

He turned and looked me straight in the eye. "Your father is dead, chap. He had me bring him here to Grand, telling me that my necklace was here. The boat went out of control in the North Sound, and he died when it crashed into the trees along the western shoreline south of where I usually kept it. Back then, there was nothing in the spot where it crashed, so I buried him on shore."

The muscle twitched on the side of his jaw.

"You're lying," I said, my voice cold with rage now.

Hoskins must have read something in my body language as well. He lunged quickly, opening a small cabinet and pulling a gun out.

Charity was faster and was on her feet, her own gun pointing at the Rogue Royal's face before he even turned around. "Move a muscle and you will die."

He froze, as did we all, then a slow smile spread across his face. "You are an American police officer, I would bet. What? FBI? DEA?"

"She's with the Department of Homeland Security," Emily said. "And you're busted, yeah?"

He stared at the barrel of Charity's gun, a nervous smile coming to his lips. "You have rules to follow, don't you, my dear?" He lifted his eyes to hers. "It's one thing to point a gun at someone, quite another to use it. Tell me, have you ever killed a man?"

"The number of men—and women—would *stagger* you," Charity replied in a low, even tone as the corners of her own mouth also turned up slightly. "Emily was wrong. DHS is just one of my covers. I'm actually a covert government assassin and I may or may not work for the CIA."

"The CI—?"

"It means she's got a license to *kill*, you wanker!" Emily hissed at him.

Nora rose slowly to her feet. "Lord Lionel Hoskins, I am placing you under arrest by authority of the Royal Cayman Islands Police Service. Put down the gun."

26

Standing off to the side as the constables were putting Hoskins in the back of a police car, I watched the others, the dynamics of their relationships and how they interacted. I'd hired AJ and her boat simply to try to try to find my father's plane and bring some closure to our family after several decades of not knowing anything. A divemaster who had a boat—that's all I'd asked for. She was standing with her friend Emily, another divemaster. Nora was with them, and as the others talked, she listened and watched, even glancing over and catching me watching them. And Buck, the enigmatic treasure hunter and ladies' man, was flirty with Charity, who, as far as I could tell, could hold her own with any man. All of them could.

And before this week, they were all strangers to me. None of them knew anything about me, my father, or what his disappearance had cost others. And yet, they'd volunteered their expertise, intelligence, and intuition, some at great cost, all risking their lives to help.

Charity broke apart from the others and approached me.

"Are you really a government assassin?" I asked.

She put a hand on my arm. "If I told you that, Eddie, I'd have to kill you," she said, every bit as stone-faced as Nora. Then she smiled. "I was just bluffing. The CIA doesn't have any assassins." She turned and looked back at the others. "You've got some *great* friends there, Eddie."

"I was just thinking that," I said, following her gaze. "I didn't know any of them until a few days ago. My wife and I run a restaurant, just ordinary people. I've never known anyone like them, and you, who will just step in and help without being asked."

She laughed and her hand made a cracking sound, as she slapped her leather-clad thigh. "Oh, I was asked, if that makes you feel better," she said. "Volun-told is what it was." She paused and searched my eyes. "Some friends only need to be informed to help. My friend, Jesse, told me what was happening and asked a favor. He doesn't do that often... er... ever. We both belong to a small group of people who believe in paying a debt forward. Jesse has known all of these people for a couple of years, I think. Buck even longer. I'd seen AJ and Nora around—it's a small island—but we'd never met. So, when Jesse asked, I dropped what I was doing and hurried over."

"So, what drives these people, you included, to want to risk your own safety for a stranger?"

"Where are you from, Eddie?"

"Originally? Key Biscayne," I replied. "But I stayed in North Carolina after college and got married. Now we live in Nags Head, in the Outer Banks. Why?"

"You're an islander," she said, as if that explained everything. "Come on. Here comes Roy."

"Pam tells me she got every word," Roy said, when we'd rejoined the group.

"What happens now?" Emily and AJ asked at the same time.

"He will be charged with the murder of Jerome Calloway," Whittaker said. "We'll have to wait and see if he tells us where he buried your father, Eddie, before we can charge him with any other crimes. In the meantime, he will be a guest in Her Majesty's cell."

Tibbetts approached the detective. "Ya know... I got a cousin who worked for Rogue Fleet back in de day—skilled tradesman, not a fisherman. I think he was 'round when dey started building over on de lagoon side."

"Is there anyone on this island you're not related to, Constable Tibbetts?" Emily asked.

He smiled down at her. "On Grand, you can't swing a fish and not hit a Tibbetts or Ebanks upside de head."

"Can we talk to him?" I asked, then looked at Roy. "With your permission, of course. I need to follow this through."

The detective nodded. "Go get some rest. Then come to my office at ten o'clock. I should have some answers by then."

We walked back toward Tibbetts's police car. AJ split off with Charity and Buck, and they were talking as AJ checked out the motorcycle.

"I don't get it," Emily said. "How did you know he didn't kill your pop over on Little?"

"I didn't at first," I replied. "But from what we learned and what Hoskins said just now, I felt certain my dad had struck some kind of deal after Calloway died. Don't you see? The Heart of Ceylon, along with the pictures of Lord Hoskins with the princess were in his safe-deposit box. Calloway wasn't trying to sell it to him. He was ransoming it. They had my dad dig the grave while they were negotiating. Calloway wouldn't be the one to do it, and if the hole was dug after Hoskins killed Calloway, it wouldn't have been him unless Dad was dead or unconscious. Dad must have told him he knew where the necklace was." I turned to Tibbetts. "What's there on the west shore of North Sound now?"

"Quite a lot, I'm afraid. Mostly new places built since de storm. A lot of de places dat were there have still not recovered. I do know, at dat time, not very much. Nothing in fact. Rogue Fleet was first to build."

"In May of 1976?" I asked, hopefully.

"Mebbe," he replied, looking thoughtful. "My cousin's first boy was born dat summer. Wit de new addition, Michael was happy to get de work. So, likely shortly after dat."

I thought about the location of Calloway's body, under a hastily poured concrete slab.

"What trade is your cousin in?"

"Michael's father, my uncle, was de first licensed plumber on Grand Cayman. Michael work for him 'til he died and took over de business. But for two years after he finish school, he work for Rogue Fleet, 'cause dey pay better."

I heard Charity's motorcycle start and turned to see Buck putting the helmet on and AJ walking toward us. Nora joined her, as the police cars pulled away.

"Looks like you're stuck riding with the four of us," AJ said. "Buck volunteered to ride with Charity on her Monster."

"I'll bet he did," Em snorted. "Monster... right proper name, that. Did you see how she shot past us in the pedal lane?"

"That's what it really is called," AJ replied. "A Ducati Monster 1200 S. We're going riding once she gets settled back in. She said she'd been gone for quite a while but plans to be around a lot more now."

We got in the car and again, Nora rode in front. I squeezed in between AJ and Emily in back and suddenly felt immensely tired— drained in a lot of ways, not the least of which was knowing what had finally happened to my father forty-six years ago. I didn't for a minute believe what Hoskins had said though. Boats don't just crash into trees. Not in the calm waters of the sound, at the end of nearly a hundred miles of open ocean. Even though I'd only been a kid then, I knew my dad was a fighter. He'd probably waited until they were close to shore to attempt an escape.

I yawned, as Tibbetts followed Charity's motorcycle back toward the south.

"I could use a kip, too, yeah?" Emily said, putting on her green sunglasses, though it wasn't yet dawn, and leaning her head back in the seat.

"If only I'd waited one more minute," I said with a sigh, "I might have gotten him to tell me *where* he buried my father."

"We'll get that sorted, yeah?" Emily said. "Oh, bugger! I better text Boone. Poor Brix is probably worried sick."

"Brix?" I asked, then chuckled, remembering their rambunctious little mutt. "Oh yeah, your dog. You didn't you call your *boyfriend* from the hospital?"

"Nah. If I had, the silly bugger would've fired up the *Lunasea* and burned up the engine racing across in the dead of night. Whatever that royal wanker gave me, they flushed it out. I didn't want to worry him."

We rode in silence for a minute, then Charity's bike turned left, as Tibbetts continued straight. "Wonder where they goin'?" he asked.

"Blimey," Emily said, looking up from her phone in time to see the motorcycle disappear into a neighborhood. "You don't think—"

"I hear people in intense situations sometimes do," AJ said.

"But it *was* a spot of luck, Charity having a gun, yeah? That pretty much sorted everything."

"That was why I arrested him," Nora said from the front seat, head and eyes looking straight ahead.

"What do you mean?" I asked, a bit puzzled.

She turned around and placed her elbow on the console, looking back at us. "I recognized that look. She's been where I was. She was just about to kill him."

27

When we arrived at the police station the following morning, I was still tired. But the lack of sleep didn't seem to bother AJ and Emily. Of course, I was probably twice their age, and though I did exercise, it wasn't even close to the level of the two divemasters. Most of my running was confined to the restaurant and kitchen.

Approaching the building, I saw Charity's motorcycle outside, and she and Buck were waiting by the door. He'd changed clothes and had his familiar backpack on, but he still looked like I felt, which made me feel a little better, since he was at least a decade younger.

Charity looked like a local, dark tanned, clothing suitable for the intense sun, and dark sunglasses perched on top of a head full of sun-streaked blond hair. Her pale blue eyes were clear and bright, suggesting that, just like the two younger women, she was able to get by on just a few hours of sleep.

"And where did you two disappear to last night?" Emily asked, bouncing on her toes as we walked toward them.

"Buck stayed at my place," Charity replied candidly with a blank stare. "Ready to go see what Roy found out?"

My gaze shifted to Buck, who let out a long yawn. He did not look very rested. Then I looked back to Charity.

"Can't have been much," I said. "They probably just booked him into a holding cell to get some rest and are starting the interview now."

"You don't know Roy," Charity replied. "He's one of the best interrogators I've ever worked with, and late nights are his specialty. He'll have something."

We went inside and after checking in at the sergeant's desk, Detective Whittaker came out of his office with Nora, who was in uniform. He motioned us to join him, as Nora started to go outside.

"You're leaving?" Buck asked her.

"Jacob and I have something to check on," she replied without looking back, as she went out the door.

We followed Roy into his office and found Emily's boyfriend sitting there. "Heya, Em," he said, getting to his feet.

The little blonde pounced on the lanky man. "Boone! Oh wow, you won't believe what happened."

"Easy now," Boone said, extricating himself from her embrace. "Roy brought me up to speed." He turned toward Buck and stuck out his hand. "That was a hell of a story you concocted. Good to see you again."

"And this is our new Caymuddy, Charity," Em said, then jabbed him in the ribs with an elbow. "That means Cayman buddy, yeah? Anyway, she and Roy are old friends, *and* she knows our old mate, Stretch."

"Charity Styles," she said, offering Boone a hand.

He shook it. "I understand we owe you one."

She looked across the desk at Whittaker. "Is he the one you were telling me about?"

The detective nodded, and she smiled at Boone. "Maybe we can call it even if you teach me some of your capoeira moves. I was once a martial arts instructor for Miami-Dade PD."

"What style?" he asked, as we all took seats.

"A mix," she replied. "Taekwondo and Krav Maga mostly."

I noticed an admiring look of approval from him as he nodded.

"What have you learned from the Rogue?" Buck asked the detective.

"Nothing," Roy replied. "And I don't mind telling you, I'm exhausted."

"Nothing?" Charity asked. "Are you losing your touch?"

"He hasn't uttered a single word all night," Roy replied. "He called his solicitor, and he will be here at noon."

"Where was Nora going?" I asked. "She seemed in a hurry."

"She and Constable Tibbetts went to pick up his cousin, Michael Lettsome. I have already talked to him, and we will meet them at the abandoned Hyatt Regency."

"Wasn't that place nearly destroyed by Hurricane Ivan almost twenty years ago?" Buck asked. "I'd heard the government was trying to force the owner to sell or rebuild for all this time."

"In 2004, yes," Roy said. "It became an eyesore and was infested with rats. The pressure on the owners finally worked, however, and they are rebuilding now. It may even reopen before the end of the year."

The cell phone on his desk rang and he picked it up, holding a finger up to us. "Are you on the way?" he asked into the phone. There was a pause, then a slight smile. "Splendid! We are leaving now."

Roy rose from his seat. "That was Nora. They are on their way to the construction site with Michael—his home is only a few blocks from here and he was waiting for them with a friend of his, a man who helped clear the first property purchased by the Rogue Fleet company, and helped lay out the first buildings."

We followed him out to a waiting van and Roy got behind the wheel, as the rest of us climbed in the back. It was a nine-passenger van, so we had plenty of room.

"You said Hoskins's first land purchase included where the old Hyatt currently is," Boone said to Roy, as he got in the front passenger seat. "And in the recording, Hoskins said that Woody died in a boat crash in North Sound, and that he'd buried his body where the boat had crashed."

"That's correct," Roy said, as he started to drive. "It isn't far."

"It's on Seven Mile Beach, yeah?" Emily said from behind me.

Boone looked back at her with a knowing smile, as if they were communicating telepathically. "On the inland side of the highway, but yeah, technically." He winked at her and turned back to Roy. "What was the first thing Hoskins built on that first piece of property he bought?"

Detective Whittaker glanced over at him, with a smile. "A large bait house."

"Ew!" Emily exclaimed. "Smelly."

I could easily pick out the resort that was being remodeled even from half a mile away. The whole thing was framed in scaffolding. Just before the construction entrance was a dirt road going back along the edge of the property. Roy turned onto the one-lane dirt road that quickly gave out to double ruts of rock.

"It gets a bit bumpy," Roy warned, as he slowly drove the van over the rough terrain.

"There they are," Boone said, pointing off to the left.

A moment later, we climbed out into the midmorning heat and started walking toward Nora, Tibbetts, and two other men. Through the trees to the east, I could see the turquoise waters of the sound. Could that have been the last thing my father ever saw? All around us was rubble. It looked like a bomb had gone off a century ago and the land was slowly retaking everything.

Overgrown as it was, I could make out several areas that were level and had familiar geometric shapes—square and rectangular— joined, but at different levels. The surface was covered with a tangle of vines, seeking out any purchase in the old foundations.

"What used to be here?" AJ asked Roy.

"That's what they're trying to figure out," Nora replied. "The last building here was a utility building for the resort."

"It was totally demolished during Ivan," Whittaker explained. "The tidal surge connected the sound to the Caribbean and most everything was washed out to sea."

"Dat was long after Rogue Fleet sold dis property," one of the men said. "Hello, I am Jacob's cousin, Michael Lettsome, and dis is my good friend, Bobby."

After the introductions were made, Bobby pointed toward what I'd already recognized as raised concrete pads all around us. "Dis de workshop," he said, then pointed to the area we'd just walked across. "And dat over dere is de old two-story Rogue Fleet Office, before dey move down to Bodden Town. De workshop needed to be deep, not tall, so dey tear it down and poured de slab bigger."

"I understand you were here when they built the first building," Boone said. "A bait house?"

"Dat was down closer to de water," Michael said. "I put all de plumbing in for de bait tanks and pumps, just pulling it straight outta de lagoon. We had to make a road. Dere was nothing here and for de first year, de bait shop only sold to working fishermen, right out at de dock."

"Surprised it not still here," Bobby said, as we stepped off the slab and worked our way slightly downhill.

"Why's that?" I asked.

"Ivan was a bad storm," Bobby replied. "Knocked down some big buildings, 'cause de waves washed out under de concrete. But de bait house only lost de roof."

"Why do you think that was?" Charity asked, as if she already knew the answer.

"Lord Hoskins was a smart man," Bobby said. "Poured de slab for de bait house twice as thick as usual."

"I was glad he wanted all de pipes above de concrete," Michael added, stepping up onto a large flat area. "Get a water leak under eight inches of solid concrete, de work get *real* hard."

"So, you didn't have to do any digging or soil compaction?" I asked Bobby.

"Soil comp—? No, sir. Dey just frame it up all level and pour de concrete in right on top of de ground."

Roy turned to Tibbetts. "Get a warrant, Jacob. We need men and equipment out here right away. There's a lot of work to be done. And tell the forensics people to be on standby for this afternoon. We'll work into the night if we have to."

28

Things happened very quickly after Tibbetts secured the warrant, which only took a few minutes talking to his uncle, the judge. Even before it came through, off-duty constables started arriving. Every cop on the island knew what had happened to Nora and two-thirds of them were off duty. They also knew how much stronger the case would be if they found a second victim of the Rogue Royal. Within half an hour more arrived, some carrying shovels and rakes.

Detective Whittaker had property records searched all the way back to 1976 and it turned out that where the Rogue's house and fleet were now located, wasn't where they'd always been. He'd purchased the land on which we now stood on May 28, 1976, when it was nothing but mangroves. At that time, he'd owned the cottage on Little, as well as a condo on Seven Mile Beach, just across from where the Hyatt stood now.

Over the years, he'd sold off parts of the property for substantial profits. The Snug Harbor community and the canals backing the new high-end homes and condos were built just to the north. And finally, he'd moved his fleet's headquarters in 1991 and had built his current home not long after that.

An ambulance pulled in and parked next to our van. Two men

and a woman got out and set up a pair of shade tents, one with large coolers of water under it, and the other with a foldable steel table. The table was quickly covered by a large black bag and a sheet.

Nora saw me staring at it. "Are you ready for what they might find?"

I looked into her eyes, usually blank and unreadable, but there was suddenly a depth of understanding there. "You've had to face something like this before?"

She simply nodded and turned toward the now cleared concrete slab that was likely my father's tomb. We stood in the shade of a group of tall palms, as several men lifted large, gas-powered circular saws out of the back of two trucks. Each one required two men to carry it to the slab, where they set up at opposite ends and began to get the machines and themselves ready.

As the others gathered around us, the sound of heavy machinery could be heard on the dirt road. We turned as one and I knew instantly that it hadn't been trucked to our location. The loading and unloading would have taken hours.

A huge track hoe came into view, little puffs of dust popping up from the treads as it turned, crushing the rocks in its path. The bucket was equipped with an opposing hydraulic grapple, to allow it to pick things up with the dexterity of the fingers and thumb of a human hand.

The roar of one of the saws quickly drowned out the approaching machine, and one of the forensic techs passed out disposable earplugs, which I gladly accepted, as the second saw started. A cloud of white dust quickly rose from the large circular blades of the concrete saws, as each began cutting through the concrete, two men in respirators operating each.

A sudden thought occurred to me, and I was about to say something to Detective Whittaker when I glanced over at Buck. I quickly realized he was just about the same height and weight my father had been and he was standing in profile, talking to Boone.

I dismissed the idea that Dad might actually be entombed *in* the concrete. It wasn't thick enough. Hoskins said he buried him, and that I believed. Besides, it would have been weeks or months before he could buy the land then start building, even with the more relaxed island regulations in the 1970s.

A man joined us, wearing a hard hat and ear covering. I glanced past him at the track hoe, which was shut down and empty, the bucket resting on the ground, like an offensive lineman's knurled fist. I hadn't even heard it over the saws, which shrieked at very high decibels, even with the earplugs.

The work continued for nearly an hour, the whole area becoming enveloped in the white dust. It settled on everything downwind, covering the field in what looked like a blanket of snow.

Suddenly, the sound stopped, and the light breeze carried the remaining dust away from the slab. The four men operating the saws were covered in a fine, white powder, wearing respirators and helmets to breathe like land-dwelling scuba divers. They moved the saws off the slab and began the process of getting the dust off and getting out of the heavy gear.

"Thanks for coming over, Gus," I barely heard Tibbetts say to the man in the hard hat, as they shook hands.

I pulled the plugs out of my ears. The silence was powerful. No birds were singing, no bugs chirping, even the gentle swish of the water against the shore seemed to have paused.

"Where did that come from?" I asked Roy, as Gus went back to his machine.

"He is the foreman of the construction crew across the road," he replied, as if it were common for workers to be pulled off a paying job.

The track hoe started up and Gus eased it toward the area where brooms had now replaced shovels in the hands of the off-duty cops. The slab revealed dozens of perpendicular lines, cross-hatching the whole foundation, creating a few dozen individual blocks.

Positioning the track hoe in front of the slab, Gus used the bucket to nudge the corner. A section moved slightly, and he repositioned the bucket and moved it some more, while tilting the bucket. The stone swung out from the slab at an angle, and he was able to deftly pick up the section of concrete with the bucket and grappler, as easily as a person would pick up a quarter from a table. The block was at least six feet long and probably three wide. It likely weighed nearly a ton.

The machine pivoted and Gus placed the block near the right rear of the track.

The removal process took over two hours, as Gus carefully removed the slab, block by block, and created a slightly distorted version of the original slab beside the machine. I could only assume it was so they could be examined for evidence.

While the work progressed, more people arrived. They were held back by the yellow police tape and several on-duty constables, but one man ducked under the tape and approached one of the officers. I recognized him—AJ's friend Reg, and beyond him was Pearl, still standing behind the tape.

Reg talked with the constable a moment and then he returned to the bystanders. The constable went over to Whittaker and said something to him. The detective looked over at the crowd and nodded at the constable who then turned toward Reg and his friends, motioning them forward.

"They want to help," AJ told me. "The people here know what you're going through."

Roy turned to the volunteer workers and all eyes were on him, as Gus continued to remove the slab, bit by bit. "Once the concrete is removed," Roy said, shouting over the machine, "the rest will have to be done by hand."

The realization of what everyone was there to do suddenly sank in, and I looked around at all of them, my eyes welling with tears. It was a gruesome undertaking, and I could tell by the looks I got in return, that it would be done solemnly and with dignity. These islands had seen loss, up close, as storms swept whole families out to sea, only to wash their bloated bodies ashore the next day.

I looked around at my new friends—some had suffered great loss as well and I could sense their pain, especially in the two tall stoic blondes, Nora and Charity. What or when it was, I didn't ask but I knew that both had suffered tremendous pain and held it bottled up inside. I was the neophyte in the group. My life until this week had been easy.

With the last of the slab removed, the engine fell silent, and exhibiting almost an attitude of reverence, the group of people began the painstaking job of removing the topsoil by hand.

It was hot, with the sun already halfway to the horizon. The forensics ambulance had more than a dozen small hand spades and while some carefully dug in the soil, others used small shovels to load the dirt into buckets, to be removed and sifted through a screen set up beside the ambulance.

Two hours before sunset, a woman shouted, "I found something!"

Everyone stopped and got out of the way, as the forensics techs moved into the shallow pit, now fifteen feet wide, ten feet long and a good twelve to sixteen inches deep.

I stood off to the side, my new friends gathered around me for support. I wasn't sure if I was ready for what they were uncovering.

The two men and one woman worked with brushes and small trowels, much like an archaeological dig. Dirt was brushed away and it was soon obvious they had uncovered a bone.

One of the men looked up at Roy. "It's human," he said. "The femur and tibia—right knee."

Roy looked over at me. "Are you sure you want to be here, Eddie?"

I locked eyes with the older man and nodded. "Have them work downward, Roy. Dad would have been wearing tan, canvas flight boots, with one of his dog tags in the laces."

The forensics team went back to work, hunched over the grim find. Finally, they stopped moving and slowly rose.

There in the hole they'd dug, lay what was left of my father's right boot, his skeletal leg protruding from the top and exposed to the hip, and a partially corroded, rectangular piece of metal in the laces.

"Dad," I croaked, and immediately felt hands on me, supporting me, holding me.

EPILOGUE

Two days later, after we'd all rested and the forensics team finished up the recovery of my father's remains, AJ and Nora insisted we all go to the Fox and Hare for one last round of drinks, before Buck had to fly back to the States. Boone and Emily rode with me and Nora in Nora's Jeep, and AJ said she'd meet us there, she had to stop and talk to someone.

A positive ID had been made, based on dental records supplied by the VA, and by the metal rods my father had implanted in his lower back—courtesy of the US Navy—the result of one too many hard carrier landings. The Navy stamped everything with a number.

The autopsy report concluded that he'd died of a single gunshot wound to the head. The bullet was recovered and matched to the gun Hoskins had pulled on the yacht.

Whittaker had made a very discreet inquiry to a contact he had at Windsor Castle. The royal family was very anxious to get the necklace back, and a finder's fee had been arranged for its return—as well as the photographs and negatives recovered at the Rogue's home. Since Winston Ebanks had been the one to find it on Jocko's body and had hidden it away in a shoebox all these years, everyone agreed he should get the money.

We headed up North West Point Road to West Bay and soon Nora pulled into the parking lot at the Fox and Hare. Two Ducati motorcycles were parked side by side and I recognized the one I'd ridden on with Charity.

"The other one belongs to AJ," Emily explained. "They must all be here, yeah?"

We climbed out and the two divemasters went ahead of me and Nora, who took her time getting out of the CJ-7.

"I'm really sorry about what you endured," I said to her, out of earshot of the others, as we followed them. "I never would have involved any of you if I thought there was a chance someone would get hurt."

She stopped and turned to face me, and once more I saw the pain and understanding in her eyes. "Each of us does what we have to do, Eddie."

"Yeah, but—"

"It's my job to find the truth," she interrupted. "And sometimes bad shit comes with that."

I looked down at the ground and moved a small stone with the toe of my shoe. "I just want you to know how much everything you, and everyone else... what y'all have done. It means a lot to me. *Thank you* doesn't even begin to cover it."

"It's enough," she said. "Let's go inside."

The old English pub feel I remembered from my first time visiting the Fox and Hare returned instantly. It was incredible how rich, dark woodwork and the trappings of another place and time could be plopped down in the middle of the Caribbean and not have a tropical flair.

"Hey, there he is," Buck said, standing at the bar with Charity, AJ, and Winston. "We have great news!"

"What's that?" I asked, accepting a beer from Reg.

"Your father's remains have been released," Detective Whittaker said from behind me.

I turned around to face him. "Does that mean I can take him home now? Back to Key Biscayne?"

He nodded. "Whenever you can make arrangements."

"Arrangements done," Buck said with finality. "We take off at sunrise. I won't even charge you the difference to Key West."

"I'll need to buy a casket," I said, suddenly thinking of all the things I had to do. "And a flag to cover it. And—"

"De man say, 'arrangements done,'" Winston stated flatly. "If you had not come here to Grand, I would never have learned who dat necklace belong to or how Jocko came to have it. Dis was de least I could do."

I looked at the two men, then glanced at the burly Reg, who was helping behind the bar. He nodded. "That's handy, Harry. Stick it in the oven."

Pearl laughed and shoved him, and he grabbed at her. I gave him a puzzled look but turned my attention to Winston and Buck. I knew neither man would accept my refusal, so I didn't even try.

"Thank you, both," I said, truly humbled at the gesture. "Your kindness means a lot to me and my fam—" My cell phone rang, and I pulled it out of my pocket. "Speaking of, this is my wife, excuse me a minute."

I pushed the *Accept* button as I stepped back outside. "We're coming home tomorrow," I blurted out, without even saying hello.

"We?" Liz asked. "They released his remains?"

"And a friend is flying us home in an antique flying boat."

I heard a bit of a gasp through the phone. "He would have liked that, Eddie. I bet he would."

"Yes, and he would have liked the people I met here. Friends like these don't come along very often. I want to bring you and the kids here one day."

"You're coming... 'home' home?" Liz asked. "We're still in Miami, not Nags Head."

"To Key Biscayne," I replied. "Mom and Dad's timeless love will be reunited."

If you enjoyed *Timeless*, you'll love *Shameless*,
the full-length novel by four more Tropical Authors.

Discover more books in the genre, and sign up for the newsletter
with new releases and great deals at
www.TropicalAuthors.com

AFTERWORD PART I
BY NICHOLAS HARVEY

Author of the AJ Bailey Adventure Series and the Nora Sommer Caribbean Suspense Series.

Nicholas wrote Part I and the flashback scenes for Part III and Part IV of *Timeless*.

In late July 2021, we'd written all four parts to *Graceless,* and the editing process was in full swing. I was incredibly excited about the project, and it had gone so seamlessly, I was dying to do it again. An idea for a storyline had been bouncing around in my head for a while, and I'd earmarked it for an AJ Bailey novel. It involved a dual timeline plot – or flashbacks as they're often called – which I enjoy writing and often use in the AJ series.

It struck me, that the idea might work for another collaboration, but location would be a problem. My characters are based in the Cayman Islands, but the other three authors scatter their stories in various locations around the Caribbean, and Wayne and John base theirs in the Florida Keys.

Hick Nick (I'm Brit Nick to differentiate between us!) had just released *Deep Devil* which concluded in Grand Cayman and featured a cameo from my characters AJ and Nora, which was great fun. In talking to Nick, he planned to move Emily and Boone to Little Cayman for his next novel, *Deep Focus*, so now we had fifty per cent of the cast in one location. Wayne's spin-off series about a former military, arse-kicking female called Charity Styles, also took in multiple tropical countries – but she kept her sailboat in Governors Creek, Grand Cayman.

Now I had something to work with. John's Buck Reilly was the only outlier, but the guy flew his own plane, so we should be able to come up with an excuse to have him zip over from Key West. Besides, that would be Hick Nick's problem to figure out in his section!

That was all I needed to get started, and I wrote the first part over the next few weeks of early August, in between working on *Deadly Sommer*, my first book in the Nora Sommer Caribbean Suspense series. And then the manuscript sat safely tucked away on my hard drive as we finished up *Graceless* and caught up on our own projects.

Around Christmas time, Hick Nick and I had just released *Angels of the Deep*, we were looking ahead to the launch of *Graceless*, and the group decided it would be great to have a pre-order link in the back for the next project. What should we do? I said, 'cool, I have it started and the cover's done, but there's one thing you should know about this manuscript... it's going to be a full novel, because my part is already 17,000 words!'

Hick Nick took the reins in January, and the master file – which we nicknamed the 'Football' – was passed around the four of us over the next eight months. *Timeless* was a far more complicated and time-consuming manuscript than our first cooperative release. Partly due to the length, partly due to the singular location, and partly due to the flashback element. But it also provided a better opportunity to blend our characters across each other's parts and keep them all involved until the end.

Of course, the first order of business for the other three was editing all my proper English spelling for the agreed upon US English... a chore they all took great pleasure in doing!

Once again, this was a remarkably fun and rewarding experience writing with friends and feeding off each other's ideas and inspirations. I hope you enjoyed our novel as much as we did in creating the story.

ABOUT THE AUTHOR

Nicholas Harvey's life has been anything but ordinary. Race car driver, adventurer, divemaster, and since 2020 a full-time novelist. Raised in England, Nick now lives next to the ocean in Key Largo with his amazing wife, Cheryl.

A motorsports career may have taken him all over the world, both behind the wheel and later as a Race Engineer and Team Manager, but diving inspires his destinations these days – and there's no better diving than in Grand Cayman where Nick's AJ Bailey Adventure and Nora Sommer Caribbean Suspense series are based.

Drawing from his own thirst for adventure, experience underwater, and a lifetime of storytelling, Nick's novels put you right in the middle of the action. Feel the ocean breeze brushing your face, the warm water washing over your feet, and the villains chasing you across the tropical island!

Find out more info, buy AJ Bailey Gear, and join Nick's newsletter at www.HarveyBooks.com

AFTERWORD PART II
BY NICK SULLIVAN

Author of The Deep Series.

Nick wrote Part II of *Timeless*.

After having so much fun with *Graceless: A Tropical Authors Novella*, it wasn't surprising that everyone was on board with writing a follow-up co-op book. What to do differently? One review we heard a number of times was that the *Graceless* novella was too short. Solution: make *Timeless* a full-length novel. In addition to making it longer, there was something else we wanted to try. If you've read *Graceless*, you'll know that our Everyman character made his way from location to location, and each of our sections was written at a separate time, in a separate place, with a different supporting cast of characters. This time, we decided it would be fun if our characters directly interacted throughout, much as they did in the Epilogue of *Graceless*. In that earlier book, my own characters—Boone Fischer and Emily Durand—were still on Cozumel, matching where they were in *Deep Devil*. But I knew by the time we started writing *Timeless*, I would have released my next book—*Deep Focus*—and Boone and Em would be on Little Cayman, just eighty miles from Nicholas Harvey's characters on Grand Cayman. Wayne Stinnett's Charity Styles often keeps her boat there in Grand, and Buck Reilly has his own plane... so it was an easy decision to set our book in the Cayman Islands. Nicholas Harvey took the reins and came up with a rip-roaring opener.

Writing each other's characters' dialogue was a challenge, but "Brit Nick" (Nicholas Harvey) and I had already had some practice. Before we started *Timeless*, the two Nicks embarked on a duo novella for the Christmas season, *Angels of the Deep*. You might have caught a little callback to that story in one of my chapters, when Em had a chat with the sculptor, Simon Morris. I just had to put that in, because the rumor is he's working hard at creating an actual *Angels of the Deep* underwater sculpture!

Brit Nick already had a handle on my characters from our collaborative work, and Wayne and John had both read my books, so I was pleased to find my characters' dialogue was nearly spot-on! Nevertheless, with so many characters, I suggested that maybe Boone would be left behind for the return to Grand. After all, some-one's got to take care of Brixton the Dog. And as many of you may know, I narrate for Wayne Stinnett, and know Charity very well. That's why I came up with "Scooter." I figured I'd throw her a bone, in the form of a big musclebound target to play with. Poor ol' Scooter.

Brit Nick had the idea of using historical flashbacks to tie every-thing together, something he does in his AJ Bailey Adventure Series. I love how it all turned out, but I'd be remiss if I didn't admit the two time periods presented a tremendous challenge! Fortunately, a few Zoom calls amongst the authors gave us a game plan, and I hope you enjoyed the end result.

One of the most enjoyable challenges in my section was to come up with what was in the case. I knew it should be something that required the particular skill set of John H. Cunningham's treasure-hunting savant, Buck Reilly. I started researching some of the biggest heists in the '70s and came upon the Baker Street robbery. For those of you who think I took that from Sherlock Holmes... I didn't. They did! The robbers themselves apparently stole the idea from "The Red-Headed League;" a short story by Arthur Conan Doyle involving thieves tunneling up through the floor into a bank vault. I watched a documentary on the actual robbery and was surprised to find it occurred in the Lloyds Bank right around the street from where I stayed in London, when I went to a British acting school in the late '80s. I believe I cashed a traveler's check there.

As I write this, we are nearing the end of our final rewrite, and I'm looking forward to narrating the audiobook. And hopefully, by the time you read this, you'll have the opportunity to pre-order the next book, with an entirely new quartet of Tropical Authors! Two of them are fellow Tennesseans, and I shared a beer with David Berens when I was home visiting family; I very much look forward to what they've got in store.

Tropical Authors continues to grow! We currently have forty-six authors, with stories running the gamut of mysteries, thrillers, suspense, action-adventure, romance... and even some tropical science-fiction! If you haven't signed up for our newsletter, please pop over to www.tropicalauthors.com and join our mailing list!

ABOUT THE AUTHOR

Born in East Tennessee, Nick Sullivan has spent most of his adult life as an actor in New York City, working in theater, television, film, and audiobooks. After recording hundreds of books over the last couple of decades, he decided to write some of his own. An avid scuba diver for many years, his travels to numerous Caribbean islands have inspired The Deep Series (formerly Caribbean Dive Adventures). *Deep Shadow* is set on the Dutch island of Bonaire and its sequel, *Deep Cut*, is set on the little island of Saba. Book Three, *Deep Roots*, takes place in Belize, and Book Four, *Deep Devil*, takes Boone Fischer and Emily Durand up the coast to Cozumel. Most recently, "Boonemily" have found themselves in Little Cayman, in *Deep Focus*.

Visit www.nicksullivan.net or www.deepnovels.com for social media links, and be sure to sign up for the author's newsletter and follow him on BookBub.

AFTERWORD PART III
BY JOHN H. CUNNINGHAM

Author of the Buck Reilly Adventure Series.

John wrote Part III of *Timeless*.

For most authors, the process of writing a book is very personal, with everyone having their own methodology, approach to considering, planning and researching a story, and then carrying through to put "words on paper." The characters we create are always an extension of ourselves, whether good or bad, protagonist or antagonist, with character arcs all their own, and often taken from real life or our observations of the world. Writing is an art form, after all, whether an author's work is compared to finger painting, or Michelangelo, and fortunately, our tropical authors have very similar palettes on which to combine our creativity.

So, when artists collaborate, it changes your entire process, but also exposes you to new forms of expression and opportunities, storylines and already developed characters from established colleagues and their popular series. Working with Brit Nick, Hick Nick and Wayne on our first full collaboration, *Graceless*, was both fun and exciting, and based on the reviews, was well received and enjoyed by many. *Graceless* was a novella, so essentially a much shorter story, and we approached it from an iterative basis where the protagonist traveled from each one of our respective worlds to the next with little overlap other than that lead character's continuous odyssey. The story covered a lot of geography, from Grand Cayman, to Cozumel, to the Florida Keys, and provided a riveting, fast-paced adventure that was almost impossible to put down, which many read in one sitting.

With *Timeless*, that formula changed dramatically. Yes, it's the same four collaborators, Cunningham, Stinnett, Harvey and Sullivan, but this was a full-length novel set primarily in one location but also contained flashbacks and a far more complicated plot. And one of the aspects I truly enjoyed writing, which I hope you as the reader enjoyed experiencing, was that our characters did overlap, in many cases, throughout the entire story. That meant we each got to portray some of the renowned characters from our collaborators' existing series. It was a real pleasure and honor to be entrusted with the opportunity to write dialogue, action, description and prose for these existing characters that I have read, enjoyed and were now interacting with my own.

In *Timeless*, Buck Reilly was surrounded with several smart, capable, gutsy and dare I say attractive, female co-characters, that I enjoyed having the opportunity to render in my section of the book. Needless to say, there was a fair amount of joking around amongst my co-writers that, for poor Buck, it was water, water everywhere, but not a drop to drink—well, maybe there was a little off-page thirst quenching—if you read the story closely, but also a lot of kidding amongst the characters. As the father of two strong women, I really enjoy portraying powerful women in my writing, and have no issue with Buck, my main protagonist, often being out-thought, out-performed and being vulnerable amongst them during the course of the story, because my goal for him is to be an Everyman character who is often in over his head, and, like so many of us, struggling against greater odds to prevail.

Albeit more complicated, the process in co-writing *Timeless* was a true pleasure, and brought me even closer to my three collaborators, who I now just think of as friends. The more we do together, the more opportunity we see for our characters to connect in our stand-alone novels, as well, so keep your eye out for more cameos in the future.

ABOUT THE AUTHOR

John H. Cunningham is the author of the best-selling, Key West based, soon to be ten book, Buck Reilly Adventure Series. John has either lived in or visited the many locations that populate his novels, and he mixes fact with fiction and often includes real people in the cast of characters. Adhering to the old maxim, "write what you know," John's books have an authenticity and immediacy that have earned a loyal following and strong reviews. John writes stories that concern themselves with the same tensions and issues that affect all of our lives, and his choices for the places and plots that populate his stories include many settings that he loves, including Key West, Cuba, Jamaica, and multiple Caribbean locations. John is also an Executive Vice President, and Regional Director of New York City for a public Real Estate Investment Trust. He splits his time between New York, Virginia, and Key West.

Visit www.jhcunningham.com to learn more, or to sign up for John's newsletter and social media links.

AFTERWORD PART IV
BY WAYNE STINNETT

Author of the Jesse McDermitt Caribbean Adventure Series, the Charity Styles Caribbean Thriller Series, and the Jerry Snyder Caribbean Mystery Series.

Wayne wrote Part IV of *Timeless*.

After the resounding success of our first effort—actually, I'm pretty sure it was even before the release of *Graceless*—the idea came up to write a sequel, if for no other reason, to motivate others in the Tropical Authors group to do likewise. Except this time, it would be a full-length novel. That meant that each of the four of us would have to write about 20,000 words, instead of the 10,000 we each did in *Graceless*. To me, that's four weeks. But after reading the first three sections in one sitting, my mind flowed right into it, and I was able to knock out my part in half that time.

We bounced ideas around before we really got underway, and continued doing that during the process, and Brit Nick even wrote a prologue to introduce us to the protagonist, which I read, but mostly I just stayed out of the outlining discussion. You see, I'm not an outliner. I write in a form some call "discovery" writing, starting with a blank page and telling the story as it's made up. Those who outline are called plotters and those of us who write in discovery manner are called pantsers, since we write by the seat of our pants. I've done a few of these before and found I work better without a net. So, I waited for Brit, Hick, and John to finish their parts. As it turned out, the protagonist was the son of the guy I thought would be the main character. But in a way, Woody Rains really is the main protagonist and Eddie was just the instrument which uncovered what happened to him.

If you're a writer and reading this, and if you're a plotter and would like to see what it's like to write without an outline, doing something like this would be great exercise.

In *Graceless*, there were more precise delineations between each of our parts and our characters. The protagonist, Nathan Fitzgerald, moved through each of our worlds and encountered our characters in separate and distant places—the Cayman Islands, Cozumel, Key West, and Marathon.

But in *Timeless*, since Hick Nick had moved his characters Emily Durand and Boone Fischer to Little Cayman, and one of my characters, Charity Styles, also lived part time in the Caymans, we decided that our new protagonist would encounter our characters there, which meant Buck Reilly, John Cunningham's main character, had to fly down from Key West and join them.

Graceless was far easier—Nathan met AJ and Nora in the Caymans, got a clue about Cozumel and met Emily and Boone there, got another clue about Key West and met Buck there, and then Nathan and Buck chased after the bad guys until Buck's plane was forced to land in Marathon, shot up and on fire. Jesse took over from there. But all through *Graceless*, Nathan was interacting with just one author's characters at a time. So, each of us were writing only about our own characters and Nathan.

That wasn't the case with *Timeless*. The new protagonist, Eddie Rains hired AJ for some dives, then Nora joined in, and in Hick Nick's section, AJ and Nora brought Boone and Emily aboard, working directly with them and Eddie. The plot thickened, and the group needed more help, so Buck Reilly flew down and in John's section, Eddie was working with Brit's, Hick's, and John's characters. You see where this is going, right?

By the time I got the "football"—that's what we started calling the many incarnations of the manuscript to avoid confusion—I would be writing Eddie's interaction with AJ, Nora, Emily, Boone, Buck, and Charity. I know some are going to ask, so I'll answer here. Yes, I know how to juggle. I can't speak for everyone involved, but I have read all the works of all three of my co-authors and hope I did their characters justice here in *Timeless*. This one was far more difficult to write, yet it was also uniquely enjoyable to work with such talented authors.

And our diabolical master plan came to fruition. Four more authors in the Tropical Authors group are nearly finished with *Shameless*, the third in the Tropical Authors Series. It's on pre-order now and will be available in late February.

ABOUT THE AUTHOR

Wayne Stinnett is an American author of more than thirty novels and one non-fiction book on writing. He's also a Veteran of the United States Marine Corps, as is his main character, Jesse McDermitt. Between those careers, Stinnett has worked as a deckhand, commercial fisherman, dive master, taxi driver, construction manager, and truck driver, among many other things. Currently, he's expanding his self-publishing company, Down Island Publishing, LLC, and is now publishing other authors' works, as well as continuing his own writing.

He lives with his wife and youngest daughter in the South Carolina Lowcountry. They also have three grown children, four grandchildren, a crazy Carolina dog, and a large cage full of parakeets. He grew up in Melbourne, Florida, and has also lived in the Florida Keys, the Bahamas, and Cozumel, Mexico, among other places. Stinnett still gets down to Florida regularly, but more often than not, it's via his imagination and writing. All his books are set primarily in the Keys and around the Caribbean. His stories revolve around a retired Marine who is a charter boat captain living on an island in the Middle Keys, where he explores, dives, and fishes the back country of Florida Bay, the Gulf of Mexico, the Florida Straits, and all around the Caribbean Sea. That is until trouble comes looking for him.

Find out more info and join his newsletter at
https://waynestinnett.com.

Made in United States
North Haven, CT
17 April 2023

35544405R00167